The Greatest Sin

Moon
Shades

Published by Tangled Sky Press
www.tangledskypress.com

First printing, May 2015
Second printing, July 2016

ISBN: 978-0-9862277-0-7

Moon Shades is a work of fiction. Names, places, and incidents are either products of the authors' imaginations or used fictitiously.

Moon Shades

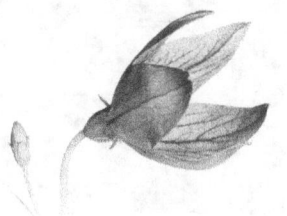

The Greatest Sin #3

Lee French & Erik Kort

TANGLED
SKY
PRESS

Acknowledgments
Lee French

For Jeffrey Cook, my ConBuddy, Connie J. Jasperson, my Chief Sanity Engineer, and Irene, whose red pen is mightier than my comma splice.

Erik Kort

People are never just one thing, but we're all trapped by the singleness of view that comes from living in our own brains. Others, just like books, can reveal things about life that we would've otherwise missed. I'd like to sincerely thank my niece and nephew, Chloe and Benjamin, for your spark, enthusiasm for life, and reminding me that it's okay to charge down the stairs even though you might fall; there'll be someone to catch you, or at least hold you when it's all done.

Alex, you're the only one I want to catch me, even if you'll mock me mercilessly later. Liz and Meghan, you both were more gentle and kind with my manic fears about the tangled thicket that formed this book.

Finally, Nanette and Rodney—you two are the best in-laws I could hope for. You've been supportive, whether I skipped family get-togethers because I was banging my head against my computer screen, or I just needed to whine at someone. I don't say it often enough (can I ever?), so I'll say it here: Thanks.

Other Books by the Authors

The Greatest Sin Series
epic fantasy
The Fallen
Harbinger
Moon Shades
Illusive Echoes

Lee French
In the Ilauris setting
standalone fantasy tales
Damsel In Distress
Shadow & Spice (short story)
Al-Kabar

Spirit Knights
young adult urban fantasy
Girls Can't Be Knights
Backyard Dragons
Ethereal Entanglements
Ghost Is the New Normal (coming 2017)

Maze Beset Trilogy

superheroes in denim

Dragons In Pieces

Dragons In Chains

Dragons In Flight

Anthology Appearances

Into the Woods: a fantasy anthology

Merely This and Nothing More: Poe Goes Punk

Unnatural Dragons: a science fiction anthology

Missing Pieces VIII: short stories from GenCon's Authors Avenue

(coming August 2016)

Non-fiction

with Jeffrey Cook

Working the Table: An Indie Author's Guide to Conventions

Erik Kort

(as Erik Marshall)

Wards of the Thicket

adventure fantasy

Children Without Faces

Children Without Voices (coming 2017)

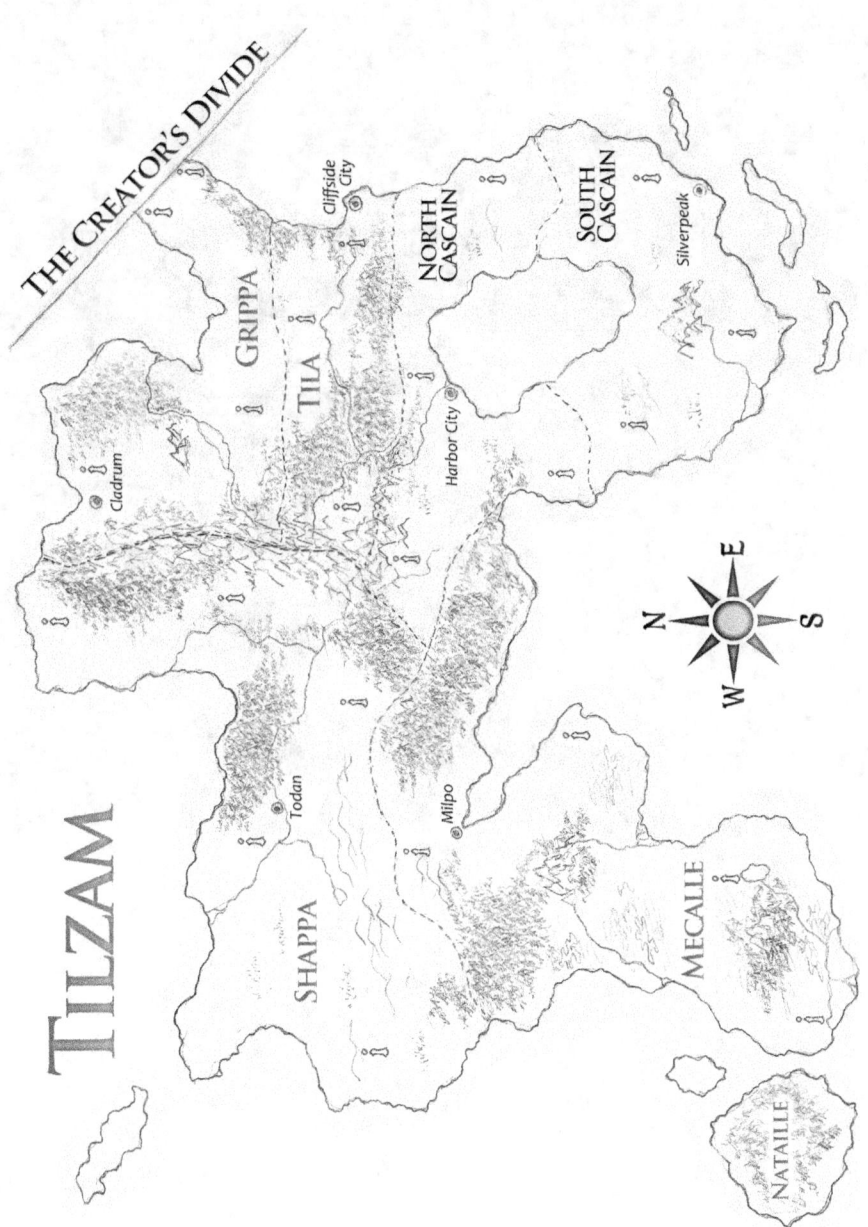

THE CREATOR'S DIVIDE

TILZAM

GRIPPA

TILA

NORTH CASCAIN

SOUTH CASCAIN

Cliffside City

Silverpeak

Cladrum

Harbor City

SHAPPA

Todan

Milpo

MECALLE

NATAILLE

N E S W

Chapter 1

Arms folded, Chavali glared at the man who had stopped her at the landing for the tenth floor. She woke only a short time ago and had been headed down to get breakfast, then to see her clan. "Who do you think you are? This is none of your business."

He hadn't introduced himself before assaulting her with his curiosity, so all she knew was what she could see: an idiot. More precisely, an inquisitive idiot who had no understanding of the difference between public and private and had managed to gain information she didn't think he should have.

The man in the ordinary, plain clothes held out his hands in entreaty. His open face held such earnest interest she wanted to hit him. "The answer could help a great many people, Chavali. Imagine the possibilities if such information could be shared."

"Shared?" Horrified by the idea that secrets of her clan would be spread far and wide, she sneered. "I don't know how you learned enough to ask about this," she growled, "but I don't care who would benefit from it. This," she jabbed a pink painted fingernail into his chest, "is not an acceptable subject for discussion."

He took a step back and rubbed where she poked him. She saw a thin scar on his wrist that disappeared up his sleeve and wondered if he got it as part of his death. "There's no need to get snippy. What difference does it make? Your clan won't care."

This stark reminder of the slaughter of her clan hurt. Chavali's nostrils flared, and her jaws clenched. To avoid slapping him and making the situation worse, she crossed her arms. "How dare you." The weight of this glare had made her clansmen flee from her wrath.

Reclaiming the step he'd retreated, he reached for her with both hands, an invitation she had no intention of accepting. "This is obviously a touchy subject, I can understand. I'm sure that if we talk this out—"

"No. There is nothing to 'talk out.' " It infuriated her that he refused to drop the subject. Worse, he had to remind her about things she ached for, things she would never have again. A memory of sitting on the back of her family's wagon with her sister as it bounced along a dirt path elbowed its way to the front of her mind, demanding she relive it now.

Everything here was wrong. The food tasted funny. Her tea had strange herbs. She slept alone, without her family to surround her. Instead of creaking wood and bare earth and lush grasses, she got hard stone. Fake light. Unfamiliar faces. That ever-present underground scent.

In private, she might weep for the loss of her clan, her freedom, and her life. Facing this man in public, all her frustration poured out into her hand. It whipped across his face in a slap that hurt almost as much as it satisfied. The brief contact gave her only a fleeting glimpse of his thoughts, and she needed no help from the spirits to know she'd surprised him.

His head snapped to the side, and he grabbed her arm—covered by her long-sleeved shirt—as she finished her follow-through. By reflex, she stepped in and jerked her knee up. He managed to shift his leg enough to take the blow to his thigh. Thanks to Eliot's training, she still jabbed her knee in hard enough to provoke a whine of pain.

"Whoa, whoa." Someone else grabbed Chavali around the waist and pulled her aside. She threw an elbow out. Her new opponent twisted out of the way and tossed her at the wall. Eliot gave her a cool stare. "While I admire you getting in extra practice time, Chavali, this isn't really the place for that. Knock it off."

Eliot held an arm out to keep the other man from moving back in. A sharp sting on her mouth made her reach up and touch her lower lip. The small smear of blood on her fingertip made her lip curl.

"She has a good hand on her, I'll give her that." Only now did the man rub his cheek, moving his jaw to make sure it still worked.

"Insufferable *bechaké.*" With Eliot between them, Chavali stayed by the wall and pushed her red-brown hair out of her face, also smoothing down the pink Seer's feather sprouted from her forehead. The three beads threaded on one lock clicked together, helping her calm down through their familiarity. "How do you even know about any of this?"

Her opponent turned and limped down the stairs, favoring one leg. Either he ignored the question or he didn't hear her.

Eliot kept his arm out to ward her off until the other man disappeared around the turn of the spiral stair. "What was that about?"

"Nothing," Chavali snapped. Her stomach growled, and she wanted to get food. To do that, she had to go the same way that idiot went.

3

"That didn't look like nothing." Eliot crossed his wiry arms.

Uninterested in explaining, she flicked her hand at him and walked away to retrieve her cloak from her room. Marcus and Penny would offer her food whether she wanted it or not. "Looks can be deceiving."

"Chavali, you're such a pain in the ass."

"So are you," she muttered. Glancing over her shoulder, she saw he hadn't followed her up the hallway. Good. A string of beads similar to the ones in her hair clacked against her door when she opened it. The room—nothing more than a large bedroom—had a paint-spattered screen blocking off the corner with her dresser and dirty clothes basket and a woven rug made from the spare ends of many different colors covering the otherwise bare stone floor in the center and under her bed. Others considered them trash. Being unable to see color, she found them interesting additions.

Her fur-lined cloak hung over the wooden chair at her desk, where she'd left it after yesterday's visit to see the children. The fresh air always did wonders for her mood, then she plodded back down here, ten floors underground. All her life, she'd lived in wagons, and now she lived in a hole in the dirt. Some days, it got on her nerves. No. All days. It never stopped grating. It never stopped reminding her of what she'd lost.

Her tiny clan of only three children expected her for lunch today. She would surprise them with an early visit, after telling Colby she needed to skip her reading lesson. Pulling on her boots and tucking her gloves into a pocket of her brown wool dress, she left the room and headed down one quarter turn on that spiral stair.

Like her own floor, Colby's had thirty private quarters arrayed in a wedge with bathing rooms, a lounge, a study, and a practice room at the far end. His room, number thirteen, sat on a side branch from the main spoke of hallway. Unlike her own floor, the numbers on this one hadn't been repainted, leaving the original stain on the stone that happened to be exactly the same tone as the stone itself. She had to count the rooms to find his.

Colby answered her knock so quickly she guessed he must have been on his way out. Towering over her at seven feet tall, he looked down with surprise. "Good morning, Chavali. I didn't expect you so early." He held the door open wide enough she could see he had no guests. Neat and tidy, nothing about the room hinted at what he might have been doing. He and his clothes also appeared to be clean and in order.

"Change of plans." She elected not to crane her neck up to meet his gaze. Instead, she looked off down the hallway. "I'm going to see the children now and will be there for a while."

From the way he shifted his weight, she guessed he raised an eyebrow. "I know this is difficult, Chavali, but the only way you get better is practice. You know that."

The cloak hanging over her arm made it difficult to cross her arms properly. She managed. It was the least she could do when he decided to chide her about something so silly. "I'm not in the mood. It will go poorly."

"What's wrong?"

She scowled. "Nothing."

"I'm not sure if I'm getting better at reading you or you're just too angry to lie well right now." Pushing the door open farther, he gestured for her to use it. "Come in and talk about it." When she failed to step in, he added, "If you're that angry, you're going to snap at the kids. I know you don't want to do that."

It galled her to admit to herself that he might be right and she might be wrong. It would be worse to admit it to him. "No, thank you. I will see you tomorrow."

He sighed. "Is this about the rumors?"

Two steps away already, she froze and peered over her shoulder, eyes narrowed in suspicion. "Rumors? What rumors?"

His face contorted with regret for asking. "It's nothing. Don't worry about it."

"You brought it up, so tell me." She pushed her way past him and into the room. "What are these rumors, and why have I not yet heard them?" Taking possession of his desk chair, she dropped into it.

He shut the door and leaned against it, reluctance obvious as he crossed his arms and pursed his lips. "There are some whispers running around about you. Specifically about where your power of prophecy comes from and how—"

"What?" She hopped to her feet, angrier than she'd been before. "How does everyone know this? It is not supposed to be known!"

"Calm down, Chavali. You're getting so worked up you're forgetting to use contractions."

"Do not tell me to calm down," she growled. "This is a disaster! It is one thing for a few people to know, but another altogether for wild rumors to run rampant. All it takes is one word overheard by the wrong person, and then *he* is drawn to me again." She paced back and forth across the fifteen feet of floor space, unable to decide if this news made her more afraid or angry. "He will learn of me, of the Fallen, of everything, and then we will all be in danger."

"I seriously doubt any of it will reach him." He stayed at the door, preventing any escape. "Even if it does, he's going to hear about a witch with the power to summon demons that whisper the future into her ears or whatever other blather they've moved on to by now."

She knew how rumors worked. Her clan had once been two hundred and thirty-one people. Everyone got bored and nattered about who did what to whom. The tales never failed to evolve until the involved parties wouldn't know any of it described them. "How does anyone even know these things? Rumors always come from somewhere. It is bad enough to have idiots asking about inbreeding in the clan without this nonsense on top of it."

Colby's brow lifted. "Ah. That's what you're bothered about."

Her eyes narrowed and her mouth went thin. "There is no reason for anyone to know these things. How do they know these things?"

He sighed again and rubbed his face. "The archives. Teryk mentioned it in our report, after the first time we met."

If he put that in the report, he put other things in it too. She wanted to know what other things. "What are these archives?"

"Every report we file goes in there. It's our history, in a manner of speaking. The records go all the way back to the founding of the Fallen."

"Every report. All of them." A week ago, she sat down with Railan and made sure the report from the mission in Ket was complete. She repeated the prophecy she'd delivered there while Railan scribbled it down, word for word. "Who can read the archives?"

"Any Fallen who wants to. When you can read, you'll be able to." He put emphasis on the second point, presumably hoping she'd changed her mind about this morning's lesson.

"So anyone could have read that report and decided I summon demons, or eat babies, or whatever other nonsense they wish to invent." She glared at him for being the messenger of this news. It changed nothing, and he bore no fault, so she crossed her arms and stopped focusing on him.

"Yes. Any Fallen could have done that. I don't think anyone would say you eat babies, though."

Something about the way he agreed, the way he chose his words or put a little too much space between the "yes" and the rest made her lift an eyebrow at him. "You know of someone in particular who seems a likely candidate."

"I didn't say that." He held up his hands in surrender. "And it doesn't matter. The damage is done, and there's nothing you can do to stop the juggernaut that is gossip here."

Taking a step towards him, knowing she couldn't do anything to harm him in any meaningful way even if she wanted to, she pointed firmly at the floor and spoke through her clenched teeth. "Tell me their name."

When she did that in her clan, the victim of her interrogation always told her. They knew she could take it from their minds if she wanted to. The fact she asked instead of grabbing and letting the spirits rip it from them meant she bore them no ill will and chose to remain relatively polite about the matter.

Colby, however, did not come from her clan. "Chavali, I don't think you really want to get into that kind of thing."

Two more steps brought her to him, and she grabbed his hand.

"Yes, I do."

He frowned and pulled away too late. Despite him trying to suppress it, the spirits snatched a picture from his mind, and it matched the man who accosted her on the stairs earlier. There could be no mistaking that head of hair short enough to be spiky and that open, friendly face. "You said you don't treat clan that way."

"This is exactly how I treat my clan," she snarled as she grabbed the handle of the door and yanked it open, "when you insist upon trying to manage me." Storming out, she slammed the door behind her. There would be no breakfast today. Her belly burned with angry fire, and she had a fight to pick.

Chapter 2

As she boiled down the stairs, people moved out of her way. She knew he went down, and given the time of day, she guessed he had been headed to the same place as she: the cafeteria. It took up half of the nineteenth floor, with the other half holding the kitchen and food storage.

A door separated the cafeteria from the never-ending stairwell. The moment she opened it, chatter and slurping and laughter and clatter spilled out, echoing off the stone walls. Poking her head in, she scanned the crowd of about four dozen humans, elves, and halfbreeds at the round tables scattered throughout the room. The object of her rage sat near the middle of the room, a woman in Healer's white beside him.

Breakfast this morning had all the usual offerings at a long buffet table: pastries, eggs in various states, potatoes, breads, fruit, and sausages. The smells taunted her, combining to demand she stop and fill her stomach before carrying on. She ignored them and squeezed past tables to reach his, where she slammed her hands down on the surface to get his attention.

"Who do you think you are?" It did not escape her notice that her action earned the attention of many others in the large room. That suited her; playing to an audience tended to sharpen her mind.

The man and Healer both flinched, startled by her approach. He coughed, and the Healer thumped on his back to help him dislodge a bit of food from his windpipe. While he stopped choking to death, Chavali straightened and crossed her arms, watching through a heavy-lidded glare.

The Healer frowned and pushed a cup of juice at him. "Good morning to you, Chavali."

"This morning *was* good, until he stuck his nose into it."

"I really don't see what the fuss is about." He cleared his throat and wiped his mouth with a napkin.

"Of course you do not, you imbecile!" Her roar quieted the entire cafeteria.

"Chavali, why don't you sit down and we can discuss the subject like rational people."

She charged forward, shoving a chair aside to reach him. There, she grabbed a fistful of his shirt and pushed her face in close to his. "Which subject is that? The one about you digging through the archives and tossing around things you find in it, or the one where you ask questions that demand—"

He surged to his feet, hitting her arm and shoving it aside while cutting her off. "Information. I only want information, and it's not a demand, just a request. You're taking this much too personally, Chavali." His expression hardened, and he took a forceful, menacing step closer.

Undaunted, she stood her ground. "It is entirely personal!"

"Chavali!" Someone grabbed her from behind and pulled her off her feet. This time, she saw Eliot and recognized his voice, so she didn't fight as he hustled her out of the room. The door swung shut behind them, and he let go, blocking her off from it. "That sure was a lot of loud nothing going on in there."

"He is trying to get me and what little I have left of my clan killed," she growled. Unable to contain her anger, she turned and ran up the steps.

Eliot followed her. "You have too much energy this morning. Sounds like you need to spar." He grabbed her arm. "Let's go."

"I do not need to be managed," she spat, shrugging to get him to release her.

He didn't. "Because all that was perfectly reasonable."

"Let go." Her voice rumbled, low and dangerous.

"Don't get pissy with me." He yanked on her arm, forcing her to face him. "Either cough it up or let it go." Her hand jerked up to slap him. He whacked it aside. "Cut it out. You're up on a horse higher than Colby's right now, and you need to settle down before you get hurt." He let go and walked away, headed down the stairs.

In a huff, she ran up the steps. She'd left her cloak behind someplace. At her floor, the tenth, she stomped to her room and tore apart her dresser, basket, and bed to find another. The manic action vented some of her anger and left her panting when she stopped. At that point, she remembered she didn't have a spare to look for and rolled her eyes at herself.

She found a brush in the pile where she'd dumped a drawer out and used it, taking care not to accidentally brush her beads or the feather strung beside them, or the Seer's feather. It took a few minutes. When she finished, she surveyed the disaster that was her room and sighed. Such a petulant display; she'd had a tantrum.

At a knock on the door, she tossed the brush into the mess and cracked it open only enough to peer through so her visitor wouldn't see the state of things. A young man in the light uniform of the Tower's servants stood there, shifting from foot to foot and biting his lip.

"Um, Chavali? Eldrack wants to see you? In meeting room three."

Of course he did. Chavali flicked a hand in irritation. "Fine," she said with a huff and breezed past him, noticing how he breathed a sigh of relief behind her back.

The primary purpose of the meeting rooms involved assigning missions. She could use a mission right about now. Beating that twit into submission would be more satisfying, but getting out of the Tower would work as a second choice. She'd been headed in that direction anyway.

When she reached the meeting room, an unadorned square with a large round table and eight chairs, it stood empty. This struck her as odd because Eldrack usually arrived first. His office was on this floor, the thirteenth, so he should be sitting there already, waiting with a folder full of information about the mission. She left the door open behind her and chose a seat where she could watch the others arrive.

Several minutes later, Eliot walked in. He stopped when he saw her and held a hand out to whoever followed him. "What are you doing here, Chavali?"

She lifted an eyebrow at him, wondering what could have prompted such an idiotic question. "The same thing as you, I assume."

"Yes," Eldrack's voice said from the hallway, heavy with an emotion she'd never heard from him before: annoyance. "It'll be the three of you. Get inside and take a seat."

Eliot raised his hands in surrender and walked in. Behind him, Eldrack shooed in the one person she didn't want to see right now. He shuffled in with a frown for the floor.

Chavali watched him with a glare. She had a thought to stand up and leave, yet she knew there was no point to making the gesture. None of them had any choice. The binding they all went through required them to take whatever missions Eldrack chose to assign. "What is the meaning of this?"

"The meaning of this," Eldrack said as he slapped his folder on the table without sitting, "is that fighting in the stairwell and cafeteria is unacceptable. I don't care who started it or who finished it or what it was about or anything else except that all my agents need to be able to trust each other enough to work together. To that end, I have an assignment that will be completed by both of you. Together. Cooperatively."

Chavali found she respected Eldrack more for knowing he could be moved by his temper. Always before, she'd found him annoyingly affable, sympathetic, kind, and as harmless as the aging clerk he appeared to be. She shut her mouth.

"Wait." Eliot looked from her to the other man. "Why am I here?"

Eldrack's expression softened to his more familiar sympathy, offered only to Eliot. "You're an experienced operator with a cool head and the ability to prevent these two from killing each other. That would be a dire waste of resources. The three of you are going to take the Courier Circuit. Chavali doesn't know what that is. Explain it to her." He walked out without waiting or asking for questions.

Eliot reached out and took the folder with a scowl. He stood without opening it. "It's a predetermined route." His words came out clipped and precise, a sure sign that pushing him would lead to a stab in the gut. "We deliver messages and packages and check up on the nearby villages. It'll take four or five days, depending on how much you two screw around. We'll walk. Be ready to go in half an hour and meet in the tavern. Sean, you take care of supplies. Chavali, just get ready without causing any more trouble. And get us a pack horse." He stalked out, folder in hand.

Half an hour barely left enough time to collect her pack and eat, let alone visit her clan. Ignoring Sean, she jumped out of her chair and hurried to catch up to Eliot. He lifted a hand to ward her off. "Not now, Chavali. Whatever you want, stuff it and save it."

She narrowed her eyes but swallowed down most of her bile. It would help nothing to spew that at Eliot. "I only wish for another quarter of an hour. To let the children know I cannot see them today. And I have not yet eaten."

They reached the stairwell, and he rounded on her, expression closed and distant. "You should have thought of that before you decided to get into a fight with someone. *Twice.*" He jogged up the stairs without giving her a chance to respond.

Taken aback by his behavior, Chavali scowled at him. This mission was clearly meant as a punishment—for all three of them—and Eliot didn't deserve it. Eldrack knew that, and so did she. Whether Sean had a clue, she couldn't guess.

His voice from behind her made her cringe. "Chavali, we should —"

"No," she held up a hand to ward Sean off and ran down the stairs, "we really shouldn't." This did not equate to fleeing. She did not flee from another Fallen. She hastened from him with purpose. Because he was an idiot and deserved nothing less.

Six flights down again, she grabbed an apple, a wedge of cheese, and a muffin, and downed a cup of juice. The food could be eaten while she walked. So focused on her task, she turned to hurry out and hit the solid wall of Colby, reaching for a slab of ham and with his mouth open to say something. He blinked at her, the impact having no real effect on him.

She, on the other hand, bounced, dropped her muffin, and staggered back a step. Her foot squished the muffin, and she growled in her throat.

"Are you alright?" Colby grabbed her arm and steadied her.

"No," she snapped. "The demons are ruining my day." Colby didn't deserve her anger any more than Eliot did. Everyone in the tower did *not* hate her, nor did they want to destroy her clan. Just Sean. She took a deep breath and shook her head. "I do not have time for this. Excuse me, Colby. I hope your day goes well."

He gave her a lopsided grin then plucked a fresh muffin from the table and deposited it into her hand. "You left your cloak in my room. Feel free to pick it up."

She took another deep breath and nodded. "Thank you. I will see you for lessons again when I return."

"Good luck on your mission." He patted her shoulder as she passed him on the way out, and she noticed people watching. Some of them had *those* looks. Wonderful. By the time she returned, there would be an affair between her and Colby, with the telling torrid and full of excessive detail.

She glowered at the wall and hurried off, running up the stairs to the eleventh floor. Panting, she jogged to Colby's room, grabbed her cloak, and kept going up to her own room on the tenth floor. It took several minutes to find her pack, already full of gear, in the mess. Then she had to stuff in extra socks and the scroll Colby gave her to work with between lessons. The sheath for her small dagger had to be buckled to the back of her belt. Sliding the plain knife into the sheath, she spotted her hairbrush and also tucked that into her pack.

Not sure how much longer she had, she dashed out and up. At the third floor, she jogged through the narrow, twisting tunnel to the next set of stairs. Halfway through, she ran into someone coming the other way at a blind corner, knocking them both to the floor in a tangle. Her head knocked on the ground, sending a jolt down her spine.

"Excuse me," Chavali mumbled as she rolled free, her muffin smashed into her chest. A tense ache built between her shoulder blades and up her neck to the base of her skull, adding to the new sharp sting above her ear.

"Goodness." A lunatic giggle followed the single word.

Getting to her hands and knees, she sighed at her muffin. "I do not have time for you, Algie."

"Oh, Chavali." The half-elf tsked at her. "I always have time for you." He picked her up by the waist. From her previous mission with him, she knew he had more strength than his loose clothes and slight frame suggested, yet it still surprised her to be set gently on her feet with no sign he'd made an effort. Producing a pristine biscuit from a pocket, he plucked the muffin out of her hand in trade, then he picked up her pack and hooked it on her arm.

Her lip curled, annoyed she had a reason to be grateful to this particular madman. "Thank you."

He flipped the muffin in the air, caught it, and giggled. "Be on your way, dear. You're in a hurry." Turning, he danced away on his tiptoes.

She rolled her eyes and returned to her flight through the tunnel. At the next floor up, a cavernous, empty space, she ran flat out from one set of stairs to the other. The other people going in both directions moved out of her way. She slowed down for the next set of stairs, a narrow spiral lit by small magical globes. As far as she knew, this stair counted as the first floor of the Tower, though she'd never found the labels for anything above the fourth.

Everyone had to turn sideways to pass on this stair, and at the top, someone else held the hidden door open for her. After doing the same for the person behind her, she rushed through the chilly provision cellar to the last set of steps. The wooden stairs took her to the rear door in the clean, welcoming tavern that sat in the center of Cloverdale. Through the windows, she saw dark clouds heavy with fresh snow.

Out of the corner of her eye, she caught a flash of movement too late to avoid colliding with a wall of muscle. The impact sent her staggering into a table, which she hit with her hip. She slipped in something wet on the floor and fell face-first across someone's lap. The biscuit, of course, flew out of her hand. It broke apart when it hit the floor, and the pieces slid under tables and feet.

"If you want to see me this badly, you could just come to my room." Harris's hand settled on her back, inviting her to stay.

Gripping his leg, she shoved herself up and rolled her eyes at the former bandit. His amused smile faltered, and she batted his hopeful hand away. That left her facing Teryk, the man she hit in the first place, looking down at her from his lofty six feet of height with an apology on his lips.

"I am in a hurry," she grumbled.

"Allow me." He ushered her to the door, cutting through the thick morning crowd.

"Thank you." With a curl of her lip for the weather, she ducked through the door when he opened it. The cold outside slapped her in the face. Five swift steps down the cobblestone walk, she slipped on a patch of ice and hit her bottom hard enough to make the tension in her neck and shoulders worse. Her apple went bouncing along the slippery path.

Growling at the world, she scrabbled to her feet and scooped the apple up. She ran the rest of the way to the stables, hitting the door rather than slowing down. Bouncing off, she spun into the tall wood building. It made her dizzy enough to need a moment to recover. Pressing a hand to her forehead, she took a deep breath and let it out as a groan. At this rate, she'd manage to kill herself by dusk.

She paced down the line of stalls, looking for an unclaimed horse that could handle carrying packs instead of people. The first stall, twice the size of the rest, belonged to Colby's massive horse, Karias. Today, she had no time for him, and breezed past, looking for an occupied stall with no tag. A tag, so she'd been told, meant the horse had an owner who wouldn't appreciate it being taken out by someone else.

The first horse she found without a tag seemed suitable until she stepped into its stall and it snapped at her hand. Rather than waste effort on such a bad-tempered creature, she moved on. Of course, for some reason, that beast had to be the only one available. Returning to it, she clenched her jaws, yanked the door open, and barged in. It bared its teeth at her, and she thumped her fist between its ears.

"You listen to me." She jabbed a finger at it. "I don't want to go either, but now we get to suffer together." Setting a hand on it, she cocked her head and listened to its uncomplicated, animal thoughts. Something had lodged in its hoof, small enough to go unnoticed, yet annoying enough to make it cranky. She stalked out to find the right tool for the job, recalling what her clansmen used to use for such a task. Whirling with the scraping tool in hand, she walked into a large white mass of muscle.

As his master had, Karias remained still while Chavali staggered from the impact. The horse stood tall and proud, his head held higher than she could reach, and blocked the hallway. Somehow, despite a lack of windows in the building, the huge beast had managed to position himself in a ray of sunshine so his white mane glowed. He stamped a hoof and snorted at her.

"I've been sent on a mission and am in a hurry. Let me pass."

He tossed his head and whickered then danced closer to her.

"Fine," she growled. She set her empty hand on his side. "What do you want?"

You've been avoiding Colby.

Her nostrils flared. "I've seen him three times in the last week."

You know what I mean. You promised to help him with his memories, with the things Pale did to him in Ket. All you've done is let him teach you to read, and he's too stoic to tell you he's been having nightmares.

"And I can do what about this right now, exactly?" She raised an eyebrow and wanted to cross her arms.

He glared at her. *Don't be a pain. Go, do whatever Eldrack wants. When you return, you see Colby and you keep your word.*

Her head hurt, her neck hurt, her shoulders hurt, her everything hurt. Snapping at this obnoxious spirit creature-horse-thing would only prolong the conversation, souring her mood further. She needed to deal with the other horse. Eliot and Sean undoubtedly already stood waiting for her at the tavern. Yanking her hand away, she waved it to shoo him to the side. "Yes, of course. He hasn't asked, and I haven't forced the matter. Now, you're making me late."

Karias bared his teeth and huffed at her, but he backed into his stall to let her pass. The whinny he sent chasing her down the hall sounded like a threat of some sort.

She smacked the gray horse on the rump then grabbed its hoof and dug out the offending rock chip. As thanks, it stuck its head into her cloak pocket and grabbed her apple. The first crunch made her turn from setting the tool aside. "I see. No, Chavali, you don't need to eat today. Just go walk several miles on an empty stomach."

It took her another few minutes to get the horse ready and convince it to move as fast as she wanted to go. This time, she paid more attention to her footing and reached the tavern door without further incident. Neither Eliot nor Sean waited outside, so she cracked the door open and peered inside. Both men stood at the bar and appeared to have been there long enough to be bored. She may have even missed them on her way through earlier.

Sean noticed her and nodded, so she yanked the door shut again and remembered she had a lump of cheese in her pocket. Eliot walked out buttoning his jacket, his fur gloves tucked under an arm. "It took you that long, and you didn't even eat yet?" He strode away, setting a hard pace.

She glared at his back. Sean saw it and smirked at her as he tugged his mittens on. Ignoring him, she hurried to follow Eliot. As they left the town square, the first fat snowflake of many landed on her nose.

Chapter 3

Walking past the farm where the remainder of her slaughtered clan lived with two former Fallen elders, Chavali sighed and scowled. They expected her later, and she wouldn't show up. The Seer took care of her clan. Along with the snow already crusting the outside of her cloak and gloves, she carried a load of guilt at leaving without even a word. It settled on her shoulders, making the tension already there worse.

Were Eliot in a better mood, she would ask to take just five minutes. Even one minute to tell Marcus or Penny and let them break the news gently to the three children would be a boon. He, however, needed to let his temper cool almost as much as she did. Walking in the snow on legs already complaining about all the stairs worked well enough for her. Too exhausted to bother with anger anymore, it took everything she had to keep up with him and Sean.

At the ground-eating pace Eliot set and kept even as the wind whipped up and drove the snow into their faces, it took them less than an hour to reach the nearest Creator's Tower. Surrounded by a forest protected by members of the Order of the Creator's Path, the black finger of glassy rock jutted some five hundred feet into the sky, tapering to a housing for a large blue crystal. Inside the wide archway at the base, Chavali knew a map was carved into the floor with levers to select which other Creator's Tower to be transported to.

Just inside the arch, two members of the Creator's Path stood guard. Cloaks and scarves covered their suits of metal plate armor. Their gauntlets gripped steel-tipped pikes, and they carried swords at their sides. The symbol of their order, a stylized Creator's Tower, had been painted on the center of their breastplates.

Stepping apart and out into the snow, they clearly noticed the trio approaching. Their armor and clothes bore no markings of rank or individuality, and full helms obscured their faces. Chavali could never tell the gender of any of these people, let alone recognize any of them.

Eliot raised a hand in greeting. "We're here to do the Courier Circuit." He pulled off a glove to show them his Fallen ring. Chavali and every other Fallen had an identical band that marked them as a particular type of agent of the Shappan Crown. She had taken to wearing hers on a golden chain around her neck along with a pendant from her first life.

"Already?" The speaker had a deep, gruff voice. "Shouldn't it be another four or five days? I thought you usually started on the full moon."

Glancing at Chavali, Eliot gave her a sour smirk. "Yes, usually."

Chavali had nothing to spare for any sort of reaction beyond gratitude for the break. She reached up to rub the crook of her neck and watched the guard shrug, making the metal of his armor clank and creak.

"Commander?" Sean perked up for the first time. "Is someone out sick? You aren't usually out here." He leaned into the conversation, and though she couldn't see his face, Chavali suspected he sucked up every detail with relish.

The guard pushed his visor up to reveal a long, serious face with a dark beard. "They're sending you out again already? But no, nothing major. Misha doesn't fit into her armor anymore, so she had to rotate to other duties until after the baby is born."

"Oh, is she doing well? I heard the father isn't very happy about her continuing to stay with the job overall or with her planning to come back after."

The Commander shrugged, clanking and creaking again. "I don't know anything about that. Tamry, get the packs."

The other guard's helm inclined in a muted nod. Tamry ducked inside while Eliot produced Eldrack's folder and handed it to the Commander. Deeper inside the Creator's Tower, a minor flash of blue light announced an arrival. They clanked and creaked, and another of the guards, helm tucked under his arm, walked out.

"Commander, a word?" The new guard had a baritone voice and an ordinary, forgettable face. Chavali could tell nothing else of interest about him.

The Commander nodded and both stepped outside, walking far enough for privacy. If she wasn't so exhausted, Chavali would wander in that direction to overhear whatever she might catch, out of nothing more than curiosity. In her current state, she leaned against the horse and closed her eyes, ignoring them.

She cracked an eye open when more clanking announced the end of their conference. The Commander returned to the Tower while the new man took the path leading away to the west.

"Is there a reason three of you are taking on this Circuit when it's usually one person?" The Commander's eyes flicked over them, in much the same way as Colby's military experience had him always scanning new people to assess them for threats.

"Oh, it's nothing. Chavali here—"

"Chavali?" Tamry, whose scratchy, alto voice marked her as female, returned with two large packs, interrupting Sean. "There's a package for a Chavali in Cloverdale. Can't be a common name, right?"

Chavali frowned, watching Tamry set one pack down and dig through it. She realized what it must be when the guard pulled out a dark pouch the size of her fist and offered it. Taking the pouch, Chavali swallowed a sigh. "Thank you."

"Oh, something for you! What is it?" Sean's reticence to address her had apparently evaporated.

"None of your business." Chavali flipped her cloak aside and stuffed the pouch inside her pack. Of course this came *today*, when she couldn't use it. She'd placed the order four days ago after asking Penny and Marcus to officially join her clan and spending an hour explaining what that meant. They'd agreed, and she'd spent the following three hours checking everywhere in Cloverdale and the Tower to find the herbs and other plants she needed for the ritual. No one had the most important ones, so she'd ordered them through the bartender in the tavern.

Here she had everything she needed to perform the ritual, and it would have to wait. No doubt, the weather over the town would clear later today to such a degree that it would be a perfect night for a bonfire, making the timing of this wretched mission all the more infuriating. She scowled at the ground, ignoring the other people around her.

"You're really far too touchy, Chavali," Sean said. "It's just a question."

Eliot cleared his throat and hefted the packs, strapping both onto the horse. "I think we're not going to have this discussion here. Thank you, Commander. Tamry. We'll see you again at the end."

Chavali looked up when she heard the Commander's faceplate clang down. He and Tamry returned to the protection of the Creator's Tower, and Eliot led her and Sean to the path heading east. Like the one that brought them here from Cloverdale, this narrow "road" had been plowed by a horse and trampled by feet. It hadn't been widened as much, suggesting less traffic.

The pace Eliot set now made Chavali have to pant to keep up. She wanted to whine and ask how much farther they had to go or even to ask for more details of what this mission involved, yet feared to rekindle his ire. Instead, she jogged along behind him, noticing neither man had to make such an effort, nor did they seem to be winded. It made her wonder if either used magic of some kind to hasten his steps. The wretched horse seemed to be enjoying it.

An eternity later, her breaths ragged and wheezing, everything aching and spent, she tripped over nothing and sprawled face first in the fresh, heavy snow. Rolling to her side, she coughed out the already melted snow in her mouth. "Eliot." Her voice came out ragged and rough.

To her great relief, he stopped and turned. "Yes?"

"You have made your point, I think." To her great annoyance, the horse stopped and whuffed at her face.

"What point is that?" he asked far too innocently, far too sweetly.

29

She lacked the energy to glare at him. "That I still need training and such things. This is too much for me today. I cannot keep going so fast. I can walk, I think, but no more of this."

Sean watched with enough interest to make her wish she had the strength to kick him in the shin. "I could carry you."

"Shut up."

Eliot's mouth twitched with a grin he only half suppressed. Returning to her side, he crouched and offered his gloved hand to help her up, just as he always did after a sparring session. "That wasn't really the point I was aiming for, but close enough. The village isn't much farther, and we can slow down. You should've spoken up before you face-planted, though."

Gripping his forearm, she groaned and let him help her sit up. "The last time I 'spoke up,' you declared I needed to go faster as we ran up the stairs because I obviously was not yet fit enough to go so slow."

He laughed. "Yes, I did. Come on, we'll stroll the rest of the way. It's maybe two more miles."

"Why do I suspect that 'maybe' means I should expect it to be closer to five?" His merriment eased her own mood, and she smirked at him.

"Because you know me well."

"Aw, you guys are cute together." Sean watched with a bemused smile.

"Don't go there." Eliot rolled his eyes and shook his head, pulling Chavali to her feet.

"Stay far, far away from there," Chavali agreed.

"Is it a crime to be interested in other people? No, of course not.

Harmless." With a light shrug, Sean turned and resumed walking.

"Ignore him, Chavali. It's the best option. I promise." Eliot let her hold onto his arm until she felt steady and took a few steps. He also did her the favor of taking the horse's reins.

She nodded too tired to care. "How do I ignore someone I must work with? I tried with Colby. It did not work." She snorted. "I tried with you. It *really* did not work."

"He's Fallen. When it comes to a crisis, you should know you can always count on another Fallen to back you up and lend a hand."

"Bah. If I only cared about crises, my clan would have been a much worse place to live." She rubbed her face, bits of snow stinging in several places. "And I would miss them less."

"So, the meddler meddles with a purpose." He grinned and let her set the pace as they walked side by side up the narrow trail.

She snorted. "Of course I do. What kind of idiot meddles for no reason?" Sean came to mind, and she jutted her chin at him. "Do you know him well?"

"I know him some...and his reputation." When she raised her brow to request more information, he continued. "He's a chatterbox. Likes to read the archives. There are a few people in the Tower who delight in spreading information, and he's one of them. None of them are mean-spirited about it. They just like to talk."

"I take it you have never been on the receiving end of this 'harmless' talk?"

"Sure I have. When you put that many people together and give them lots of free time, it's inevitable. Sometimes, I think Eldrack comes up with unnecessary missions just to keep us busy. Sure, most I've been on were important, but a few have left me scratching my head. He's got to be making stuff up part of the time. Can you imagine having to manage a hundred and fifty people, all worthy of being raised from the dead as Fallen? Not to mention all the Healers and servants. It must be a nightmare."

Chavali had considered some of this before, though not in such terms. She did have to admit that fighting with Sean had been, at best, ludicrous. Nothing positive had been accomplished, especially the second time. That first time, she could claim that Eliot's training had sent her following through after that initial slap. The second time, though, she went looking for him, on purpose, to cause trouble. Like a bratty child.

"I am sorry to have dragged you into this."

Eliot shrugged and watched the path, dodging an overgrown shrub with all the grace she already knew he had. "You're a prickly pain in the ass. It was bound to happen eventually with someone."

Since she could tell he meant nothing by it, she stuck her tongue out at him. "You are wrong. I am difficult. Everyone knows this, or they should."

He chuckled. "Yes, well, whatever word you want to use, I'm not actually the one you should apologize to."

Her lip curled. "A punishment beyond anything you would usually devise."

"At least say something about letting your temper get the better of you. You can word it as a warning instead of apology. That should appeal to you."

At last, she found the energy to laugh.

Chapter 4

The village ahead reminded Chavali of a thousand other places she'd been before. It had few enough people that her clan wouldn't bother to set up their carnival, but they might stop for trade. Passing up such places often meant missing out on provisions they wouldn't otherwise come across. She remembered picking up herb plants in villages this size, for the wagon rooftop gardens they kept.

Trennis consisted of a collection of small homes clustered together around a well and surrounded by trees. These people probably subsisted on small gardens and hunting forays. Chavali often wondered why anyone would decide to settle in this kind of situation. Some wanted to escape the bustle of larger towns and cities, and that made sense to her. But why here? Perhaps when the ground had no snow cover, it sparkled in some sense. To these people, anyway, or to their ancestors who settled it.

Sean reached the town well before them, and they found him inside the tavern. He sat in the center of a handful of elder locals, all of whom turned to look when Chavali and Eliot entered. It seemed clear he'd already ingratiated himself with these people from how they all leaned towards him and returned their attention to him quickly.

"Is the mayor available?" Eliot set the one pack he'd removed from the horse on the bar.

"That's me." One man straightened, joints creaking, and hobbled behind the polished maple bar, gripping the edge and leaning against it for support. While Eliot pulled packages and letters out, the mayor rooted around under the bar. "Here, son. Not much to go out so soon after Sean's last visit, but there never really is. I suppose that's good for your back, eh?"

"Yes, it is." Eliot grinned and passed over two wrapped paper packages and four envelopes, taking three envelopes in return. "Can we trouble you for some lunch? Whatever you can spare."

"Sure, sure. Poke your head into the kitchen and get Marya to make you up a bite." He peered at Chavali. "What're you here for, then?"

Surprised to be asked, Chavali blinked. "I'm here with them."

"Three people for courier? Huh." His eyes bounced from Eliot to Sean and back to her, then he gave her a knowing smile. "I see. Clever girl." He winked and hobbled to his chair.

Chavali had no idea what to make of his words. "I'll go see about the food." Since Eliot didn't object, she wandered away and found a small kitchen in the back. The plump woman working there pushed bread and cheese into her arms while chattering about people Chavali would never meet about their uninteresting romantic escapades. The cook swept Chavali along in her wake to return to the bar with glasses and a pitcher full of warm cider.

"...interested in how contained populations manage the problems

34

of inbreeding that can produce such tragic deformities. Tila, for example, has a village with the practice of sending their young women out to find husbands and bring them home. Their biggest problem seems to be the tendency of young men to follow young women without truly considering the permanence of the situation."

In the titter of laughter that followed Sean's statement, Chavali set her burdens on the bar and sat beside Eliot. She started with the bread, finding it plain compared to the usual fare available at home.

"And Chavali's clan is even more intriguing." Sean pointed to her, and she froze with a piece of bread halfway to her mouth. "They use a mystical connection to each other, made through some kind of pact with magical goats."

"What?" Bewildered by this interpretation of her clan, Chavali stared at him in disbelief.

"Is that not how it works?" Sean gave her a pleasant, inviting smile. "Maybe you could explain it for us."

She glared daggers at him. "No, I won't discuss this here, now, with you."

"We could take the conversation outside."

Eliot nudged her thigh and flashed a warning glance at her. She took a deep breath to calm her temper. "Or not have it at all."

"I'd like to hear about magical goats." The mayor's grin spread wide across his face. "Do your men use them as replacements when your women get surly?"

"I think we should get going." Eliot slid off his stool and flipped a silver coin onto the bar. "Thank you for the hospitality." He grabbed the pack and gave the room a strained smile before walking out.

Jaws clenched shut, Chavali hopped down and followed him, carrying the food again.

Behind her, Sean sighed as he stepped outside and pulled his cloak close. "This is what happens when you leave people to come up with their own explanations. It would be simpler if you just explain, Chavali."

She growled in her throat. "It's none of your business! How many times must I say that? This is a subject I won't discuss. You have no right to poke and prod into this. I am a person and a fellow agent, not an interesting thing to poke and prod!"

With a roll of his eyes, Eliot strapped the pack onto the horse again and pulled the reins off the branch they'd been lashed to. Handing the reins to Chavali, he turned and set a more sedate pace for the rest of the day's walk.

"But you can't just leave it at that," Sean whined. "Imagine how this knowledge could help us stop crossbreeding! We could prevent halfbreed births. It could bring the Creator back, then we'd be free, and there would be no more of this. Depending upon what it is, you could possibly even help solve infertility problems. Did you know that some people who have difficulty conceiving turn to elves *on purpose* for breeding? The practice is entirely barbaric, and you could help stop it."

"Stop." She shoved a chunk of bread at his face. With Eliot here and glancing at her, she kept a grip on her anger. "First, I don't care. Second, *I do not care.* This doesn't affect me, and the truth of the subject won't help anyone else. It's not...transferable. Leave it alone and look elsewhere. There are no answers for you within the secrets of my clan. To anything."

"I know you think the greatest sin is about stagnation, or something like that." He waved to dismiss this as foolish. "But what if you're wrong? I can admit that I might be wrong about the halfbreeds, but until we manage to succeed at eliminating them, we'll never know for sure."

"It's so refreshing to find someone who knows me so well." She gave Sean yet another glare, despite the previous ones having had no effect. "You're an idiot."

Sean sighed. "Just tell me the idea of it. Please? Only the broad strokes. Never mind the specifics."

Baring her teeth at him, she still managed to sneer. "Magic."

"I knew it!" He pumped his fists in victory. If only the subject had nothing to do with her, she might find his antics amusing.

"Don't be stupid. Of course this is magic."

"Am I going to have to listen to this sort of thing for the next few days?" Eliot turned around to walk backwards, one side of his mouth twitched in bemusement. "Because if I am, I can find a way to plug up my ears."

Chavali snorted. "Find this for me too. It would make this much more pleasant a journey. How far to the next village?"

"Shelton is a few hours' walk. We should be there by dinner. There's no inn at any of these villages, so we've got to take whatever space they offer for us to sleep."

Still walking beside her, Sean sighed. "Fine, fine. I can see you don't want to talk about that."

Chavali raised an eyebrow. "It's a miracle," she told Eliot. "He noticed."

"How about your prophecy powers? It's remarkable how precisely the predictions came true in Ket. How does it happen? Can you produce one now?"

"Eliot, what happens if I kill him?"

"Well, first, we'll have to stop you, which would add to your existing aches and the bruise I think you're going to have on your hip from the way you've been favoring it since you fell earlier. Then, if you manage to succeed anyway, it would probably trigger the Wasting we're all informed we can acquire when we pledge our souls to the Fallen for five years."

"Your arguments are persuasive. May I hit him in the face to make him stop instead?"

Sean sighed melodramatically. "This is why no one likes you, Chavali. You're so mean-spirited."

"I don't care if people like me or not," she grumbled. She had her clan, after all. People cared about her.

Eliot chuckled. "I never would have guessed that. But don't worry, Chavali, I like you. You're the most interesting sane person I know."

"Thank you."

"You two really are good together. Have you considered—"

"No." Chavali and Eliot spoke at the same time, both emphatic.

"Friends do make for a good pairing."

Chavali rolled her eyes. "How did you die, Sean? Did someone strangle you for asking too many personal questions?"

He stuck his tongue out at her. "No. I was wrongfully executed for stealing from a Tilan noble."

"Wrongfully." Chavali snorted. "As in you didn't steal it, or as in you don't think it was a fair sentence?"

With a sly smirk, he said, "I didn't steal it. The thing I stole was something else entirely, and they probably haven't even noticed the fake I put in its place yet, five years later. I was executed for someone else's idiotic blunder, which is horribly unfair. Especially for the fact I have to bear the indignity of having my name slandered with a crime far beneath my skills."

Eliot barked out a laugh, and Chavali found herself snickering.

"Ah ha! The lady isn't all slapping and snarling." Sean grinned and poked Chavali in the arm. "It's your turn now, though. How did you die?"

Chavali's amusement disappeared, replaced by the empty spaces in her heart she usually could ignore. "My clan was attacked and slaughtered so a man could take possession of me for my prophecy gift. I killed myself to prevent it." The words became a bit easier to say every time she repeated them.

Sean stopped and put a hand on her shoulder, giving her that awful sympathy she hated to see. "Oh, I'm so sorry. I had no idea. I thought— And you haven't been with us long, so it's still fresh. I am really, truly, so very sorry, Chavali. I never would have pestered if I'd known they were all dead."

"That's not in the archives?" Not wanting to deal with his apology right now, she shifted her attention to Eliot.

"Ah, yes, it is," Eliot nodded, "but they generally keep any information surrounding the death circumstances of active agents restricted, at least until we're done with our term of service or get killed a second time. It's done out of politeness, so far as I understand."

"Oh. I see. How interesting." She gave Sean a sidelong glance and saw he still had his apologetic sympathy face. The urge to strangle him still gripped her. "I accept your apology." She saw Eliot's mouth twitch. "It's possible I may still need to work on holding my temper in check."

Sean smiled and patted her shoulder. "We're going to be friends. I can feel it."

"Delightful."

Chapter 5

Shelton had nothing more of interest than Trennis. A group of hunters formed the core of it, and the place had no tavern or other communal building. The three Fallen split up for the night, each sleeping on a couch in a different cottage. Chavali found this to her liking, as the woman running the house she stayed in offered a delicious soup with expertly made biscuits for dinner. It also kept her from having to listen to Sean.

The next day, aching from exercise beyond her usual routines, Chavali limped down the path. Eliot forced her to keep to a faster pace than she found comfortable and chose to lunge in attack at random moments as a replacement for their usual sparring practice. They passed through another tiny village, then stayed the night in yet another one. At each stop, Eliot traded packages and letters with someone.

On the fourth day, under assault by Sean's incessant chatter about the birds he'd observed in his three years as a Fallen agent so far, Chavali rolled her eyes for the five hundredth time today and found herself staring at a gruesome sight. She sucked in a breath and grabbed

Eliot's shoulder, pointing at a dead body hanging from a rope tied to a tree branch. With the continued cold, it gave off no stench and had minimal damage from insects and wildlife.

"Sean, stop." Eliot directed the other man with a nod of his head.

"Oh, my." Sean stepped into the underbrush and approached the corpse. "Is that Jack?" He closed the distance and stared up. "Creator bless, it is. Why would they hang Jack?"

"Who's Jack?" Chavali asked. "Should we cut him down?"

"Jack is—" Sean sighed. "Well, *was*, I guess, what passes for a sheriff in Eagle Falls. He kept law and order. Good man, as far as I know. I can't imagine what he might have done to deserve this."

Chavali grimaced in distaste. "Yes, we should cut him down. Bodies should not be displayed this way. It's disgusting. If it cannot be properly burned or buried, at least let it touch the earth."

Eliot climbed a nearby tree and slashed the rope with his knife. The corpse dropped to the ground with a crunch, frozen and blue.

"How long do you think he's been dead?" Crouching beside the body, Sean turned Jack's head. His thick, purple tongue hung out.

Eliot scuffed a boot in the snow, frowning down at the ground. "There's no way to know for sure." He bent and batted at small lumps of snow. "There are some signs of people here, but they're indistinct. It must have happened before the storm ended. That would be at least three days ago. I'm sure the people of Eagle Falls will know."

Chavali turned away from the sight, uninterested in examining him closely. "Was he well-liked?"

"Respected, I'd say." Sean sighed and she heard crunching as he prodded the corpse. "These look like bruises to me, and this definitely happened before he was strung up."

Compelled to look and see what he referred to, Chavali forced herself to focus on Sean's hand. Her gaze skipped to what he pointed at, and she furrowed her brow, unable to decipher the ragged wound on the man's leg. "What could have done that?"

Eliot stooped and poked his knife into the wound, wedging apart the purplish slabs of frozen meat. "A large dog, maybe, or some predator about the same size. I agree it happened before he died. He was also beaten, so this is probably the work of a lynch mob situation. It's not really our job to investigate this. Whether we like it or not, they have the authority to execute people for committing crimes."

Chavali elected to regard a tree instead of the grotesque body. "If it was a lynch mob, these people will be on edge, even a few days later."

"Yes, they probably won't be precisely chatty." Sean grabbed the corpse by the arm and dragged it farther from the road.

"And keep in mind that some kind of crime had to have caused this. Probably something very serious. There could be another body." Eliot sheathed his knife and gave Chavali a hand to return to the path. "I haven't mentioned it before because it didn't seem to matter, but we also do this route to keep tabs on these villages. They're near to our tower, so it's important to make sure they aren't stark raving mad or sheltering lunatics out to get us. That sort of thing."

"I see. So, it does matter to us why he was executed, but not because we need to second-guess the judgment."

"Yes."

Sean rejoined them with a grim nod. "There's an agent living here, a researcher. We should speak with her first." With his gesture at the path and no disagreement from Chavali or Eliot, they continued on their way. Jack had been hung a mile from the outer edge of the village, where a ring of cleared land covered by a nearly flat blanket of snow suggested farming fields. Less than forty buildings huddled together in the center.

"Ramelia's house is there. Oh. Hm." The windows of the house he pointed to looked strange. As they approached, it became clear the house had been boarded up. "That's unexpected."

Chavali flicked her eyes over the scene, confused and concerned. She noted deep scratches in the wood of the frames and could tell the boards had been applied recently. "Should we break in or continue on?"

"Continue on," Eliot said. "No reason to break in. Yet."

As they walked, Chavali noticed smoke coming from most of the chimneys, and no one out and about. This matched what she expected, given the snow still on the ground; most people in these northern climes had indoor pursuits to keep them busy until spring. She suspected the folk here had plenty of reasons to be subdued besides the weather.

This place had no indoor tavern, only an old stump in a clearing to be stood on and shouted from. The closest building, one with a large bell hanging from the side, had a shingle out, proclaiming it to have sewing thread, hammers, and wedges of cheese. Sean chose this place, opening the door and leading them inside. Shelves and tables filled with neat rows of various supplies—including those promised on the sign— lined the walls and formed an island in the center of the shop.

"We're here for the Courier Circuit," Sean said with a pleasant smile.

The gentleman behind the counter, a balding, middle-aged man, mustered up a strained smile in response. "I'm afraid we don't have anything right now. You could have just passed us by."

Eliot pulled off his pack, now much smaller and lighter, and retrieved a single letter, offering it to him. "We could have, but then we'd have to come back later to drop this off."

"Where's Ramelia? She promised me a cup of tea the last time I was here," Sean said.

Chavali pretended to peruse the wares while watching the shopkeeper. She did have some small amount of curiosity about what sorts of items people bought in a place like this, but not enough to take her interest away from whatever had happened here.

"Oh." The older man's face fell. "It was terrible, terrible. I'm so sorry to be the one to have to tell you. She's dead. It happened a few days ago."

Sean seemed to be genuinely upset to learn this as he covered his mouth and blinked. "Creator watch over her. What happened?"

The man's eyes darted around. "I wasn't there."

Chavali raised her brow at his blatant lie. "But you're the most important person in town, of course, so you've heard things."

"Well, sure." He toyed with the letter, running his fingers along the edge. "It's not that big a place. Everybody hears a little bit about everything."

"How did Jack kill her?" The leap seemed obvious to her. Eliot and Sean each gave her a quizzical look, suggesting they hadn't made it yet.

The man shrugged his shoulders, rolling them in discomfort. "If you really want to know, you should go talk to Kember. She'll be at home, third house up that way, the one with the green door and rosebushes."

"Thank you." Sensing his reticence to say more, Chavali left the store and gathered the horse's reins. "Curious."

Eliot shut the door behind them. "Agreed."

"Kember is what passes for a mayor here. We could go see her, or we could talk to Lilly instead." Sean shrugged. "I've met her, and she's a friendly sort. Likes physical activity—running, climbing, that sort of thing. Her son is cute as a button."

"With an agent dead, this is officially our problem." Eliot sighed and looked up at the streaks of white marring the late afternoon sky. "Which means we need to find a place to stay here tonight and go home tomorrow whether we know what happened or not. But we can't say that. Chavali, quick: reasonable lie."

"Sean considered Ramelia a friend and is too stricken by her death to continue on today without being able to properly mourn. If he can, he wishes to see the inside of her house, because he left a personal possession with her on his last visit that she thought might relate to her research." She gestured with her palms up, asking without words if this suited the situation.

Eliot smirked. "Knew I could count on you."

"You just thought that up? On the spot?" Sean blinked at her in surprise.

"Yes. I was a fortune teller before my death."

"Really? That's fascinating." His mouth curled into a bemused grin. "Can I ask you about that profession?"

"Some other time, perhaps. Let us meet with this Lilly. It shouldn't be suspicious, because Sean knows her, and this is, presumably, not a secret."

"No, not a secret at all. I actually met her through Ramelia. They weren't exactly friends, but both of them knew Jack well." Sean's face fell into a frown. "As I recall, Ramelia considered Jack a friend. It's a shame something happened to make him want to kill her."

"If there is anything I have learned, both as Fallen and before, it's that the first impression of a situation is rarely as interesting as the truth." Chavali gestured for him to go, which he did. They followed channels of packed snow between the houses, a testament to the fact the populace did move about despite the weather. Her clan preferred to do their hard work in the morning and settle in time to make dinner. These villagers probably felt the same way.

Sean took them to a house no different from its neighbors, save for the snow-cleared wood bench in front of it with a row of empty clay pots. He walked up to the door and knocked. Intrigued by the pots, Chavali peered over the two-foot snowbank flanking the narrow walk. Each pot had a word painted on it in some dark color, and she squinted, trying to puzzle out what it all said. The letters swooped and whorled, unlike the straight, blocky ones Colby had been using to teach her. Shadows obscuring parts of them didn't help.

The man who answered the door wore a thick, knitted sweater and dark pants with fat, fluffy slippers. Squinting at Sean, he snapped his fingers, trying to remember his name. "I know you."

Offering his hand to shake, Sean sighed. "Hello, Andrew. It's Sean, I'm a friend of Lilly's. Really more of Ramelia's, actually. Is your wife in? I've just learned about—the news. I was hoping that she would help me understand. It sounds like a mess, and no one is around to talk about it."

Andrew gave Sean an unhappy look that he extended to Eliot, but not Chavali. "It's cold out there," he said with a sigh. "Come on in."

Chavali led the horse into the yard and tied its reins to the bench.

"I'm sorry for the imposition." Sean stepped inside, with Eliot and Chavali following. The small house had clutter everywhere, a mess reminiscent of Chavali's room back at the tower. The probable cause streaked past: a naked child shrieking with delight from one room to the next.

"We're having a rough day today." Andrew shut the door and sighed, rubbing his eyes with a finger and thumb.

A woman stopped in the doorway and leaned against it, every fiber of her being exhausted and ready to give up. Her short, dark hair stuck out at odd angles and food stained her ordinary linen clothes. "Sean? What are you doing here?"

"We're running the Courier Circuit. This is Eliot and Chavali." Sean offered her a hand, helping her step over the debris covering the floor.

Chavali noticed Andrew giving Sean a dirty look, and took his arm. A husband rarely glared at every man stopping by to see his wife unless he had a reason to, or *thought* he had a reason to. That kind of tension now, after the death of two people, struck her as interesting. Did Lilly have an affair with Jack?

"You must have seen—the house, they boarded it up already." Lilly sank into a battered, old couch with Sean. For a moment, she leaned on him for support, then her eyes flicked to her husband and she stiffened away from him. Chavali watched her face shift from exhaustion, through grief, to a muted kind of despair.

"Yes, we saw and heard about both Jack and Ramelia. I was hoping you could explain what happened, because I hate to bother people I don't really know." Sean reacted to her signals and offered comfort only through the warmth in his voice.

Lilly sighed and looked to Andrew, who huffed and left the room. "It happened three nights ago, right before that last storm. There were screams and howls. It was awful. Everyone heard it and rushed out." Lilly covered her face, which Chavali found interesting. "She'd been thrown through the window, and a monster crouched over her. Someone hit it in the head with a rock, distracting it long enough for someone else to run up and crack a thick branch across the back of its neck. When it fell to the ground beside her, unconscious, it...*changed*." Looking up, she strained to hold tears in check. "It was Jack."

Sean sucked in a shocked breath. Eliot rubbed his chin thoughtfully. Chavali knew a liar when she saw one. None of the emotions rang false, though. This woman had an attachment to Jack of some sort and tried to keep that hidden. Her husband wasn't fooled, and neither was Chavali. Beyond that, she couldn't tell for certain how inaccurate the depiction was, nor could she pluck the truth from any of it.

Now sitting on the floor and with her gloves off, she considered offering the woman some words of sympathy. It might provoke her into revealing more truth. On the other hand, she had no need to stir this household's pot. If Lilly wanted to pretend she only cared as much as an acquaintance or friend, Chavali had no compelling reason to contest it. "It seems strange that a man with so much trust and respect here could hide a secret of this magnitude for what must have been a relatively long time."

"He was private." Lilly pushed her bangs back in what appeared to be a nervous gesture. "No wife or children, and he didn't have an eye for anyone that I know of."

In the face of this bald-faced lie, given away so subtly she barely caught it, Chavali chose her words carefully, selecting the right amount of vagueness to hopefully pluck out some unexpected detail. "What about Ramelia?"

Lilly's face closed down, and she took a deep breath. "If he was seeing her, they didn't advertise it."

"I did think she had someone special," Sean offered, "though I couldn't say who."

"No? I suppose with a little one, you have no time to watch your neighbors and notice who mourns most deeply." Chavali turned to see Lilly's son poking his head into the room with a cheerful smile on his face, the kind that spoke of a young boy who'd just done something he knew he both shouldn't have and wouldn't be punished severely for. With his large, dark eyes and unruly mop of dark hair, he reminded her of Danel.

"Ah, this is that little one, yes? Come, don't fear us. Your mother is sad, and we have come to cheer her." She beckoned to the boy, and he looked to his mother, who nodded.

With her permission given, he stepped out, now covered from neck to toes in fleece. The house needed to be heated more, she thought, and wondered if Lilly had been letting the hearth fire fail. In her experience, women in these small places often took the responsibility of cooking and keeping the fire banked while the men tended to hunting and other physical labors. Only in the larger towns and cities, where magic or conveniences could handle the simpler chores, were duties split in other ways.

"I have a child, a boy, and he's the same size as you." Chavali could call him her son, but that felt wrong to say, even to a stranger. Most things she had no difficulty lying about, yet an unequivocal confirmation of motherhood bothered her. "He also likes to run around without clothes on." She smirked at him and held out her hand. "His name is Danel. What is yours?"

The boy smiled wider, now delighted, and ran to her, grabbing her hand and flinging himself into her lap. His thoughts showed her nothing unexpected. He wanted his mother to be happy, the way she was before, and he didn't know what had happened to make her sad. If she could fix it all, he would be happy too.

"I'm Joey. You sound funny when you talk."

"Joey." Lilly used his name as a warning.

"It's fine. I've been told this before. My family lived in a wagon instead of in a house. We rolled from place to place, always moving. After doing so for long enough, we picked up pieces of how people speak in every country and region, and all of it is mushed together in how I talk." This, so far as she knew, was true. The phenomenon merely had happened many decades ago, well before her grandparents had been born. "My accent is unusual for being familiar and strange at the same time. I say some things exactly the same as you, yet everything else is quite different. It's confusing to your ears."

"That's fascinating," Sean breathed.

She ignored him. "We have customs for these beads too." Leaning forward, she let her hair fall in front of Joey's face, the three beads clicking together where he could see them. "You see this?" She pointed to a tiny, finely carved rune in the bottom bead. "Its meaning is a secret," she whispered, well aware Sean would pester her to learn what she told him later.

"Really?" To her delight, he also whispered. "What kind of secret?"

"It holds a key to the soul of another. When I was about your age, my grandmother gave it to me. She said that it belonged to her grandmother, and to her grandmother before her. It was made a very long time ago. Touch it and see how smooth the edges are. Many have touched it before you, and many more will touch it after you. By letting you do this, I give you an honored place in my clan's history, as a boy allowed to brush against our story."

Eyes wide and round with wonder, his small hand reached up and took the bead in his thin fingers. "What happens if you lose it?"

"Then I lose a piece of my clan. My ancestor will wither to nothing in my memories. Because of this bead, I know her story. Guard this knowledge, Joey, for it could cripple my clan to lose something so precious."

He looked at her, solemn and earnest. "I promise I won't tell anyone except Mama. I don't keep secrets from my mama."

"As well you shouldn't. Keeping secrets from your mamá is a bad thing. She is your anchor and foundation, and never forget that." Chavali wished she still had her own mother to speak to from time to time. Right now did not happen to be one of those times, because that insufferable woman would see Chavali with a child on her lap and natter on about how precious the scene was, and how much she knew Chavali ought to delight in becoming a mother.

The thought of carrying her own children made her want to shudder. For the benefit of the boy, she clenched that urge down. The joy of entertaining someone else's offspring gave her as much as she needed. At least, she told herself that. To have one of her own, she would have to bear it herself, and that would mean sex with someone's noxious, needy, selfish thoughts pressing on her. Then would come the horror of having a child in her womb and learning when, exactly, it became capable of thought. She had no interest in discovering whether that would drive her mad or not. It probably would.

Joey nodded and gave his mother a smile bright enough to bring sunshine on a dismal day. "Mama, can they stay tonight? I want to hear more stories."

Eliot cleared his throat. "We do actually need a place to stay for the night. It's too late to return before nightfall, which is a lousy time to be traveling when it's this cold. But we don't want to cause a problem. We can split up—"

"No, it's fine." Lilly seemed cheered for having someone else to take care of Joey for a short while. "So long as you don't mind sleeping on the floor, we won't turn you out to find someone else who can spare the space."

Joey clapped and grabbed Chavali to hug her. Eliot dug into a pouch at his waist. "I know this is short notice, so let me help with the expenses. Sean here eats a lot."

"That's not necessary." Lilly held up a hand to refuse the coins he pulled out.

"No, of course not. I still insist. We're a strain on your resources." He set the coins on the nearest side table. "If it was only one of us staying here, I wouldn't make the offer, because I know it would be rude."

Lilly sighed and gave him a sad smile. "Very well."

With Joey in her lap, Chavali chose not to ask further questions about Jack or his death. This mother, she thought, needed time to herself, or perhaps with her husband. Since she'd offered that to the women of her clan often enough, she had no compunctions about offering it here. "Go and do whatever you wish," she told Lilly. "I have plenty of stories."

Sean squeezed Lilly's shoulder as the woman stood and walked out of the room. "Your mother will be fine," he said to Joey as soon as she disappeared from sight.

"Tell me, what is your favorite animal?" Expecting to be sitting here for a while, Chavali shifted enough to be comfortable. Eliot handed her a cushion.

The boy thought for several seconds. "I like all kinds, but wolves are my favorite. Or maybe kittens. No, wolves. They're big and furry, and I saw one out my window once in the light of the full moon. It looked like a protector of the woods."

"Very well. Then I will tell you a story about wolves."

Chapter 6

Joey's appetite for new stories parched Chavali's throat until dinner, then after. He fell asleep in her arms. Never did she have the time to allow this to happen with Danel or Haizea, or even Biholtz. Her own clan couldn't have this much of her, yet she offered it to a stranger for no reason. The first day she could, she would give them all she had for as much of a day as she could manage. Training and learning to read were both important. Clan was important too.

She carried the boy to his bed with Lilly's help and backed out of the room. On their way down the short hall, Lilly stopped her and put a hand on her arm.

"Thank you so much," she murmured. "You didn't have to do that."

Chavali glanced at the door. "He reminds me of other times and places."

"He's the most precious thing I have."

She put her hand on top of Lilly's. "You need to care for yourself or he will devour you. I've seen this." The other woman's thoughts danced from moment to moment with Joey in her past. Chavali recognized Jack in them, and Lilly's fondness for the man came through loud and clear. She lingered on a recent, cherished memory, of Jack tousling the boy's hair and telling him to go play. "Did Jack help with that sometimes?"

Lilly pulled her hand away and sighed, nodding. "He was good with children. I considered him a dear friend." She held something back, and Chavali suspected an affair. It would be an old story, that one: the rightful father of a child hangs around, pretending to be an uncle for the benefit of the mother's reputation or marriage, or whatever else they might feel required it.

"Do you think he killed Ramelia?"

In the dim light, Chavali thought she saw Lilly's expression harden. "I don't know. The man I knew wouldn't do such a thing, but you never really know what's in someone's heart, do you?"

Given such a lie, Chavali wanted to know more. She caught Lilly's hand, squeezing it in an effort to appear to be offering comfort. "No, I suppose not."

They'll get the bastard. Before any more have to die. She squirmed her hand free again and used it to point at a cupboard door. "You can find extra blankets there. I'm sorry I can't offer more than that. Good night."

Chavali let her go without further delay, returning the well wishes. After pulling three thin blankets from the cupboard, she returned to the family room and stretched. Eliot stood and helped her reach higher and farther than she otherwise would. As always with his touch, he thought only about his concern that she could accidentally hurt herself by doing it wrong or not doing it at all.

"You two really are a startlingly good pair." Sean watched them with the stupid, dreamy gaze of a busybody matchmaker.

"I'm a trainer." Eliot waved him off with a roll of his eyes. "She's my pupil. Since we're going to spar tomorrow, I want her to be in good form for it."

This came as news to Chavali, but she put her effort into reaching where he wanted her to. Sean could say or do or think whatever he wanted, so long as he didn't go spreading some noxious rumor of a relationship in the tower.

"Of course." Sean gave them both a wry smirk. "Chavali, can I ask you to talk about your accent some more?"

She took a deep breath and straightened from the last stretch. The room still had a great deal of mess, and it didn't seem reasonable to ask Lilly or Andrew to come clean it all up for them. Crouching to the floor, she picked up toys to arrange them in a tidy pile. With her example, both men also bent to the task.

"It is as I said. My ancestors traveled just as the clan did during my life with them. At some point, they decided to be different on purpose and took to changing the sounds a bit more. By the time I was born, we sounded foreign everywhere. It marked us as different, exotic. Since our livelihood depended upon that, no effort was ever made to change it again."

"Really." Sean deposited a handful of wooden blocks into a bin, holding it out to take hers. "Did you develop your own words for things to keep secrets from outsiders?"

"My clan has our own language. Before you ask, no, I will not teach it to you. Should the clan ever fully die, our language will die with it, and that is the way I prefer it to be."

He stopped and stared at her. "But how will anyone read your histories?"

"There are no histories to read. None of it is written. We did not learn to write in Shappan, nor did we use lettering for our tongue."

"No...writings?" He gasped hard enough to be melodramatic and gaped at her. "Then how do you know the stories? You're awfully young to have memorized every tale your clan had to offer."

Chavali frowned and shook her head. "I do not wish to discuss the subject."

"Can I ask a question?" Eliot arranged the wood pieces of a chess set on their board. "When we visited, I got the impression you had people leave the clan infrequently and didn't keep track of them. Was that true?"

Dropping blocks into the bin, Chavali took a deep breath. "I'm sure it seems ridiculous to you both, but although my clan numbers only four now, I am still inclined to keep its secrets close. This is my duty. I am the Seer of the Blaukenev clan, which means a great deal more than it appears. This feather is grafted into my skull for a reason. It is a reminder and a connection, a visible mark of my status and my promises. Those promises were not made to the elders, to my predecessor, or to my parents and siblings. They were made to my clan. So long as I have clan, which I will until the day I die, I will hold the secrets close."

Sean smiled at her. "I understand. I do think that's a little ridiculous, but I have to respect your customs and sense of duty. Whatever you feel you *can* talk about, though, I'd be delighted to listen. If for no other reason than because you're obviously good at telling stories." He winked at her.

"Thank you." At least now he'd stop pestering. She still needed to deal with whatever preposterous notions the rest of the Fallen had come up with about her, but that had little to do with this.

Eliot grinned. "I'm glad this moment didn't take a third fistfight. Let's get some sleep. We have work to do tomorrow morning."

"You can have the couch to share if you want it." Sean's eyes sparkled with mischief.

Eliot ignored him and patted the couch. "Go ahead, Chavali."

She also ignored Sean and laid herself out on the cushions. As much as she needed sleep, she dreaded it tonight. The two men settled on the floor, and Eliot doused the light, leaving her staring into the darkness, waiting for the nightmares to begin.

Chavali found herself in an icy wasteland, on a flat plain of unrelieved snow. It had no trees, no mountains in the distance, no structures, nothing but frozen water and sky, monochrome as always. Barefoot, she walked alone, her body so cold she felt nothing. Light shone from nowhere, reflecting off the white ground to blind her.

Hugging herself, she stumbled through the snow, determined to get somewhere without knowing where that might be. The ground had an odd pattern stamped into it, that of a wagon wheel. The wheels connected together, forming never-ending figure eights no matter where she looked. With each wheel she stepped on, a hiss escaped the snow, whispering voices she couldn't make out.

Something gave her a flickering shadow, and she turned to see the glow of fire, marching in a line towards her. It would consume her if she didn't outrun it. Despite that, she couldn't go any faster. Her foot struck something hard enough to make her toes crunch, and she fell. Where she hit the ground, spikes of ice pierced her hands, making them bleed frozen crystals, each in the curled shape of her Seer's feather.

She looked down through a frigid puff of her own breath and saw a face under the ice. Though she knew him, she couldn't remember anything about him, not even his name. He stared at her, eyes glassy and flat and empty. His mouth hung open in surprise. When he blinked, she jumped with fright and scrambled, wanting to be anywhere but here. Behind her, the flames kept coming.

He needed to be saved from the flames. Throwing herself forward again, she pawed at the ice, her fingers tearing apart on the jagged shards. She felt the heat creeping closer, warming and warning at the same time. Frantic, she raised her fist and slammed it against the ice, causing a tiny crack. Again and again, she pounded her hand against it. The crack grew bit by agonizing bit.

The flames closed in, heating her frigid limbs. Pain shot through her body, threatening to overwhelm her, yet still she pounded on the ice. It shattered, and she plunged her shredded hands through the clumps of ice to reach him, to touch him. The flames licked at her feet, burning with heat so intense she cried out, and still she dug through until she found his face and recognized him.

"Turn around," he breathed.

Her head snapped around, and she saw the flames weren't fire at all, but water that burned. The moment she saw it, the wave crashed down on them both, flooding into her mouth and everywhere else. Its force smashed her eyes to oblivion, and its heat boiled her flesh.

Chavali sat up, panting and clutching at her blanket. How did

Keino get into her dream? The most irritating of all her clansmen found a way to worm into her nightmares somehow, and the thought of it concerned her, but not more than the fact the flames changed to water. They'd never changed to water before. They'd never caught her like that before either. In the normal dream, she saw the face and knew it meant she had to keep running. The wagon wheels and whispering were also new.

She should have run until her feet froze and broke off, then crawled until her hands froze and broke off. The flames should have swept over her, burning with a fire so intense she felt it in her bones. That dream should have ended with her flailing her charred, blistered arms and sinking into the ice, where silvery fish snapped at her and devoured her flesh.

For the last ten of her twenty-five years, she'd had the same nightmares, over and over, none of them changed in even a single detail. Everything happened exactly the same, one nightmare per night. As the years passed, she learned to live with them. By the time she died, she had no particular reaction to them anymore and could roll over and go back to sleep without issue.

Now, she lay there, shaking and sweating, gasping for breath and afraid to close her eyes again. The pale glow of the waxing moon cast deep shadows about the room, and she imagined tendrils of fire writhing inside them, snaking their way up the sides of the couch to force her mouth open and drown her. It would boil her flesh and turn her into soup, her eyeballs bobbing in the pot and her teeth collecting at the bottom.

She curled up into a ball, pulling the blanket tight, and stared into the darkness with more fear than she'd felt in a long time. Something changed her nightmare. Something pushed Keino into it. Something *changed*. She recalled cryptic exchanges with that mysterious woman in Ket and the admonition to "tend to her dreams." These words still meant nothing to her.

A noise on the floor made her jump and let out a tiny squeak. Her heart racing, she caught sight of a dark shape rising up and leaning towards her.

"Chavali? Are you alright?" Eliot asked in a whisper.

His voice startled her, then she berated herself for not realizing it had to be one of the two men. She pushed hair out of her face and wiped sweat from her brow. Unable to catch her breath or stop shivering, she shook her head.

He rubbed his face and crawled to her side. When he took a good look at her in the dim light, he hopped up to sit beside her. "What happened?"

"Nothing."

"I'm starting to think that when you say "nothing," you mean "something awful I don't want to talk about.'" He offered her the shelter of his arm over her shoulders.

"It is too much to explain right now. Later." She took the comfort he offered and leaned into him. Even in this condition, she took care to keep the blanket between them so she wouldn't catch his thoughts through his flesh. At a time like this, she preferred to hear the calming words that came from his mouth, not the disparaging things she expected from his mind.

"Good plan." He yawned and pulled his own blanket up from

the floor. Having his body there reminded her of home, of sleeping in a pile. He drifted back to sleep. She lay there, sharing his warmth. Staring into the darkness, she picked out Sean's slumbering form, his breaths loud enough to hear and soothe her with their regularity. Eventually, once the rush of fear abated, her eyelids grew too heavy to stay open, and she found dreamless sleep.

Chapter 7

Morning came too early. Chavali woke when Eliot shifted, and she opened her eyes to see Sean watching them with a wistful smile. With Eliot's hand on her hair and her clutching his shirt, she knew what Sean thought. She glared at him for taking what he saw and deciding what it must mean.

"Did you sleep well?"

Chavali had a thought to slap that look right off Sean's face. Of course, that impulse got her into this duty in the first place. If she hadn't been here, the nightmare wouldn't have changed, and if the nightmare hadn't changed, she wouldn't have needed anyone to sleep with her. Obviously. Getting in deeper with Sean would only mean more of this sort of nonsense.

"No." She grabbed the brush out of her pack and used it while Eliot stood and made his way to the privy. "It's not important."

Joey ran into the room, adding his joyful cheer to the warm sunshine streaming in through the windows. Still dressed in his pajamas, he leaped at Chavali, throwing himself into her lap. "Good morning! Can

I have a story before breakfast?"

His infectious smile banished the last vestiges of her night's terror. "I'm not really awake enough for that yet." She settled him onto her lap and held him close, finding him a balm to ease her worries. "Perhaps you can tell me one."

"Oh! Once upon a time, there was a..." He frowned and nibbled on his thumb.

"That can wait." Lilly, dressed for the day and looking much fresher than she had last night, stepped into the room. "Daddy's already out with the sheep. We need to get you dressed." Her gaze shifted to Chavali. "There's some breakfast out. Take your time. We have chores to do, even in the winter, but you're welcome to stay as long as you need to."

"Thank you." Pushing Joey off her lap, she tousled his hair. "You can think about your story all day and tell it to your mother tonight."

He kissed her on the cheek, giving her a brief flash of a child's boundless trust and affection for anyone who treated him well, then ran to his mother. Chavali suspected he promptly forgot about her.

Eliot gave Lilly a smile as he returned then followed Chavali and Sean into the kitchen. They'd left out enough food that Chavali marveled at how they all slept through its preparation: pancakes, apples, raisins, cheese-laden flatbread, coffee, and juice. The trio sat to eat. Chavali found her stomach wanted as much food as she could cram into it and dug into the meal with enthusiasm.

Keeping his voice down, Eliot said, "The village already executed someone, and from what Lilly said, they probably got the right man. It's our responsibility to check into this, but I'm hard-pressed to think of an excuse to linger and investigate."

Chavali frowned. "Lilly doesn't really think Jack did it. She's lying about what happened that night too. I'm not sure how, precisely, but I felt she perhaps recited someone else's account, filling in with nonsense."

"That changes things."

Sean swished his pancake in a glob of syrup. "I haven't done many investigations in my time. What do you recommend we do from here?"

Eliot looked to Chavali. "Not really my best skill either."

Accepting that she had some small amount of expertise with this sort of thing, Chavali nodded. After unraveling the mess in Ket, a large city, she felt confident she could handle a murder in this tiny village. "We need to get into Ramelia's house and try to get access to any items that may have been removed from it. Ideally, we would see her body, as well. Other residents should be questioned about the incident and about both Ramelia's and Jack's life."

"And we need to do all that without giving away the fact we're doing it for the Crown or the Fallen." Eliot scratched his scalp. "Let's attack this one step at a time."

Chavali paused, about to take her first bite of the flatbread that smelled delicious. "First, the house. We may need to steal Ramelia's body, if we can determine where it is. Sean has declared himself her friend. We can push that one step further to being a friend of her family, which is true. From a particular point of view. He can ask to see the inside of the house under the pretense of...trying to find a keepsake for her...mother? Brother? Uncle Eldrack?"

Eliot chuckled. "Let's go with uncle and not mention his name, just in case."

"That might get us access to her body as well," Sean said, "and then we could remove it for Eldrack."

"You know as well as I do that they don't just revive everyone we come across," Eliot said.

"Yes, but it's not up to us to make that determination." Sean stuffed pancake into his mouth and shrugged.

"True enough," Eliot said. "See if you can convince whoever we get referred to that you want to take her body home to her uncle. That should get us everything we need."

Chavali hadn't yet learned what price the Fallen paid to bring people back from death. She guessed it must be a significant, substantial sacrifice. Prior to being revived, she had no idea such a thing could even be done. The research that must have gone into discovering the process would be fascinating and probably also quite grim. At the least, she doubted that one life could be traded for another, as that made no sense.

"We may be able to use Sean's relationship as a cover for discovering everything else we need to."

The opening and closing of a door deeper in the house made the three of them turn their attention to the food. Lilly popped her head into the kitchen as the front door opened. "We're going out. Like I said, take your time. No rush. And don't feel like you need to clean up."

"We appreciate your hospitality. Thank you, and I hope your day goes well." Eliot lifted his cup to her, a gesture Sean and Chavali echoed.

"Good speed to you." Lilly gave them a curt nod, her features still taut with grief she refused to show. She waved and ducked out to chase after her son.

The door shut, and Chavali shook her head. "She had to have been having an affair with Jack. Have you seen how Andrew looks at her and at the two of you? And the strain she's under. Something was definitely going on between them. That's more than just the ache of losing friends." She knew all about the kind of pain Lilly chose to hide. Chavali pursed her lips as she tried to ignore her own losses.

Of all the members of her clan to appear in a changed dream, why did it have to be Keino? Even in death, he still plagued her as a lovesick puppy that would never give up, all because she loved him but couldn't handle the things in his mind. Women were not meant to know what men think, her mother had told her. Such painful truth. She sighed and shuddered at the memories crashing down on her.

"Chavali?" Eliot's concern made her look up. "What happened last night?"

A shiver ran down her spine. "I had a nightmare."

Sean reached over to pat her hand, which she pulled out of his reach before he could. "About dying?"

She blinked, wondering how he knew that. Then she remembered being told that nightmares were common for a few months after waking up, and she had a perfect way to not go into detail. "Yes. It was especially vivid and seemed quite real."

"I remember having those," Sean said with a knowing nod. "My execution was particularly gruesome, from my perspective, and my head remained alive long enough to see that it had been detached from my body. I used to have very troubling dreams about that. I think the mind just needs time to sort it out. Eventually, your brain gets over it and you move on."

"So I've been told," Chavali said. Though Eliot had a good heart and wanted to see her do well, neither of these men needed to know what had happened or help her determine what it might mean. Her Healer would listen. For whatever reason, Kelly's job seemed to consist of being available to Chavali at any time with no notice. It boggled her mind that each Fallen had their own personal counselor. Since Kelly had sworn to keep any secrets told to her, Chavali thought she could probably trust the woman with this sort of thing.

"Are you going to be alright today?" Eliot asked. "We can take things easy, stop for a break later if you need to."

"I'll be fine. And I won't tell anyone you offered to be gentle."

He and Sean both laughed. "Good." Standing up, Eliot grabbed a piece of the bread and nodded towards the door. "No time like the present to get moving. We'll take everything with us and plan to sleep at home tonight, though we may need to come back tomorrow."

Chapter 8

Adjusting her cloak over her pack, Chavali stepped out into a morning much warmer than the one before. The sun beamed down at them, making every surface sparkle. The juxtaposition of this lovely weather with her night's trauma made Chavali kick a small pile of fluffy snow out of spite. "How much more of this wretched cold will there be?"

"Another month or so." Eliot flashed a grin. "Then the snow will melt, and everything will start growing. You'll switch to complaining about the stench of horse dung or the clashing aromas of the flowers."

"Very funny." She stuck her tongue out at him and followed along as they wound between the houses. Here and there, townsfolk braved the cold to take care of morning chores or to bring food to the communal brick ovens to bake all day. She waved to a few, curious to see what they would do, and found that they returned the gesture.

At the house with the green door and large clumps of snow that might be rosebushes, Eliot nodded for Sean to take the lead and waited at the end of the stone walkway with Chavali. It took a short time between Sean's knock and the door opening, then a middle-aged woman bundled against the chill answered. Only her face could be seen under all the knitted wool, and her wrinkles spoke of a hard life.

"Good morning, Kember. I'm sorry to disturb you, but I was hoping to get permission to have a look inside Ramelia's house."

The woman frowned. "Why would you want to do that?"

"Well, as you know, she considered me a friend. Something I learned after I met her is that I'm actually a good friend of her uncle. He'll be heartbroken to learn of her death, and I'm hoping I can soften the blow with some kind of keepsake or other close-held belonging. If we could also prevail upon you to allow us to transport her body to him, that would be appreciated."

From ten feet away, Chavali watched Kember think about the requests. "The matter is closed, so if you want to look through the house, go ahead. The body's been buried, though. If you want it, you can dig it up. Nobody's going to object to that."

"You dug a grave in the middle of winter?"

Kember gave Sean a flat look. "No, it was dug months ago. Before the ground froze. We always dig one in the fall in case it's needed."

"Oh." Sean nodded. "That's very sensible. Could we borrow a sledge to transport the body? It would be returned within a day or two."

"Sure." Kember waved the matter off. "We don't need that kind of thing much this time of year anyway. My boys'll set it up for you later. Be ready to go by dark."

"Thank you," Sean said with a polite nod, "I appreciate it. Could you possibly tell us more about what happened that night? No one really seems to want to discuss it."

"Not much to tell." Kember stepped far enough outside to shut the door behind her. "Jack killed her. It was plain to see he'd been hiding what he really is from us."

"And what is that, exactly?"

She shuddered. "A monster. Scariest thing I've ever seen. He ripped Ramelia's throat out with his claws, and we managed to knock him unconscious before he hurt anyone else. Still having nightmares about it."

Remarkably, this tale rang true. Chavali detected no hint of deceit about Kember. It correlated with Lilly's story, so why had the other woman's recounting been so false? Aside from her belief in Jack's innocence, they said nothing truly different. Intrigued by the small mystery, Chavali wanted to question Lilly more. She'd have to think about how to phrase questions to get the answers without Lilly realizing it.

Sean patted Kember on the arm. "I'm so sorry. That must have been horrible. To think he'd been living among you."

"That seems the worst part to me," she nodded. "Other than his obviously monstrous appetites and urges. Poor Ramelia. I didn't know her well, as she kept mostly to herself, but she was always nice and pleasant and never asked for anything that was a hardship to give. Always paid for everything without delay and helped anybody who needed it when she could. Creator watch over her." Opening the door again, she stepped inside.

"She was a good person," Sean agreed. "Thank you for your time." He gave Eliot and Chavali a quizzical raise of his brow as the three of them walked away from the house. "How disturbing. When Lilly said 'monster,' I thought she meant that he seemed wild and feral."

Chavali nodded. "Kember made no effort to lie. She really did see that or thinks she did. With the way the shopkeeper acted yesterday, I'm inclined to think it really happened. I do know some stories about people who can change their shape but always assumed them to be allegories about the perils of letting one's inner beast be in control."

"I can't imagine what kinds of problems that could cause," Eliot said dryly.

"Shut up." She thumped him in the arm, earning a smirk. "I would prefer to see the body before we leave, but I think that will be too disturbing for our stated purpose, so we can let someone with more expertise take a look at home."

"Agreed."

Sean led the way to Ramelia's house again. Eliot used two of his daggers to pry the front door open. Standing at the threshold, all three stared in disbelief at the level of destruction inside. Furniture lay in pieces, ripped and smashed. Broken glass littered the floor. Papers had been thrown about. Feathers, disturbed by the door opening, swirled and settled all over the place. Random splashes of dry ink—and other dark liquids—stained the floor and walls. Flies buzzed in small swarms.

Chavali entered first. Gouges in the floor and walls suggested the claws of the creature Kember described. Taking care with each step, she still managed to crunch glass and other debris under her boots. She found the bedroom had a similar mess. The other, smaller room had been some sort of lab, with an overturned and broken table and significantly more glass and stains. Only the kitchen had been left untouched.

"A tornado blew through here," Sean murmured. "I wonder if they found..." He bustled to the bedroom and pawed through the rubble, shoving broken furniture aside. Chavali and Eliot followed him, watching from the doorway. "We talked a lot, and I stayed with her the last time I was here. Not *with* her—my wife would kill me. I mean on her couch."

"You're married?" The idea made Chavali smirk, imagining him somehow courting a woman with incessant questions and gossip.

"Yes, to my Healer." He waved that off as unimportant. "I didn't really understand most of what she talked about with her research, but I still listened. It had to do with some kind of unusual flower that grows near here. Ah, here we go." He pushed down on a floorboard. They heard it click, then it popped up. Removing it, he revealed a storage area with a leather-bound notebook.

"She was working with someone else on the subject, another woman here in town I haven't really had a chance to get to know yet."

Chavali snorted. "Slipping in your old age, apparently."

He made a face at her. "She's new to the village. She and her husband both. They've only been here for a couple of months." Flipping the notebook open to the middle, he showed the final few entries to Chavali and Eliot. "Maybe one of you can puzzle this out?"

"I cannot read," Chavali said.

Eliot took it and scanned the entries, his brow furrowing deeper and deeper as his eyes moved lower and lower on the page. "I think I'd need to read it from the beginning. And get used to her handwriting. This is awful. You know what else is awful?" Shutting the book, he flicked a hand at the main room. "That."

"There's a lot of blood," Chavali agreed.

"There's a lot of everything." He nudged some glass with his

75

boot. "There's no obvious path or course of the fight. The destruction is too complete, like it was done on purpose, either to hide what really happened or," he lifted the journal, "because someone knew about this and was looking for it."

Chavali raised an eyebrow. "I cannot imagine what a flower could have or do that would be worthy of murder over it."

"It could be about the soil, or the water, or something else near these flowers. Who knows? What about this other woman she worked with?"

Sean pulled his head out of the storage area. "She's a mage. Her name is Candace."

"Better a mage than a telepath," Eliot muttered.

Chavali rolled her eyes. Doing so let her notice a silver glint across the room. She moved to investigate it and found a silver necklace. The pendant strung on it had a carved, wooden flower. "This looks the same as the one in the book, yes?" She ran her fingers over the wood, finding it irregular.

Eliot nodded. "Interesting coincidence."

She snorted. "Someone made it for her. Ramelia had a lover or one who wished to be this. He either had no money to get her an expensive gift or wished for it to be personal."

"It doesn't really matter," Eliot said with a shrug. "Let's go talk to this mage friend." He tucked the journal into his pack and strode out with the other two following him. Five feet from door, he stopped abruptly enough that Chavali walked into him. She flung out one hand to stop Sean and reached for her dagger with the other.

Another man stood in the gap between the next two houses,

carrying a stack of firewood and staring at Eliot with his mouth hanging open. Eliot appeared stricken, unable to speak. Chavali had no idea what to make of this reaction from the man who never missed a beat and never lost his footing.

"What is it?"

"A ghost." Eliot blinked and regained his senses. "You two go ahead and talk to Candace." He shooed them away without breaking eye contact with the other man. "I'll catch up with you later."

"Are you alright?" Considering the effort he put into making sure she had what she needed, she felt compelled to offer the same in return.

"No," he breathed, then he shook his head. "What? Yes, of course, I'm fine. I just...need to...do something. Go find the mage."

Chavali watched him walk to the man with the dark hair and beard, his stouter frame better suited to grunt work than Eliot's. They stood at near the same height, and she wondered if this other man had been part of his past somehow. She recalled that part of the vow to join the Fallen included renouncing one's former life, and she had no idea what happened when it crossed their path by accident.

"Come, he obviously needs to deal with this privately, whatever 'this' may be." She tugged on Sean's arm, pulling him around Ramelia's house.

"How do you think he knows that man?" Sean tried to peer around the corner at the two men, but she yanked him back and restrained herself from smacking him for stupidity.

"We don't have time for that." She somehow kept herself from adding "you idiot" to the end of the statement. "Not with having to dig up the body and get home tonight. So, Candace. Where does she live?"

Chapter 9

The house had nothing to mark it as special or different compared to the rest of the village. Sean knocked on the door, with Chavali standing behind him, ready to kick him in the leg if he needed it. They waited long enough for her to notice this house did have one unusual feature: no smoke coming from the brick chimney.

The man who finally opened the door wore a flour-dusted apron over wool pants and a single shirt with a thin pair of socks, unlike everyone else in this village so far. "Can I help you?" His hair, face, and even stature were all bland and average, forgettable in every way. With him came the smell of baking bread.

"Excuse us for the interruption, but I was a friend of Ramelia's, and I've just learned about her death, and I recall meeting Candace at her house once." He paused for a beat too long.

Chavali stifled a roll of her eyes. "This is Sean. He's upset and reaching out to the people who knew her here, hoping to make sense of this tragedy."

"Oh, I recall her mentioning your name once. Candace is busy, but I'm sure she can set it aside for a little while. Come in."

One step inside the small house and Chavali hit a wall of warmth. It made her pull her hood down and gloves off. They must use magic to heat the building, instead of the fires everyone else employed. Sean shucked his cloak and pack, leaving both by the door, and Chavali followed suit.

"Candy! Sean's here to see you." The man left them alone in a cozy room with a couch against the wall and a low table in front of it.

Before they had a chance to do more than take in the sparsely appointed room, a thin, waifish woman stepped out from a side door, her narrow face full of sympathy. "Oh, Sean, I'm so sorry!" She rushed to him and took both his hands, closing in and delivering fake kisses to his cheeks. "You were so fond of her. I hadn't really gotten to know her terribly well yet, but I think of her as having been a friend in a place where we have so few of them."

Sean squeezed her hands and walked to the couch with her. "It's always terrible when people are taken from us too early."

"It really is." They sat together and cooed at each other.

Happy to be ignored by this kind of nonsense, Chavali leaned against the wall and waited for Sean to get to the point. She knew she'd have a hard time determining if this woman lied or not, since her entire demeanor felt fake. Beyond that, people who insisted upon behaving like twits generally annoyed her. Somehow, though, she would have to interject and manipulate the woman into taking her hand and holding onto it long enough to get useful information.

If she thought of Candace as a prospective client who needed to be coerced into allowing her to read her fortune, the task felt less onerous.

She focused on reading Candace, on picking up her quirks and tells, her interests and dislikes, and waiting for a good moment to jump in and take control.

Sean's voice rose again. "I'm having such a hard time getting a straight answer out of anyone about how she died. Were you there? Did you see it?"

Candace sighed and deflated. "I only caught some of it. The whole thing happened at night, of course, and we live on the other side of town. I've put up a number of enchantments to give us privacy and comfort, so we didn't really hear anything until it was all over. I've heard all the chatter, of course. Who would ever have guessed about Jack? Not me. He seemed so reasonable and stalwart, I would never have believed he could be hiding an awful secret." She poured words out, barely pausing for breath.

"Really?" Sean squeezed her hands again. "What awful secret?"

"Oh, Creator bless," Candace gushed. "I'm surprised people aren't shoving that part down your throats. It's got everyone all atwitter. There's talk about hunting the wolves around here to safeguard the village. He was, so it seems, a werewolf."

Sean slapped his hands to his chest in shock and horror. "I thought those were just stories."

"So did I! I've studied magic most of my life, and I never had any idea they might be genuinely real. Imagine having your life ruled by the moon and having to find ways to hide it. Of course, in hindsight, he spent a lot of time alone, didn't he? And his duties let him wander off into the forest whenever he wanted to and do other strange things without anyone asking questions. Right up until Ramelia must have figured something out in her research, the poor dear. I'll bet she confronted him and he tore out her throat in a rage."

Chavali cleared her throat. "Why would she confront him in the middle of the night?"

Candace blinked and stared at Chavali, as if she'd forgotten about her. "I'm sure I don't know. People do strange things sometimes. Maybe she couldn't sleep."

"The poor dear." Sean recaptured Candace's attention by opening his mouth, it seemed. "Can I ask you about something else, though? We just saw a young man who I think was here the last time I came through, but I don't remember him. He's got dark hair, green eyes, a full beard, and has lots of muscles. We saw him over by Ramelia's house, but he moved so quick that we couldn't tell which house he went into before we got there."

Chavali quirked an eyebrow, wondering why Sean would ask about that of all things. Eliot would tell them if he wanted to, and as much as she wanted to poke and pry, she knew better than to do it behind his back.

"That sounds like Patrick." Candace's husband stood in the doorway to the kitchen, wiping his hands on a towel, the apron gone. "I hired him a while ago as security on my trading trips. He settled here before we did, but he's kind of a private person. What about him?"

"He's a very capable man," Candace said. She waved to indicate her husband. "I never worry about my Grant being out in the wide world without me so long as he takes Patrick along."

Sean beamed. "Does he live near Ramelia's house? Maybe he saw something and can explain it better."

Candace and Grant glanced at each other. "I doubt he saw anything." Candace flipped her hand to dismiss the subject.

It annoyed Chavali that Sean's sidetrack took them someplace worthwhile. Candace and Grant didn't want them talking to Patrick for some reason. "Do you know anything about what Ramelia studied? Her uncle is Sean's friend also, and he may be interested in her notes or whatever small thing we can give him to ease the pain of loss for a dear niece."

"Sorry to interrupt," Grant said, not sorry at all. "Candy, I think lunch is ready for your special touches before I set it to cook and bake."

"Oh, excuse me." Candace jumped up and fled to the kitchen, squeezing past Grant and disappearing behind him.

Chavali pursed her lips, finding the timing excessively and suspiciously convenient. "We can wait a few minutes for her. Our time is not spoken for."

Grant failed at suppressing a frown. "Candy really doesn't know much of anything about it. They shared tea sometimes. She does that with a lot of people. They natter about this or that." He threw such strong signals for them to leave that Chavali perversely wanted to stay.

"I see. Still, anything she can tell us would be a great boon."

Sean stood up. "We should go find our own lunch."

Chavali shrugged. "When Candace is done using magic on the food."

"She's not using magic on the food." Grant chuckled nervously, making it clear he lied. "She's just, er, better with herbs and spices than I am. You should try the slop I eat on the road when I have to cook for myself! It's awful. Edible, but awful."

Head tilting to the side, Sean asked, "Doesn't Patrick help out?"

"Oh, yes, but he's not much better than me. Or, maybe he likes his food bland. I don't know. No complaints from him, so that's probably it."

"Maybe Candace could make you up packets of herbs to take along."

Chavali forced herself not to let her boredom show. Cooking held no interest whatsoever for her, and knowing Candace had talent with magically enhancing the flavor of food didn't help them discover what really happened that night. One thing she knew for certain: everyone who lied about that incident had a stake in it. So far, Lilly and these two people had made it clear they all knew or did or saw *something* they refused to divulge.

Grant and Sean blathered more about cooking and spices until Candace returned, her smile dimmer than before. "That was fun," she said with too much gusto. "I don't really know much about what she was doing out there." Gesturing towards the door, she tried to herd them out.

Sean obediently went for the door. Chavali reached out and took Candace's hand, shaking it. "I appreciate your time, nonetheless. If you think of anything about Ramelia's research or perhaps discover notes of hers in your things, please send a letter to Sean in Cloverdale."

I don't know what to think of you. Why won't you leave? An undercurrent of mild panic chased the thoughts in Candace's head. *I'm not going to talk about those flowers.* Chavali saw a flower, so blue it defined the color and glowed from within. She took the image and cherished it, a bright spot of glorious color in her memory. Then Candace pulled her hand away and stepped closer, trying to get Chavali to move without being too aggressive.

It amused her that Candace stood shorter than she, by a good two or three inches. "Do you think it had anything to do with a sketch of a flower we found part of in her house?"

Candace blushed. "I beg your pardon?" So close, Chavali could feel the heat radiating from her cheeks.

"A scrap of paper, torn in half, had part of a sketch of a flower." Warming to the fib, she carried it through where it needed to go. "Her handwriting is difficult to read, but it seemed to say the flower glowed blue. That's unusual, is it not? Did her research involve determining how it made the glow?"

"I...well...I mean to say...she didn't really— There *was* a flower, I think. I suppose. I recall finding a flower like that once, while strolling with her in the evening. We discussed all kinds of things, of course, and she had a scientific mind. It's so rare to come across people like that and such a joy to be able to chat with them."

"Can you show us where to find these flowers? Do they bloom in the winter?"

"I, um, you know, I don't know." Candace squared her shoulders. "That would be interesting to find out, wouldn't it? Of course, they're much easier to find in the dark, so it would be better to go looking at dusk. Meet me over by Ramelia's house then, and I'll show you where they grow."

Finally taking the step back that Candace wanted her to, Chavali nodded. "Thank you, that would be nice of you. I'm sure her uncle would appreciate having one, if that's at all possible." As she turned to go, she noticed Candace's face twitch in distaste about that idea. Too bad for her. The door slammed shut behind her.

Twenty feet from the house, Sean beamed. "That was great. How did you know to ask about a flower?"

"The demons I talk to suggested it."

His jaw fell open. "You talk to demons?"

"No. But for some unknown reason, people at the tower seem to think I do."

Sean sighed melodramatically. "Chavali, I have no control over the insane things people decide to think when you leave a knowledge vacuum. I said I was sorry for pressing about your clan. I meant that. I'm not sorry for reading the archives and discussing what I found with others who have similar interests as me. Your gift is amazing, it's impossibly useful. Imagine what the King of Shappa—"

"I have imagined this." Chavali cut him off with a slash of her hand. "Because I was forced to. The man who murdered my clan wanted to control it for his own purposes. He's still out there, and he still wants it. The how and why of this thing you feel is a gift are questions I will not answer. I do not appreciate people deciding I must consort with demons or whatever else they choose to fabricate, and they do this because of the information you passed on to them."

She stopped and poked him in the chest, forcing him to stop too. "No, it isn't your fault they make up such wild things. It is, however, a result of your actions. I live with the knowledge every day that someone out here wants me under his thumb. When he finds me again, and I have no doubt he eventually will, especially when people whisper about a woman with a feather who can do impossible things, he will torture me until I break. He will put this thing you feel is such a grand gift to use for his own benefit. And on that day, no one who stands in his way will ever be safe again."

Sean blinked at her for several seconds. "How can someone be so unpleasant and so selfless at the same time?"

Chavali rolled her eyes and walked away from him. Only an idiot would accuse her of being selfless.

Chapter 10

The sounds of anger led Chavali to Eliot, still talking to Patrick. They'd wandered a good distance from Ramelia's cottage, and Chavali threw out a hand to stop Sean before he blundered into the argument. Both men gestured with sharp, precise movements. That they flung words at each other instead of fists told her these two men had a relationship of some kind, one both felt deeply.

Curiosity sent her hurrying to the other side of the house she'd shoved Sean behind. Their voices cut through the air, clipped and harsh yet pleading. In some ways, the tone reminded her of Keino, trying to tell her what she wanted. Edging closer, she finally made out words.

"Why can't you just tell me?"

"It's not—Patrick, I have to—" Eliot made a noise she'd never heard from him before, of frustration so deep and monumental he had no other way to express it than a primal sound somewhere between a roar and a grunt.

"Go ahead, run away," Patrick spat after him.

Sensing Eliot would be storming in this direction, Chavali chose that moment to "accidentally" walk around the corner. She made sure her expression showed surprise when she walked into him.

In a measure of how distracted he was, Eliot stumbled to the side and had to catch himself against the wall of the next house. He wore a scowl so deep it made her flinch. "We're leaving now," he growled. "We can reach home by nightfall if we hurry." He threw himself away from the wall and devoured the ground with strides Chavali had to scramble to catch up with. Even Sean had to jog to keep up.

"We cannot leave now." She reached out and grabbed his shoulder to make him slow down. "The mage is taking us to see a flower we know to be important, and Ramelia's body won't dig itself up. We have to deal with these things."

Eliot stopped so abruptly she ran into him from behind. This time, he remained rock-steady, and she bounced off and to the ground. "Dammit."

"What's wrong?" Sean caught up and put out a hand to keep Eliot from taking off again. "We can't help if you won't tell us."

Glaring at the snow on the ground, Eliot snapped, "I don't want your help."

"That much is clear." Chavali stayed sitting in the snow, ready to out-stubborn him if he needed her to. She crossed her arms. "Go if you wish. We have a duty here and I will stay until it is complete."

Pressing on his eyes with a thumb and forefinger, he scowled. "I hate you."

She snorted and brushed snow off her skirts. "Now you know how I feel much of the time."

Sean looked from one to the other and sighed with his

infuriating, dreamy smile. "You both—"

"Stop. Now." Chavali grabbed a handful of snow and threw it at him. It sprayed out in a shower of sparkles.

Eliot narrowed his eyes. "I see we need to work on your throwing skills." He crouched and scooped a ball of snow up, then hurled it at Sean. It hit him in the face, leaving the other man sputtering. "It's all in the wrist." Though he still wore an irritated grimace, she saw the tension easing in his shoulders.

Getting to her feet, Chavali brushed the snow off her dress and cloak. "We can leave after we see this flower. It seems important. For the promise of my own bed, I'll run all the way home to get there before the cold is too much to bear."

Eliot rubbed his face, showing a rare moment of weariness. "Fine. Let's go dig up a body. It'll be fun." He turned and trudged away, head down and movements lackluster.

Sean held a snowball, ready to retaliate. When Chavali arched an eyebrow at him, he shrugged and dropped it. "What was that about?" he hissed.

"I don't know, but you shouldn't pester. He will speak of it whenever he's ready to. Go be useful and find us shovels." She followed Eliot from a distance, letting him have space to breathe. From behind, she watched him kick a pile of snow, rake a hand through his hair, narrowly miss walking into a villager, and recover gracelessly from tripping over a rock. Whatever he argued about with Patrick, the encounter rattled him to the core.

He stopped at the edge of a small birch and cedar grove, staring into the graveyard. The snow had been trampled. Since the snow at the hanging site had been dusted with fresh snow, they'd hung Jack, then buried Ramelia after the storm passed. Fear of a rampaging werewolf must have spurred them to act quickly with Jack. Chavali walked up to stand beside Eliot, wanting him to know of her presence.

Several pine boughs lay in a neat pile over a thin layer of churned snow at the foot of a cedar tree. From memories taken in her first life, she understood this practice. To show respect for the dead, each griever selected a sort of plant not available in the graveyard grove. It meant the person had spent a moment in thought before arriving and taken the time to choose a gift to honor the passed soul.

"In my clan, we burn our dead. It releases their soul to wander, where being shackled to rotting flesh would doom them to eternal stagnation. I've been aware that is unusual for some time, yet this practice of burial is still strange and barbaric to me." She paused to offer Eliot a chance to speak. Dead leaves scraped across the snow in a breeze, and he remained silent.

"When a Seer dies, we have to retrieve the feather from her skull to pass on to the next Seer, so her head is cracked open. This is done by the clan elders, who squabble among themselves over who gets to perform the duty. Since her head is opened like a ripe melon anyway, we also bathe wooden beads in her brain matter." Her hand flicked the beads strung in her hair, making them click together.

Eliot grimaced. "That's disgusting."

"It is, yes." She smirked because he'd let her distract him. "I had to do this myself, before they chipped a hole in my skull to insert the feather. There is a story that the feather actually grew out of the first Seer's brain, coaxed out by our clan's founder. It punched its way out of her skull in this very spot." She touched the base of the feather in her forehead.

"That sounds unpleasant."

"I agree. This is why the feather is thin and curled instead of thick and straight."

He blinked a few times and looked at her. "Is that actually true?"

She shrugged. "Perhaps. It's as likely as any other possibility."

For several seconds, Eliot stared at her, his brow slipping upwards. "You just shared a clan secret with me."

"Yes." Her smirk grew. "But it's a little one, and I doubt you can cause any trouble with it." Crunching in the snow behind her alerted them to Sean's arrival. "Unlike *some* people."

"Three shovels, as requested." Sean handed them out.

Chavali hefted hers and approached the grave, patting Eliot's shoulder on the way past him. She picked up the pine branches and set them aside. The sooner they began, the sooner they would finish, so she got to work. Sean followed suit.

Eliot took a deep breath of the frigid air. "Thanks. I trust you too."

Sean tossed a shovelful of snow to the side. "I swear, if you two don't at least hug, I'm going to be very disappointed."

"Disappointment is good for you," Chavali said. "It builds character."

"Oh, for goodness' sake," Sean groused. "Both of you are the most stubborn, bullheaded pains-in-the-behind I've ever met."

Eliot managed a small snort. "You don't get out much."

Pleased to see Eliot's mood lifting, Chavali laughed and applied herself to the gruesome labor. She supposed that the Fallen benefited from the custom of burial. It still struck her as grotesque. That thought led to wondering why all the rest of the world chose burial, when her clan found it so distasteful. One small group of people had completely different ways from all the rest of the cultures.

She paused with a frown. "Explain to me why burial is the one, true way to dispose of the dead."

Eliot shrugged and looked to Sean. "You handle that. I'm not much for this kind of discussion."

"Explain why? Oh. Well. It's giving back to the earth that sustains us. We eat plants and animals all our lives, then when we die, they eat us while our spirit moves on. It's the most respectful to bury a person under a tree, to provide for it. It's said that the memories of the people buried under it live on in the rings. The worst criminals, of course, aren't buried, as the ultimate form of rejection."

"Which is why they left Jack hanging." The dirt here, so recently churned, proved no more difficult to move than if it had been warm. It still would take them a fair amount of time to dig deep enough. Chavali paused and rolled her shoulders, not used to this kind of work. "Should we have left him strung up?"

"Personally, I'd say no." Eliot shrugged. "It sounds kind of like he killed her in a fit of uncontrolled rage. Given what he was, he may not have been able to help himself. That's clearly different from a person who murders in cold blood."

"He was still a monster," Sean said. "Imagine if Ramelia had carried his children without knowing. Abominations."

Chavali took a deep breath and looked off into the woods. "I know clan stories of these creatures; we called them a different word. It translates roughly to 'hidden wolf horrors.' " For a moment, she thought she saw someone—or some *thing*—staring back at her, deeper in the trees. She blinked and peered closer. Nothing met her gaze. It had, perhaps, been a trick of the light.

Chapter 11

The sun settled low before they found the body, wrapped in enough layers of white gauze to obscure her features. It took all three of them to haul the limp corpse out of the deep hole, then carry it to their horse. As promised, they found a sledge with the beast. A feed bag had also been slung on the horse's head, which Chavali chided herself for not thinking of on her own.

She pulled the bag off while Eliot and Sean set up the sledge and offered the horse an apple she still had from the meal provided to them earlier. Chomping the fruit, it brushed its head against her. She rubbed its nose with her bare hand and reveled in the uncomplicated affection it felt for her. "Yes, you're a good horse," she told it. "I appreciate you too. Without you, Eliot would undoubtedly make me carry all these things."

Eliot tightened a strap with a smirk. "You're right. I would."

"You see?" She ran her fingers through its forelock, combing it, then scratched at the roots. It huffed what she knew to be a deliriously happy sigh. "We'll leave soon but not yet. When we get home, you can kick in fresh hay and sleep in warmth again. Soon." She pointed to the ground. "Stay. We must see a woman about a flower."

The trio left and the horse stayed. Sean let out one of his annoyingly dreamy sighs. "That's amazing, Chavali. I think it wanted to follow you, like a puppy. You're great with horses and children. Don't you want to have—"

"No," she snapped, cutting him off.

"You're so sour," he huffed.

"There's Candy." Chavali pointed the woman out for Eliot's benefit.

Dressed in rabbit fur, the woman met them at the edge of town and held an unlit lantern in one gloved hand. Sean cheerfully introduced Eliot, and they crunched through the fresh snow of a path through the trees. With wild abandon, the pair of them plunged into chatter about nothing of interest. Chavali ignored them, her thoughts straying from the horse to Karias to Colby.

To herself, she had to admit she had been avoiding him. Delving into his thoughts with the purpose of prodding and nosing around bothered her. She accepted the Fallen as a sort of clan to which she belonged and chose to treat them accordingly. This meant avoiding contact, to keep the spirits from drinking down their thoughts.

She missed having someone she could say anything to. Pasha took whatever fell out of her mouth in stride. No matter how angry Chavali got, no matter what awful thing she said, her little sister hugged her and made her smile. Healer Kelly purported to offer this, yet it could never be the same. With Pasha, she could have moments of complete honesty, with nothing hidden or guarded. No one here offered such an opportunity.

"You're loud enough to wake the dead."

Torn from her thoughts, Chavali looked up to see a man blocking the path. He wore leathers and a wild beard. One bare hand held a bow with an arrow ready. His other hand warded them off, held up with his palm out.

"Hello, Ander," Candy said with a strained smile.

Sean took a step toward the man, hand out to greet him. "Oh, Ander, it's nice to meet you. I've heard about you. All of it good, of course."

Ander's craggy face scrunched into a frown, and he looked at Sean's hand. "It's not safe to be wandering around here now."

"We're not wandering," Candy sniffed. "We're going to the waterfall."

Faltering under Ander's withering gaze, Sean let his hand drop. "Ramelia was my friend, and her uncle is too. I just want to take as much to him as I can. So he can mourn her properly."

"The wolves are restless lately, and there seem to be more than before. You should go back to the village." His head snapped to the side, though Chavali heard nothing.

"You seem to be doing fine." Peering in the same direction, Chavali saw a branch quiver. Had those eyes been a trick earlier? Perhaps she'd seen something that ran off when she noticed it.

"I live out here. I know the woods, and the animals know I won't harm them if they don't harm me."

"What about the monsters?" Sean asked.

Ander snorted. "Monsters? There are no monsters out here." He inflected "out here" in a way that made Chavali think he considered the villagers to be more monstrous than anything found in the woods.

"Don't be ridiculous," Candy said. "Everyone knows Jack was a werewolf. We all saw him."

Lifting his bow, Ander gave his attention to the nocked arrow, running his fingers over the stiff, white feathers of the fletching. "People sometimes see what they want to see instead of what's there."

Intrigued by this man, Chavali asked, "Did you know Jack?"

He nodded. "Good man. Took care of Eagle Falls until it turned on him."

"We're just going to the waterfall." Candy held up her lantern and walked past Ander. "We'll be fine."

Sean edged around Ander to follow her. Eliot nodded to the man on his way past. Chavali wished she could find a simple, harmless way to touch Ander. He'd refused Sean's gesture, so she felt confident he'd do the same to her. She let the others get ahead of her and stopped where she could speak to him without being overheard.

"Why do you think the town turned on him?"

Ander looked down his nose at her, mouth a thin slash. "Don't know. These woods do feel less friendly than usual since it happened, though. There's anger bubbling here, looking for someone to lash out at." He glanced up the path. "They left you behind, miss. I'll walk you there. It's on my way anyhow."

"Thank you." She matched his pace, surprised by how slowly he chose to walk. "Does the waterfall area have some special significance?"

"They say the founder of Eagle Falls chose the spot for the town because the waterfall was so breathtaking. He went swimming with his young wife and babe not long after putting down roots. An eagle swooped down and tried to carry the child away, then a wolf lunged out and saved her by ripping the eagle's talon off."

She'd never before heard a tale with a wolf as the savior. "Do you believe this story to be true?"

"I was told it is, but no, I don't think so." He smirked at her. "It catches the kids off guard, though. Makes them think about wild animals differently."

"No doubt." The story certainly cast a different light on the name of the town. "Do you think Jack was involved with Ramelia?"

"I think he'd been spending more time in the town than the woods lately. Man makes a change like that, it's usually about a woman."

Agreeing with him, Chavali echoed his smirk. They remained alone, though she heard the splash of water and murmur of voices filtered by the trees. "Do you think Jack killed her?"

"I wasn't there."

"That's not what I asked."

He stopped and pointed up the path, where it curved. Pine trees flanked it on both sides, obscuring what lay ahead. "We're almost there."

Narrowing her eyes, Chavali wondered if this man hid the same secret as Jack. They lived in the same circumstances and had a similar build. All this talk of the forest being "angry" and living in harmony with wolves built her suspicion. "You question what those people saw."

"Of course I do." He crossed his arms and stood tall yet kept his voice down. "They went mob on him. He spent years keeping their peace. Feuding families turned to him, and he kept them from killing each other. Without him, there would be five times as many bodies buried in that grave grove. He was fair and honest. He deserved better than a botched hanging. They stayed and watched him suffocate to death without ever waking up, or I'd have cut him down before he died."

Her eyebrows climbed as he spoke, certainty growing that this man must also be a *yekalta*, a werewolf. "Yet you didn't cut him down after."

He shrugged. "No point then. Dead is dead."

This sentiment she understood and felt no need to question it. "You sound as if you speak of your brother."

"I would've been grateful to have a brother like Jack." He turned and swept up the path.

Not wanting to be left alone here, she hurried to follow him. Around the corner, she found a frozen paradise. The last light of the day hit the water at the top of a wide cliff as it tumbled over the edge and into a wide pool. Dark vines hung from cracks in the rock, studded with small light and dark flowers defying the cold. Smooth rock formed the edge of the pool and the mouth of a brook. Snow covered the branches of short evergreen trees and the ground. Small mounds suggested plants or rocks scattered about.

Something threw a weak glow on the scene, and it took Chavali several seconds to notice the delicate flowers matching the drawing in Ramelia's journal. They grew in random clumps around the pool. Eliot crouched beside one bouquet, poking a flower with his finger. Sean and Candy stood a few feet away, watching him and nattering to each other.

Approaching a different group of the flowers, Chavali noticed a ring absent of snow surrounded each stem, and each of the blooms faced the same direction. Following it to the sky, she saw the moon, hanging fat and bright in the darkening sky. It would be full tomorrow, she thought, or perhaps the next day. Did they face the moon specifically, or did it happen by chance?

Chavali turned to Ander. "Will you object if we take one? For Ramelia's uncle."

"Not at all."

"Are you sure you want to? They're probably delicate and won't travel well." Candy clasped her hands together and bit her lip.

"We don't have far to go," Eliot said with a shrug.

"Take a full bulb," Ander suggested. "I've done that for Ramelia. They don't live very long, but they'll last longer without cutting. You can probably get four or five more days if you take a bulb with one that hasn't opened yet."

Sean nodded and bent to help Eliot dig a plant up.

"That doesn't seem right," Candy protested.

Chavali raised an eyebrow. "What interest do you have in them?"

"She's been out here with Ramelia," Ander supplied, "several times. These flowers are, of course, unique to this area."

Having traveled extensively all her life, Chavali believed that. More interesting, Candy made semi-frantic gestures to suggest she wanted to interject. "I wonder what makes them glow?"

"No idea," Ander said. "I suspect that's what Ramelia was trying to discover. What I find more interesting is how they always face the moon. When the moon sets, they close up, and when it rises, they point at the horizon and open, then track it across the sky."

"Fascinating." Turning to Candy, she stifled a smirk to ask, "Did you have any findings yet?"

"No, no, I really didn't do much." Candy tried so hard to project ignorance that Chavali knew she had to be lying. It came from the way she waved the conversation off, trying to shut it down, and the nervous warble to her voice. "I liked Ramelia a great deal, so I came to help her. She did all the work and came up with all the conclusions."

"And what conclusions were those?"

"I couldn't say."

Chavali arched an eyebrow. "You assisted her, yet she never discussed her ideas with you? Asked your opinion? Had you organize her notes? What exactly did you do to help?"

Candy blushed and averted her gaze. "Well, I mean. I carried and fetched things for her."

"I imagine your command of magic assisted with such things." Chavali threw the statement out as a net, casting for whatever fish she might catch.

The woman's mouth fell open, and she stammered for a second or two before managing to say, "I don't command magic. I just know a few things to help out. That's all. It's nothing, really. Hardly worth mentioning."

Chavali found this reaction interesting, since all the mages she'd known—including the one in her clan—considered magic a precious gift of the Creator, no matter how small or limited. She opened her mouth to attempt to draw more from the woman, only to stop as a howl rent the air. Full of rage, the sound rang out nearby, close enough they had cause to worry.

Ander's head snapped around, and he raised his bow, pointing it at the trees. "That's no wolf."

"No, I don't think so either," Eliot said. He passed the bulb to

Chavali and pulled his blades out. "Set it someplace," he suggested to her.

Sean pulled a short, thin blade out from under his cloak and gulped. "I wonder if it's true they can infect others with a bite?"

"Let's see about not finding out," Ander murmured.

Cracking and crunching announced a large creature crashing through the trees to the left. Chavali looked for someplace to set the flowers as she drew her dagger. Before she saw anywhere appropriate, a monster stumbled into the grotto. "*Yekalta*," she breathed, awed by the sight.

Dark fur covered its entire body. Both hands and feet ended in sharp claws. Instead of a man's face, he had a shortened wolf's muzzle with excessively long fangs. Everywhere, it had thick bunches of muscle, and it stood at least as tall as Colby. Wild, dark eyes roved over the group as he roared and flung himself at them.

Ander let an arrow fly, sinking it into the creature's shoulder. It howled and lunged, backhanding the man aside. Eliot dropped into his fighting stance, waiting for it to come to him. Sean made a small noise in his throat and scrambled back, bumping into Chavali and nearly stabbing himself on her knife.

Chavali snarled and shoved the plant at Sean, annoyed beyond words when he stepped on her foot. Too close for such blundering, Eliot danced around the creature's first strike and had his counterstrike batted aside. Chavali shouldered past Sean and scraped a handful of snow up.

"Hey!" she called out. Eliot stood a better chance of harming it with his weapons than she did with hers. With no one else able to assist, that left her to distract it. This thing had size, strength, and probably speed on her, and it might be better equipped. She pinched the clasp on her cloak and hurled the snowball at its head.

The glob of snow hit the creature's shoulder, attracting its attention. Tossing the cloak so it fluttered to the ground, she tucked her shoulder down and somersaulted away from where Sean had tripped and landed on his side. As she'd hoped, all of this served to confuse the creature. She heard it yelp in pain as she sprang to her feet and saw Eliot ripping his sword out of its body.

It staggered back a step, panting and gripping the fresh gash in its side. Chavali watched in horror as the wound stopped bleeding. The stories said these things took a great deal of effort to kill, and now she knew why.

"It's healing itself," Chavali said.

Eliot gritted his teeth together. "Great." With a jerk of his chin, he asked Chavali to join him in assaulting the thing.

She wanted to run. That would leave it to devour Sean, who apparently had the self-defense skills of a toddler. Ander rose to his hands and knees, shaking his head. She had no choice. At her nod, they both darted in. The large claws swung. Chavali threw herself to the side, diving under a swipe. Her blade sliced through the air, managing to cut a line up its arm with the tip. With the werewolf's attention on her, Eliot drove his sword through its leg.

It threw its head back and yowled, both arms flying out. One claw clipped Eliot's shoulder, knocking him aside. He lost his grip on his sword, leaving it in the monster's flesh. Chavali ducked under the wild swing and jammed her dagger up into its armpit. It drove its elbow down into her neck, sending shooting pain through her body and knocking her to the ground.

With his second, smaller sword, Eliot slashed across its belly. "Ander," he barked, "on your feet!" He leaned away from a swipe of the werewolf's claw, then to the side so its jaws crushed empty air.

The archer rose to one knee, still unfocused, and loosed an arrow into its chest. Chavali rolled to her knees, ignoring the pain to hurry to Sean's side. He'd managed to scramble to the cliff wall, his stiletto held out defensively. Behind her, Eliot continued to fight the thing. She swooped down on Sean, snatched his thin blade, and charged the monster.

Like every other large wall of muscle she'd ever run into, this one barely noticed. She hit its side and stabbed the thing repeatedly while it staggered in circles. The hilt of Eliot's sword ground into her hip, and she yanked at it. The damned monster had healed around the weapon, and she groaned with the effort to wrench the blade down and free. Gobs of flesh clung to the steel, and she put all her weight into shoving it into the werewolf's chest.

Her grip on the blade kept it in her hand as the creature fell, and she saw Eliot hop out of the way. Panting, he held out a hand for his sword, and she passed it over. Sean's thin blade felt inadequate after holding such a substantial amount of steel. She watched the werewolf writhe and whimper. Perhaps it would revert and come to its senses so they could question the person it pretended to be.

Eliot wiped his sleeve across his face. Chavali doubled over to catch her breath. The werewolf surged up and at her. She froze in a moment of panic and blinked in shock when a blast of fire caught it in the chest, lifted it up, and threw it into a tree. Its hair caught fire, and it spasmed, yipping with agony while it burned.

Horrified by the sight, Chavali turned to see Candy with her teeth bared and eyes locked on the werewolf. The clearing filled with the smell of burning flesh and the body shrank to human shape and size, toppling into the snow.

Candy met Chavali's gaze and the mage crumpled into hysterics. Chavali stared at her, not sure what to think of that display. Whatever reason Candy refused to acknowledge her power, it had saved her life. She sat and watched Ander get to his feet, holding his head. Sean kept his eyes on the ground as he moved to Candy's side, trying to comfort her. Eliot scraped one blade against the other, slicing the still-stuck flesh off.

"I know this man." Ander crouched beside the smoking corpse, using the hilt of a dagger to lift his face. "Owen. He lives out here in the woods with his son. I hunt with him too."

"Do you believe there are werewolves now?"

Ander glanced up at Eliot. "Yes. I do. But I don't understand any of this. Both Owen and Jack were trusted, valued friends. Hunting partners. Men of integrity."

"Except for one minor detail." As Eliot spoke, he produced a cloth from his pack and wiped his blades clean then sheathed them.

Chavali shook her head. "In the stories, werewolves go mad under the full moon."

Sean looked up from Candy with a frown, nodding. "Yes, I've heard that too. Though, it's strange it would only happen now and not, say, last month or the month before."

Eliot waved off the small mystery. "We need to take Ramelia's body to her uncle," he told Ander. "Escort Candy back and rouse the village. They need to know and prepare for more of these things. Have them send a message to me, Eliot, in Cloverdale if they need help preparing defenses or if anyone else goes missing. The bartenders at the tavern can find me."

Ander nodded. "I'll see to it. Thank you for your help here. I would be dead were it not for the both of you." He returned to Chavali's side, offering her dagger to her, hilt first.

She took it and let him help her to her feet. "Sean, do you still have the flowers, or must we dig up another?"

Sean held up the bulb, all three flowers still intact. "May I have my stiletto back?"

Chavali considered throwing it at him. In her mind, it sank into his chest as revenge for his inability to use it. She clenched her jaws and flipped it around, handing it over hilt first. He'd defended himself against her in the Tower, though when she thought about that, it really had been two very short, non-life-threatening scuffles.

"Let's go," Eliot said. "If we hurry, we can make it home by midnight."

Chapter 12

Snow began falling five minutes after they left town with the horse. Aches and pains sprang up across Chavali's shoulders and hips, tensing muscles and souring her mood. Despite the pain, she pushed herself to walk as fast as she could, with a hand on the horse's neck to keep her balance and motivation. Eventually, it all faded and she stopped noticing it. They reached the Creator's Tower a few hours later.

It seemed that no one stood guard until they walked through the archway and found a lone Creator's Path guard leaning against the wall, covered from head to toe. He took the packages and letters in need of further transport, handed over a few more for Cloverdale, and scribbled a note on his clipboard about the exchange.

"Hey, what's that flower? I've never seen anything like that before." His voice held genuine curiosity.

Tired and longing for her warm bed, Chavali ignored him and led the horse out.

"It's remarkable, isn't it? We found it at Eagle Falls."

If Sean wanted to stay behind and chat, he could walk the rest of the way home by himself. She trudged through the snow, now with fat flakes falling steadily enough they would need to plow the paths again after the storm passed. By the time she hit the edge of Cloverdale, Sean and Eliot had caught up to her, and the soft glow of the flower showed the way again.

At the town square, already covered with a foot of fresh snow, Eliot stopped and patted Sean on the shoulder. "Sean, I'll take the flower and do the report. You go ahead and get back to your wife."

"Are you sure?"

"Yes, I'm sure. Go get some sleep."

"Good night, both of you." Sean handed the flower over. He paused with his mouth open, then shook his head, shut it, and hurried inside the tavern.

Not caring about anything to do with Sean right now, Chavali led the horse to the stable. She pushed the door open and walked into a wall of warmth that made her consider dropping down here to sleep. Someone shut the door behind her, and she turned to deal with the buckles holding the sledge to the horse's harness. Eliot stood there, already doing the job.

"I thought you might need some help."

"Yes. Thank you. The walk to my room seems daunting enough without this on top."

"I also wanted to ask you a favor."

She rubbed her face, unsurprised. "What do you need?"

"I'm hoping you'll come to deliver the report with me." He stood in profile to her, dealing with the buckles on the harness, and she could see tension across his entire body.

"I thought you would ask me to do it myself."

"No. I need..." He pulled the harness off and set it on a rack to be checked over in the morning. Fishing around in the stable master's desk, he found a piece of paper and a pen to write out a note. "Would you please come with me? There's— I'd just really appreciate it."

The horse rubbed its head on Chavali's arm. She brushed snow off its mane and noticed Karias standing at the half-door of his stall, watching her. "Yes, of course." Eliot had never asked her for a favor before, and she had no reason to refuse. "Will he be up now, or do we wait until morning?"

"He's probably up now." Rolling Ramelia's body off, he leaned the sledge against the wall. "It's not actually that late, and he always seems to be available whenever someone needs him anyway."

"I have also noticed this." She led the horse to its stall and rubbed its nose, then shut it in. Someone would take care of the beast in the morning. They'd probably curse her for leaving so much undone. She could live with that. Returning to Eliot, she picked up the pack with deliveries for Cloverdale.

Eliot handed her the flowers and hefted the body over his shoulder. "I swear he's magically fused to the tower."

She opened the door with a snort and shut it after them, the cold harsher for the respite from it. They trudged in silence through the driving snow, fighting for each step. Inside the tavern, the thin, spindly bartender stood watch over the room. Several patrons sat at windows, watching the storm with steaming mugs.

Walking through with a corpse insured no one bothered them, and Chavali hid the flowers under her cloak to avoid curious questions.

She opened the doors for him along the way until they reached the main spiral stair. He stopped immediately on the fourth floor, the first of those connected by the wide stairwell, and dropped off the body with a tower servant. Later, Chavali decided she would come up and ask questions there, to learn about that process.

As they descended, Eliot fidgeted. He tugged on his jacket, rubbed his nose, raked a hand through his hair, scratched his cheek, and repeated all the gestures over and over. The movements gradually became more wooden, betraying tension as it screwed tighter. At the landing for the thirteenth floor, he paused and took a deep breath, then plunged down the hallway.

This behavior, so bizarre for him, made her watch him carefully. Nothing had been strange about him until he ran into Patrick. Why would meeting someone he must have known from his first life set him so on edge? The oath she swore to the Fallen popped into her head.

I renounce my former life with all its trappings of individuals and wealth—lovers and enemies, plenty and poverty, friends and foes—I renounce them all. I give myself to the Fallen and their pursuit of the greatest sin and the hope of Reunion. I will repay the Creator and Shappa for my rebirth with five years of faithful service, and may I be struck down with the Wasting should I violate the terms of our agreement.

That explained everything, and she felt stupid for not realizing it sooner. He cared about Patrick, that much she already knew. This tension had to come, at least in part, from not knowing how to handle running into him by accident.

She touched his shoulder. "There is a way, I'm sure of it. If you need my help to find it, I offer it."

"What?" He stopped and furrowed his brow at her.

"Don't act dumb." She rolled her eyes and walked into the only briefing room with the door standing open. Unsurprised to find Eldrack sitting in a chair at the table, she set the pack beside him. "I did not kill Sean." The flowers she laid gently on the table.

"Good to know." Eldrack stared at the flowers, showing the most confusion and surprise she'd seen from him so far. He reached out and picked the plant up by the stalk. "What's this?"

"The thing Ramelia studied in Eagle Falls." Chavali sat down and watched Eliot jump into a chair. She also saw Eldrack notice his behavior. Concern settled on the Administrator's brow.

Without preamble, Eliot launched into his report. He had little to say about the early parts, offering a brief overview of the uneventful stops. Eagle Falls took longer. Chavali noticed he skipped over meeting Patrick to plow through the rest of it. "We brought her body, and it seems prudent to have someone skilled examine her injuries. I don't doubt Jack killed her at this point, but it would be best to make sure."

"I see." Eldrack's eyes slid to Chavali, who had remained quiet through all of this.

She shrugged. "Something else is going on in that town, but I don't know what. I suggest sending someone to check on Eagle Falls again soon. He told them to send for help if they needed it." She waited for Eliot to cough up the reason he dragged her here. As the seconds ticked by with nothing but silent uncertainty from him, she realized that reason may have been to stand in for him when he lost his nerve. "Eliot encountered someone from his first life. The man is named Patrick, and they had a close relationship."

Eldrack's brow raised, and he gave Eliot his full attention. "Ah. There are, of course, rules for this sort of thing. Let's hear the specifics so we can determine what should be done."

Eliot covered his face and sighed. "He knows I died. He went to the funeral and watched my parents bury my body. I thought he was dead too. Then there he was, carrying firewood in Eagle Falls. He just happened to wind up in a town less than ten miles from here."

"What kind of relationship did you have?" Eldrack at his most sympathetic grated on Chavali's nerves.

Eliot looked up at Eldrack, his expression raw and pleading. "I love him. Creator help me. I know I took that oath, but Eldrack, I can't. Knowing he's there, so close, I can't walk away and never look back. He saw me too, and I even tried to talk to him."

This explained everything, and Chavali had no idea what to suggest for resolving it. "That argument happened because he wanted to know how you live and breathe now, and you couldn't tell him, yes?"

Eliot nodded. "He wouldn't tell me how he was alive either. Because I heard he'd been killed. Since I couldn't talk, I couldn't press him."

Fingering the flowers, Eldrack picked up the pack and pulled the letters out. "I'm glad you restrained yourself in offering explanations. Chavali, I'd like your opinion of Patrick."

"I have none. We did not meet, and I saw him only briefly."

He flipped through the letters and stopped at one that he then plucked out of the small stack and set aside. "I see. In that case, Eliot, you need to think long and hard about what we should do here. There are protocols for this sort of thing, but I'd rather handle it individually, with a solution that works for everyone whenever possible, instead of following impassive rules." Setting aside the stack of envelopes, he picked up the separate one and ripped it open.

Eliot blanched. "I understand."

With his reaction, Chavali also understood. "Letting me rescue my clan was against those 'impassive rules,' yes?"

"Yes. Quite." Eldrack scanned the letter, frowning deeper with each passing second. "The Lady of Ket is dead."

Chavali's head snapped to attention. "What? How?"

"The third fish swallows whole, I'd guess." At his mention of her prophecy in Ket, Chavali scowled. Eldrack continued, "Her daughter found the body, and no one saw anything, though it's clear she was murdered. The Regent hasn't been announced yet. The leading candidate is the Lady's brother. Strange. I would expect the husband."

Chavali, Colby, Harris, and Portia had each come close to death at least once to prevent that murder. For nothing. Granted, they did accomplish other things. It still galled her to know how futile those efforts had been.

"You did important work there, Chavali. That mission was *not* a waste of time or of blood. " Eldrack turned his thrice-damned sympathy on her.

"Of course not," she snapped.

Beside her, Eliot sighed and stood. "I'll...figure things out, Eldrack."

Eldrack nodded and gathered the letters. "I appreciate your telling me about Patrick instead of trying to keep it a secret. You have good judgment, Eliot. Use it."

Chavali's irritation faded. Some idiot woman died far from here, probably from her own stupidity. It happened every day. Eliot, though, stood here now. She touched his shoulder, hoping to provide some measure of comfort as they walked out.

"I'm fine. I'll be fine. Plan to spar tomorrow."

"As you say. We did well against that werewolf, yes?"

"Yes." A smile ghosted at the corners of his mouth. "You're better in a real fight than practice, which is good. Most people are the other way around."

She grinned. "Perhaps I should practice less."

"Nice try." They reached the landing for the stairs, and Eliot pointed down. "Are you hungry? I'm going to grab a bite before heading to bed."

As much as she wanted to offer her shoulder and ear, she knew Karias would be even more unpleasant tomorrow if she failed to see Colby tonight. Even if they accomplished nothing of value, she needed at least to be able to say she started working on it. "I must tend to other things. Until tomorrow afternoon."

He nodded and walked down the stairs, giving her a wave. As she turned with her own wave, she caught sight of Eldrack standing in the hall, watching them from a distance. He smiled at her, and even from a few dozen feet away, she could feel his smug satisfaction. It made her roll her eyes and climb the steps. That man paid too much attention to everything and everyone.

After a brief stop in her own room to drop off her pack and winter clothes, she went to Colby's room and stood outside his door, staring at it. What she'd offered to help him with would require her to delve deeply. She'd never done that before. It meant picking through his thoughts and memories. This ought to be handled by someone with skill and experience.

She was stalling. This task promised to be unpleasant, and she had no desire to do it. A week ago, she made the offer because he seemed upset and disturbed, and she wanted her clan healthy and whole. That want had not changed. She needed to either knock on this door or go tell the horse she changed her mind and withdrew or postponed the offer, for whatever reason she thought the horse-spirit would accept.

Annoyed at herself for considering the coward's path, she knocked on the door. Colby opened it, barefoot with a book in hand. His shirt hung loose, and she saw past him to the rumpled bed. He smiled at her. In the next moment, his face fell into concern.

"Are you alright?"

She schooled her expression down, chiding herself for not doing it before knocking. This place made her comfortable enough to drop her guard. Parts of the tower did, anyway. This part, for example. "Is this too late? I can come in the morning."

"No, it's fine." He stood aside. "I was only reading." He shut the door behind her and set the book on his table. "What's wrong?"

"Nothing." She waved off his concern and plunged in. "I returned not long ago and am wide awake still, so I thought perhaps it would be a good time to see about the things Pale did to your mind."

"Oh." His face fell with disappointment. "I'm not sure I'm up for

119

that right now."

"I suspect—" Someone else knocking on the door interrupted her. She sighed and dropped into the chair at his table while Colby answered the door again.

The new visitor surprised her. Railan stood there, the slashed scars across her face marring an amused smile. "Oh, that's funny. I was looking for you, Chavali, but that's not why I'm here. Looks like I can get two birds at once."

Colby let her in and leaned against the door, arms crossed and expression closed. "I guess two telepaths are better than one."

"Better than two cooks, at any rate." Railan's favorite loose pants, the fabric dark with a geometric pattern in a lighter shade, swished as she crossed the room. Colby's room had only one other chair, sitting at his desk, and she took it. "Chavali, I'm sorry I haven't had time before this to work with you about Pale's memories. Since you're here, though, let's work on his." She jerked a thumb at the big man, making him frown.

He rubbed his eyes and sighed. "Ladies, I know this important, but I'm actually pretty tired."

"That's fine." Railan shrugged. "You don't have to do anything but stay still. Lie down and fall asleep if you want. We'll be doing all the work." She beckoned to him, inviting him to sit on his bed. "Chavali's never done this before, so you might experience some of the memories again. Can't be helped. Since hers only works with physical contact, you can hold onto her hand and squeeze it if things get too difficult."

"You mean if I want to stop and give up."

"No," Railan said with a sigh, "I mean if you're experiencing significant mental anguish. We're here to help, not to make things worse.

If there's failure here, it'll be on our part, not yours."

Chavali gave Railan a flat look. "This makes me feel so much better."

Barking out a laugh, Railan hopped up and grabbed Colby's arm to goad him to his bed. "Meddling in the mind is a tricky thing. Even those of us with lots of practice fail for one reason or another, all the time. Have you been able to read every single person you've ever touched?" From her intonation, she had a clear expectation for the answer to be "no."

"Yes."

Railan stopped and stared at her. "Really?"

"Yes." Chavali turned to examining her fingernails. "I cannot turn it off. You already know this. Nothing can stop them."

"Them?"

Scowling at her slip, Chavali growled in her throat. "It's not important. What was your point?"

Railan shoved Colby, and though he could have resisted, he sat on the edge of his bed. She shrugged. "Don't feel bad if it doesn't work right."

Such a statement deserved no response. "What will we do, exactly?"

"I'd like to know that too," Colby said. "Since it's my mind."

Railan pushed on Colby's forehead, trying to make him lie down. "Relax. You might pass out, and neither of us can catch you, so let's prevent head injuries. We're going to dive into your mind and poke around to see if Pale left anything behind. If all goes well, you'll feel nothing. If not, you'll get to experience some memories over again. Odds are good they'll be the worst of the worst."

"This might be unnecessary," he protested.

"Lie down, you big, stubborn oaf." Railan pulled a chair next to the bed and patted it, inviting Chavali into it.

"What is it you fear we will see?" Chavali moved to stand beside the other chair. She understood his concerns and had to make him want to push past them. He'd spent his life relying on physical strength and faith, neither of which would help him through this. Finding himself in the position of damsel in distress had to grate for such a stalwart defender of others. It probably also terrified him. "I made this offer, Colby, and you accepted it already. You hoped it would be only me, only one person, and for this," she gestured to Railan, "I am sorry. I don't know how to do this yet, and so I need a teacher."

"Colby," Railan held up a hand in a solemn oath, "I swear that nothing we do here will end up in the archives, and neither of us will talk about any of it with anyone but you, each other, and possibly our Healers. They've all already pledged to hold our secrets close, so you can count on them."

Chavali nodded. "I also swear this, and you know that if there is one thing I can be trusted with, it's secrets."

Railan smirked. "So annoyingly true."

"I will, of course, use all of it against you but only in private." Chavali gave him an encouraging smile, one she hoped would ease his concerns more.

Colby huffed and squirmed. "Alright, I just— It's my mind. I kind of need it." He meet Chavali's gaze, and she saw pleading, to be gentle perhaps, or to not judge him harshly.

"I promise we won't break anything," Railan said.

"Nothing important, at any rate." Chavali sat beside his bed and took his hand. The spirits surged across the link formed by the contact, feeding her his thoughts.

This is the strangest thing I've ever done, aside from waking up after dying.

"It's strange for me too."

Chavali, you can hear me?

"Yes. If you prefer, I can avoid answering. I know it calls attention to my intrusion."

No, it's okay. Thank you for being here. Under his thoughts, she noticed Karias's thread, radiating approval and providing a solid, steady core of confidence for Colby to lean on.

"You're welcome." She squeezed his hand, and he returned it.

"Chavali, I'm going to take your other hand." Railan sat beside her, bracing herself between the chair and wall. Her hand slipped into Chavali's. Railan's mind felt ordered and calm, reminding her of Robin's. Where that despicable man had used his abilities to hide his desires and intentions, she kept hers tidy as a matter of course. The spirits flooded through pathways left open to them and found themselves blocked from others.

"Whoa." Railan let go, cutting them off from her. She took a few deep breaths. "Damn, Chavali. You're a tidal wave. No wonder no one can resist you."

This is going wrong already.

Chavali ignored Colby's miserable thoughts. "Will I need to do this alone?"

"No, I just wasn't expecting that." Railan shook out her hands and took another deep breath then settled her hand into Chavali's again. *Here we go. I'll pull you in deeper. Pay attention, and you should be able to do this by yourself.*

Once before, a velvet whisper had threaded through her mind. He'd used it to violate her mind and leave a stinking, oily stain. Chavali flinched and recoiled, seeing his face again, feeling his touch again, hearing his voice again.

"If you are very, very lucky, we will kill you." His fingertip *caressed her skin, somehow jolting her entire body with wracking agony.*

Grinding her teeth together, Chavali forced the memory away. That vile man wasn't here, and Railan wouldn't intentionally hurt her. The Order of the Strong Arm had no more sway here than any other order. She took a deep breath and focused on how Railan's mental touch differed from his. Where he'd slithered in and sought every corner, she flowed through and pooled in the center. She carried no filth as he had.

This experience, she noticed, felt like a partner asking to dance, and not a master subjugating a slave. Railan waited with a patient, encouraging smile instead of grabbing. The difference eased her, and Chavali directed her thoughts to accepting the invitation. A piece of her touched the piece of Railan, the same as two people holding hands. Then, Railan pulled.

The sensation reminded her of falling, without the fear of landing. They flew through billowing, white clouds, puffy and soft. Chavali watched all around and paid fierce attention to the sensations. Colby's mind had no defenses, she realized. This outer layer served only as a boundary, not a barrier.

With a flash of white, Railan set her bare foot down in a field. "We're in."

Chavali surveyed the scene, dismayed to discover the sky here had silvery-gray cloud cover. At least she could bask in the lush yellow-green of the tall grasses. Her own dress, she saw, matched the dark red-brown of her hair. Railan wore clothes in a warm honey-brown with golden yellow accents.

"Your eyes are green." The minds of others always taunted her this way. "I don't remember the word for that shade."

"I think most people just say 'green.' Come on. Let's not waste time here."

"Of course." Duly chastised, Chavali hurried along with Railan. She schooled herself to focus on their purpose: looking for any taint left behind by Pale. "Can he hear us?"

"Unless I've messed up, he should be unaware of us. We can communicate with him if we want to, which you might want to do to direct him to think about a specific thing."

The meadow stretched into infinity, as did the cloud cover. "Does this mean his mind is empty?"

"No. It means he's not experiencing any strong emotions or having especially coherent thoughts. Every mind is different, and there aren't any hard and fast rules, but based upon this general paradigm, I'd say the sky means he's not having a sunny day."

"It represents his unease and dislike of the situation?"

"That's my guess." Railan nodded and scanned the scene. "We have to determine what mechanism his mind uses to link his thoughts to his memories and use it to find something we're not sure exists that could be connected to anything."

"So this will be easy." Chavali sighed and applied herself to the puzzle. "Would that be based upon his personality? Or does this have more to do with us?"

"His mind, his rules. We *can* bend it to our will. We're not going to, because that's subverting his will in favor of our own. It's wrong, remember that. You can look, you can touch, you can fix, but you never, ever change it to how you want it. That's the same thing as holding a knife to their throat."

Chavali shuddered and hugged herself. "This is what Robin does as his primary weapon."

"Yes, that seems to be the case. And then he taught Pale to do it too." Railan stopped and settled her hands on her hips. "You know Colby better than me. What do you think we should do here? Think metaphorically and symbolically."

Metaphors and symbols had been Chavali's tea and cake for years. She crouched down into the grass, thinking about what she knew of his past. He'd been a soldier, a mounted knight for some lord in Grippa. Putting her hand on the ground, she scooped up a handful of the earth and let it fall. He'd been around riding horses all his life. Karias bonded to him several years ago, and he thought duplicity to be the greatest sin.

This man had shown that, as much as he hated lies, he told them to himself often enough. His mind would follow that pattern, she figured. That meant the meadow had to be a lie. Grass and dirt and clouds showed him as he believed himself to be. The true man lurked underneath.

It seemed that things often lay beneath her feet in these

mindscapes. If she counted her dreams, the ground nearly always concealed something or proved to be the way out. While that might be her own mental paradigm, she imagined there could only be so many ways for a mind to defend itself. Besides, the only other option seemed to be the clouds, which had no real features.

She looked up at Railan to see her smiling down in approval. "You already knew where to look but wanted me to think it through and figure it out."

"Most people learn best that way."

Chavali's lip curled. That truth never failed to irritate her. "How do we break through the ground without harming him?"

"What's your best guess?"

"I see how this will be." She sighed again and thought about it. "Digging seems intrusive, but I see no other way, unless we are capable of things I'm not aware of. I don't really understand my surroundings."

Railan nodded and crouched beside her. "How do you normally get what you want out of someone's mind?"

"I say things to make them think of the subject I want more information about. Often, I compare what they say to what they think and derive more this way than from one or the other alone."

"So it's all passive for you. That's interesting. I'm an active telepath, and the fact you can enter mindscapes means you have the capacity to be one too. Maybe that's why you can't control what you've got: because the passive side is so much stronger than the active side."

Chavali felt confident the spirits had more to do with that than any latent abilities she might have on her own. If she had any at all. Everything came from the spirits, so far as she knew. She never sensed thoughts before she became the Seer and had no ability to craft illusions or spew accurate prophecies then either.

"Perhaps. What does this mean here?"

"It means that I can do, for example, this." Railan touched the ground and melted. Her form oozed into a puddle that sank into the ground. Before disappearing completely, she put a floppy, squishy hand on Chavali's arm and sent a jolt through her. Her body lost its shape and slid to the ground. She found all the gaps and cracks and tunnels to pour through it to the other side.

Her body solidified on new ground, kneeling on a landing of the stone spiral stair in the center of the Fallen tower. In Colby's mind, the number one stood out starkly as an orange stain on the blue-gray stone. She'd never seen it before and had to agree that it seemed quite obvious to someone without her colorblindness. The archway it indicated opened into a stone hallway resembling those in the Fallen tower.

"This is Colby," she said without waiting for Railan to pose a stupid question. "He is honest and straightforward, so I expect his memories to be laid out either from newest to oldest, or least important to most."

"Most people put their darkest, most intense memories as far away as possible, but I think you're probably right about him. He might have managed to stow them inside boxes or some other closeable containers." Railan took the first step down and beckoned Chavali to come with her. "We won't find anything up here, that's for sure." She smirked. "Nothing of relevance to our actual purpose, anyway."

Following her down the steps, Chavali touched the stone wall and trailed her fingertips along the cool surface. "Is this common? For one's home to affect how the mind works to this degree?"

"Yes. Watch out what you touch. You can cause changes by accident."

Chavali stuffed her hands into her pockets. "What should I look for?"

"Things that feel out of place or strange. His mind knows what belongs and what doesn't, so even if the insertion was deftly done, he knows, and that'll show. Do you know if he's been having nightmares?"

"What difference does that make?"

"There are a few different kinds of nightmares. One of them is your mind trying to tell you something's wrong."

Frowning, Chavali tried not to think about her own bizarre nightmare last night. Mucking around in Colby's mind wasn't the right time to discuss her problems. "I seem to recall—" Did Railan know about Karias? He had given her the impression he'd never spoken to anyone else before, so probably not. She might know what Eldrack knew, which amounted to being aware he had some form of specialness to him. "Yes, I think he mentioned nightmares. We did not discuss them."

"You said you saw his memories when you found him in that cave. What were those about? Nightmare-worthy stuff?"

Chavali remembered flashes of fire and agony, confusion and smoke. "Yes. Quite. It was his death, only I had seen it before, and this was different. It had grown more intense and destructive."

"It'll be about fire then, and failure. We'll try the bottom first and see what's there."

They hurried down the steps, Chavali watching for anything out of place. As they descended deeper and passed more archways, the stone grew warmer yet darker. At the level labeled with a ten, she paused and peered through the archway, wondering if she might be wrong about the organization here.

"Railan, perhaps we should stop and take a look before we go too far. I would hate to walk all the way down only to discover we need to be closer to the top. We both walk up enough stairs every day with our legs."

"Have you noticed the intervals between levels get longer as we go?" Railan stopped and nodded. "Yes, let's take a look here. Before we walk through this arch, though, let me tell you one more thing. His mind will work actively to defend sensitive memories. It doesn't look like he cares that we're here, but he may very well object to us actively rifling through certain memories."

"Which means what?"

"I'll go first. You tell me if you see anything weird. Basically, nothing changes except we may meet active defenses." Railan stepped through the archway and walked down the hall.

Following her, Chavali swept her gaze back and forth, checking the walls and ceiling and doors. As they passed door number seven, the same as her own room number, she noticed a string of pink and maroon beads hanging from a hook at her eye level. She stopped, confused. Why would he have this here? A memory of this should be new and of passing interest.

Compelled to find out, she put her hand on the knob and turned it, ignoring the fact that Railan kept going. Behind it, she found a perfect copy of her bedroom in full color. She saw the multicolored spatters of paint on the screen in the corner and the hideous pattern of her rug for the first time. Likewise, the pot she used to cover her magicked light stone at night had been poorly glazed with strange colors.

Stepping inside, she took it all in, wondering what this meant and why he had it in his head. He'd only been there twice that she knew of, and both visits had been brief. As a result, the level of detail astounded her. Her table had the three scratches exactly where she remembered them being.

When she peered around the screen, she came face to face with a wagon from her clan. He'd noticed, along with the general details, the brush strokes of the paint and the imperfections in the wood. It had been ten years since she saw the bright blues and reds and greens they'd been painted with. This particular one had belonged to Keino's family, and Colby must have gotten very close to it. Some parts remained fuzzy, and she found it fascinating to see what attracted his eye and what didn't.

She put her hand on the wagon her entire clan had expected her to move into at some point. Keino had pressed her up against this wheel once, trying to force her to kiss him. He knew she wanted to, but she wouldn't do it. She hated listening to his thoughts more than anyone else's. His acceptance and desire bothered her more than her mother's rejection and fear. Mamá's issues made sense. Keino's never did.

It felt wrong, blank. This wheel should feel sturdy and strong, capable of carrying dozens of generations of her clan. It should be smooth, with seams where parts had been replaced, and thick and solid. The strangeness reminded her where she was. Colby must not have touched any of the wagons.

Pulling her hands away to avoid sullying her own memories, she paced to the end of the wagon. The door stood shut, and a book with a red-brown leather cover lay on the platform. It struck her as so incongruous to have a book, of all things, connected to her clan that she picked the slim volume up. On the side, a silver lock with a keyhole held it shut.

"I can appreciate why this particular room would grab your attention, but I'm pretty sure it's not what we came for."

Railan's voice behind her made Chavali jump, and she dropped the book. It tumbled through the air to land in the same spot she'd picked it up from. "No, of course not."

"It's alright." Railan put a hand on her shoulder and squeezed it. "If I saw a big sign pointing to what he thought of me, I'd be tempted to take a look too."

Chavali nodded and took a deep breath. "It seems safe to say his thoughts aren't organized by date. Room seven on the tenth floor is mine, and here I find not only his memory of my room but also my clan. The two locations are connected in his mind, with the obvious link of me. I'd guess all his memories of moments and events are in books."

"It's a fairly common metaphor. Books hold stories, and many people think of their memories as stories. I'm kind of interested how you do it, but that's not really any of my business. We're both telepaths. We can delve into the memories you pulled from Pale without having to do this kind of thing. And, if we did try it anyway, it would be easy to accidentally wind up in a fight to the death. Best not to chance that."

"Agreed." Chavali followed Railan back to her room, then out of that door. She shut it and noticed the hanging beads clacked against the door. The sound seemed off somehow. Perhaps it came from his height. Things might sound different from seven feet than they did from five and a half.

"This wasn't a waste of time," Railan assured her. "We learned something. Let's go try his room."

If they found what they needed in his room, what would they find at the bottom? Chavali paused, staring at her door and frowned. If he put his books in their proper locations and linked the locations by people, then she should have found other things in there. "Wait. Why is there no link to Ket in that room? We went on that mission together, and we had a heated argument, which should be a strong memory. I saved his life, twice."

She grabbed the handle and opened the door again, bustling inside again. It made no sense to link some things one way and other things a different way. He had more logic to him than that. As much as he might want to suppress such unpleasant memories, they should be here. Stalking around the room, she opened and shut drawers. She found another red-brown book inside one, a thicker tome with a more substantial lock.

It held almost no allure. Brushing her fingers across it, she found herself with nothing more than the plain curiosity of seeing a closed box. The other book caught her attention more. She wanted to see her clan, not herself. Colby would have memories of Papá different from her own. He'd have memories of many people whose loss ached most when she lay at night in an empty bed.

Shutting the drawer, she whirled to face the room and glared at it. "There is a link here, I know it. Colby is an idiot, but he's not a flighty twit."

Railan smirked. "If he doesn't want to think about it every time he sees you, the link here will be hidden behind or under something." She leaned against the shut door and nodded towards the bed. "Try under there."

The implications of her suggestion arched one of Chavali's eyebrows up. She supposed that offering to help him with memories and giving him a person to speak to about spirits had been a rather intimate proposal. In the mind of a man, one type of intimacy could easily be interchanged for another. It made a kind of sense.

She flung the covers aside to peer under the bed and found water. At least this hadn't been between the sheets. "Yes, this must be it. I cannot imagine any other reason to find the ocean here."

Railan moved to Chavali's side and took her hand. They dove in together. On the other side, Chavali landed on her feet in the basement of the Lady of Ket's estate. Jail cells lined the walls. The particular one they stood in front of had blood splashed across the walls and pooled on the floor. A red-brown book sat on the bench inside the cell.

"This is not the right place." When he thought of her and Ket, he remembered her killing that guard in cold blood instead of their conciliatory conversation about it later. Wonderful. At least he'd hidden it. "But it *is* Ket."

"Then we should be able find a connection." Railan tugged her to the door.

Chavali frowned at what they found on the other side. A blanket of snow covered the outside of a sheltered, stone nook. A pool of blood lay atop a frozen puddle outside it. Inside, rocks ringed a firepit in the center with an emerald green book instead of a fire, and a spike had been hammered into a crack in a large boulder. More blood covered the inside, in spatters and clumps.

"I have no idea what this place is."

"Not Ket?"

"No, there was no place like this near the city. That means what happened here must be similar to what happened in that cell." No wonder he reacted so harshly, and no wonder he jumped to the conclusions he did. "I saw no sign of a triggered memory when we argued about that moment, either time." She'd missed it. What else had she missed? Were her skills slipping, or was she never as good as she thought? Had she misunderstood everyone in her clan?

Railan nudged her arm. "Focus, Chavali. Do you see anything weird here?"

Reminded of their goal, she rubbed her face and took a deep breath then scanned the scene. She could ignore her own self-doubts long enough to do this. Her second clan needed her, and she would do whatever she had to.

Flicking her eyes from one blood spray to another, she searched the rocks and patterns. Nothing stood out at first, then she let her gaze linger over each significant object. One piece gave her a strange itch inside her head. "The spike." She gathered a handful of her skirt and stepped gingerly over the rocks, avoiding the still-wet blood. "It's...not right. I cannot explain this."

"Try."

She threw a glare back at her teacher, getting a smirk in response. Closer to it, she examined the spike and tried to put what she noticed about it into words. "It's subtle. Small. I think the spike belongs to the scene, but it doesn't belong *here*. It's in the wrong place. Could this be Pale's trigger?"

"I doubt it." Railan shrugged. "This memory is probably pretty traumatic, but it's got no fire. If he had fire on his mind, then she mucked with a fire memory. Doesn't mean it's not her work. Do you want to try to deal with this?"

Chavali reached up and stopped short of touching the spike. "I don't know what to do. Show me, please. The last thing I want to do is make things worse here."

"You know, Chavali, for someone with such a low opinion of Colby, you're very concerned about his well-being." Stepping up beside her, Railan examined the spike. "A person could get the wrong idea about your feelings for him."

Chavali arched an eyebrow again, eyes narrowed and flat. "I am everything he despises. It's natural we should grate against each other."

"Yes. Except you don't. You call him an idiot and sneer at his beliefs and ideals, then you bend over backwards to help him with this and ask him to teach you to read. You fought with Sean, not Colby." Railan took Chavali's hand and touched her fingers to the spike.

"I have fought with Colby."

"Not in the cafeteria."

This conversation reminded her of one she'd had with Mamá several times about Keino. "What difference does that make?" The spike felt frigid and rough on her fingertips. "Colby has never tried to pry about the clan or spread information about me. He is too stupidly honest to do such things."

"Mmhmm." The corner of Railan's mouth quirked up, and Chavali got the impression she found all of this highly amusing. "Focus on the spike. Think of it as a picture broken into pieces, a jigsaw puzzle.

You have to put the puzzle back together."

Chavali frowned at it, happy to abandon the other conversation. "How can it be many pieces? It's one—" She sucked in a breath as Railan shoved her fingers into the spike. In flashes, she saw Pale's cold, hard glare from the spike's point of view. It knew it belonged in the blood on the frozen puddle. Pale had torn it from its rightful place and jammed it into the stone.

"She must have used this as an anchor point." Railan covered Chavali's hand with her own, curling her fingers around it. "By removing the anchor point, we'll make it easier to remove the trigger in the fire memory. Feel the spike. Let it tell you what to do. It's a memory in itself, a detail Colby remembers for a reason. Pale picked it for a reason too."

Chavali nodded, too breathless to speak. She stared at the spike, holding it tighter than Railan's hand forced her to, willing it to show her what it meant to Colby. Bits and pieces flashed for her, of a man with emerald green eyes, of five people stained with the filth of poverty, of a sword dripping with blood, of soldiers.

What she saw made her want to let go and flee. Railan held her in place. "It's got to be a bad memory, or Pale wouldn't have used it. Stay strong, Chavali. Let it guide you to put it back where it belongs."

Her eyes burned with tears that belonged to Colby. "It killed a child."

"Where, Chavali. Focus on where, not what. You can do this."

Gritting her teeth, she growled and yanked the spike out of the wall. The movement knocked Railan's hand away. Chavali held on, certain she needed to. It dragged her to the puddle and threw her to her knees. She drove the spike into the blood and ice and knew too much about how it had wound up there and what part of the child it had pierced.

"Good." Railan lunged in and wrapped her arms around Chavali, holding onto her while she slumped to the ground. "You did good. That was rough, but you did it."

"Stop it!" Chavali wriggled and squirmed. "Do not touch me!" She needed to breathe. She needed time. Sympathy and pity did her no good, not here and not anywhere else.

Railan let her go and gave her space. After several seconds, she said, "We should stop for today. You need a break."

On her hands and knees, Chavali wanted to throw up and cry and hurt something and curl up in a ball and run forever. She nodded. "This is difficult."

"Yes. Give me your hand, and I'll show you how to leave."

Chapter 13

Chavali found herself slumped across Colby in a world once more devoid of color. He must have shifted her body, because her head lay on his chest, nowhere near the chair. He'd fallen asleep and now dreamed of that scene at the rocks. "Wake up," she croaked out. Letting go of his hand, she cleared her throat and sat up on the edge of his bed.

"I think you probably can spend more time on this than me." Railan stood and brushed herself off, with no sign of lingering effects from the jaunt. "As much as my experience would make it go faster, you're capable enough to handle it, and having another person who can do this is a benefit to the Fallen in general."

"You want me to continue on my own and take care of it myself." A tiny thrill coursed through her, for the time she'd be able to spend surrounded by colors. The dull, harsh weight of the duty and the awful things she'd see blunted it.

"Yes. Are you up for that? It doesn't need to be done in a rush. Space the sessions out so you can recover between them. Once or twice a week should get it taken care of without stressing you too much."

Nodding, Chavali rubbed her face. "Yes, I will handle it. I already gave my word that I would." She paused and huffed in irritation. "I apologize for—" Unable to find the right word, she waved a hand and shook her head.

"Don't worry about it. When you inspect memories, you're bound to get caught up in them. Remember that."

Chavali nodded, grateful the matter could be closed without ill will. "Should I wake him up? He's in that memory."

Railan shrugged. "If you want. His mind might resolve part of it if you leave him. Or he might just stew in the parts about it that horrify him the most. Hard to tell. You've got good instincts, so let them guide you. Also, make sure you eat before going to bed. Doing this stuff sucks the life right out of you if you let it."

"I will. Thank you." She turned to watch Colby twitch, and she frowned at the sight of him in obvious distress. If she chose not to wake him, she needed to leave rather than witness this. It would be a retreat, of course, to abandon him after causing his nightmare in the first place. She gritted her teeth and patted his cheek, catching part of that awful scene as his mind replayed it. "Wake up, Colby. It's a dream."

He sucked in a breath and grabbed her arms, eyes wide and wild and unfocused.

His fingers clamped so hard around her that he threatened to break her bones. She gulped at this reminder of his size and strength. Though she knew he'd never purposely hurt her, anything could happen with him in this state. "Colby, you're safe. This is your own bed, in the tower. That was a nightmare and nothing more."

Finally seeing her, he relaxed and let her go then rubbed his face while she sat up and gave him space. "Thank you. Did you succeed?"

"Yes. And no. I have begun the process but will have to continue it. Railan showed me what to do, and now she need not be here. Unless you wish her to be."

Sitting up, he shook his head. "She's busy, and it's disturbing enough to have one person in my head, let alone two."

"Did you feel any of it?"

"I think I fell asleep right away, then I had a dream about the stairs, and your clan's wagons and your room. It segued into something else. A nightmare, I guess." He shrugged.

"A memory." She considered reaching out to offer comfort, yet he kept shifting away from her, inch by inch. "Do you wish to speak of it? This man who murdered a child and four other people?"

He frowned and looked down. "Before I died, I was a soldier in the Queen's Guard in Grippa. Laren was a member of my squad, and he —" Sliding his feet off the other side of the bed, he shook his head. "It's an unpleasant story."

"All the more reason to speak of it. Pale was able to use it against you for the very reason that you refuse to discuss it. Besides, I have been told, over and over, that the more times I tell the tale of my death, the easier it will be to deal with. In following this advice, I have found it to be infuriatingly true."

He smiled at her, weary and amused. "Only you would hate that."

"Perhaps." She stood and smoothed her dress down. He chose to evade the subject, and she chose to let him. "I have been instructed to eat after doing this. Do you wish to join me?"

Straightening, he raked a hand through his dark hair and breathed deeply. "No, I had a good meal before all of this. Go ahead. I'll see you soon."

"Sleep well." She let herself out and hurried downstairs to grab a quick meal. Walking through the cafeteria, she noticed people watching her and muttering to each other. They had so many rumors to choose from. In light of that, she sat at an isolated table and ate swiftly. Instead of lingering and enjoying tea there, she took a mug to her room and let it help her relax in privacy. Someone had tidied the mess she made without putting things away. It could wait until tomorrow. She climbed into bed when she felt settled and tired enough to sleep.

When she woke, she heard the remnants of a strange scream echoing in the room. Her throat felt raw, and her heart raced. Another changed nightmare haunted her as she dressed and hurried down the stairs to get breakfast. The food, delicious as always, turned her stomach, and she sat staring at the wall and sipping hot tea until someone sat beside her.

"Chavali?" The pretty young woman with the light hair frowned at her, oozing concern.

She blinked and turned to regard Kelly, her Healer, her assigned confidant. She barely spent any time with the younger woman and had a thought to wonder what she did all day. It also struck her that she'd never heard anyone refer to a Healer as male.

"Yes?"

Kelly carefully kept her hands to herself, already aware of Chavali's preferences and abilities. "Marjeline, she's in room number eleven, next door to you. She came to see me and said she heard you screaming during the night. I know you have nightmares all the time, but I'd gotten the impression they don't really bother you."

That noise she heard when she woke up had come from her own mouth, which explained her throat. Chavali sipped at her tea and looked down to watch the brown water swirl in her mug. "What of it?"

"Chavali." Kelly fixed her with a stern, brook-no-nonsense look. "This is exactly the kind of thing you should come to see me about."

"I seriously doubt you are capable of assisting with this matter."

Kelly clasped her hands together and made a noise of frustration in her throat. "Please let me try. You know I won't tell anyone else what you say to me without your permission, not even Eldrack. Come up to my office and talk about it. If you don't want me to say anything, I'll just listen. Everybody needs someone to listen to."

Chavali stifled a scowl. She had things to do today. She also missed Pasha, who had been about the same age as Kelly. This business of Eldrack choosing who she ought to confide in grated on her, yet she could only say so much to Eliot and Colby, and they were only men anyway. Penny could help her but did enough for her clan already by taking care of the children. Besides, as she'd been told over and over, Kelly had training for this sort of thing.

"Fine. I'm not hungry anyway." Grabbing her plate of barely eaten food, she stalked to the bin for dirty dishes and shoved it in then refilled her mug and stormed out. Kelly followed her up one flight of the stairs and hurried ahead to open her office door. She'd rearranged the furnishings, probably to suit Chavali's preferences.

She dropped into one of the two soft, cushioned chairs, both facing a painting of intriguing whorls and spirals. Facing Kelly distracted her, causing her to focus on her Healer instead of on the subject she came to talk about. This arrangement meant she might be able to forget about the other person in the room and actually talk in a location designed to insure privacy. In her own room, she could be disturbed by a visitor at any time. Here, no such thing would ever happen for any reason short of an attack on the tower. Even Eldrack had to wait until she left this room.

Despite having been the one to suggest this change, it irked her that Kelly had done it. The girl wanted her secrets, Eldrack wanted her secrets, everyone wanted her secrets. "I hate this."

"I know. I'm not asking you to like it." Kelly shut the door, locked it, and slipped into the other chair. "I'm asking you to use it."

For several minutes, Chavali traced the design of the painting in her head and sipped her tea. To her satisfaction, Kelly remained silent and still. "My nightmares are changing."

"They haven't changed in a long time, right?"

"They have *never* changed before. I have had all the same dreams since I became the Seer. Ten years ago."

"What do you think that means?"

"I don't know." Chavali clutched at her teacup and glared at the painting. "Many of them seem intended to be warnings, and as they change, that could mean the things they warn about draw close. I do not understand any of the warnings, though, if that's what they are. They're cryptic at best and absurd metaphors at worst. No sane person could interpret such things. The prophecies, at least, are intelligible. These are madness."

"Did the previous Seer have them too?"

"Yes. We spoke of them and of the spirits in general. She wanted me to know what to expect, so I wouldn't think myself insane."

"Spirits?"

Chavali pursed her lips and cursed on the inside. She never intended to use that word with anyone here. Colby got an exception because of Karias. No one else needed to know the source of her power. "This is probably the wrong word. It's the thing that makes me able to form illusions and read thoughts. I have noticed there are curious holes in my vocabulary."

"Ah. I see. I think we'd just put that under telepathy. Did you like the old Seer?"

Relieved the girl accepted her excuse, she paused and furrowed her brow. "Like her?"

"As a person. Did you like her?"

"What does that have to do with anything?"

"I'm just curious."

Chavali sipped her tea in silence for several long seconds, composing her thoughts on the subject, before setting the cup in its saucer. "I was chosen to be the next Seer when I was ten and had only five years to learn the trade before she died." Unpleasant memories of Marika's shaking hands filled her mind. "She explained many things and still managed to leave me to flail on my own well before I was ready for the duty. Did I 'like' her? No, I did not."

"Maybe your memories of her would change if you forgave her for not being everything you thought she should be."

"Memories do not change. We only decide to forget parts of them to better suit our conscience. It makes no difference anyway, she's dead. The dead don't care if they're forgiven or not."

Kelly left a long pause. "You don't forgive people for their sake. You do it for your own. To release the anger or hate they inspire."

Nostrils flaring, Chavali sipped at her tea. "This is a distraction and has nothing to do with the nightmares. Something changes, and I do not know what or why."

"And that uncertainty bothers you."

"Of course it bothers me," Chavali snapped. "What daft moron wouldn't be bothered by that? She said they would never change. Seer Marika lived with these for more than twenty years, and never once did they change for her. They have been the same for our Seers for hun—for a long time. That they should change for me either means something has happened or I am going insane. So yes, it *bothers* me."

"Chavali," Kelly murmured after a few seconds of quiet, "I'm on your side. We want the same thing."

"Do we? What is this magical thing we both want?"

"For you to be content enough that this second life isn't more a curse than a gift." The warble in Kelly's soft voice made Chavali glance to the side in time to watch her wipe her cheek.

Wonderful, now she'd made her Healer cry. The woman had, for some reason, devoted her life to Chavali's well-being without ever meeting her, and deserved more from her than misplaced anger. Someday, she would discover this mysterious reason. For now, she sipped at her tea and used the painting to settle herself.

"It's vexing to be surrounded by Outsiders, but I would rather be here than dead."

Nodding, Kelly flashed her a small smile. "Will you tell me about these nightmares? If they *are* warnings of some kind, maybe I can help decode them."

"I am not ready to share them yet. I am, however, ready to induct Penny and Marcus into the clan tonight. The incense and herbs I needed have arrived."

"Are you still sure you want to?"

"My clan is four people, and these two have proven themselves willing and able of taking care of the children in my stead. I have no reason not to. It would be better were they younger and able to bring children of their own into the clan, but I recognize the value of elders and their wisdom."

Kelly nodded again and looked down at her hands as she laced them together. "Would you consider letting me into your clan?"

Chavali did have to admit that she needed more people. Inducting someone whose entire job involved dealing with her held a certain allure. "Perhaps. It would mean any children born to you from that moment on would also be part of the clan."

"I'm infertile. I can't have children."

Jealousy jolted across Chavali. No one would have pushed her at Keino so hard if she'd been unable to have babies, and he might not have been half so interested. Then she wouldn't have to now think about him and wish he'd show up so she could slap him one more time.

"Ah. I will think on it. That in itself is not a reason to refuse." To consider Kelly for the clan, she'd have to get to know the woman better, which meant coming to see her more often. Papá would scoff at bringing a barren girl in. Dead men, however, did not get a vote. "This is not to be done lightly, and it is not a thing that can be undone, much like the whole Fallen enterprise."

"I understand." Kelly gave her a small smile. "I'm here whenever you want to talk about the nightmares or anything else."

"Yes, I know. Thank you." She left, her stomach growling, and found breakfast much more appealing the second time.

Chapter 14

"Again." Eliot held his swords ready, goading Chavali to attack him.

It amused her to have gone from Kelly to Eliot. The former wanted to force her to talk, and the latter needed to be forced to talk. "No." She sat, panting, holding her thigh where he'd cut it and blood stained the cloth of her skirt.

"It's minor," he growled. "You can handle it."

"Of course I can," she snapped. "You, however, came close to cutting my leg off. You're unfocused, and it made you too sloppy to prevent this. If all you can think about is Patrick, then you need to find an activity without sharp blades."

He scowled. "I'm the teacher, you're the student. *You* don't tell *me* when I've had enough."

"Perhaps not." She let go to pull her skirt up and took a good look at the cut. He'd kept it shallow, at least. It still stung and needed to be wrapped. "I, however, did not come here for lessons on how to fight while injured. I came here for practice to keep myself from getting injured in the first place. I am not your sparring partner. I'm not good enough for that, and you know it."

His eyes flicked to the tip of his second blade, the shorter one, and watched her blood slide down the edge. He let out a heavy sigh and let his shoulders sag. "You're right. I'm sorry. Go ahead." He nodded to the closed door and sheathed the clean blade.

"Don't be stupid." She flipped her dress down and squeezed the wound again. "I will not bleed to death from this. Tell me what the problem is."

Pulling a cloth from his pocket, he shook his head and cleaned the blood from his sword. "I need to go see him again, but I don't know what to say. He wants to know why I'm not dead. He knows my family, my friends, everyone. He's a link to my past that I can't afford to have."

"And yet, you love him." She sighed, wishing she could fix this for him as much as she wished she could fix things for herself. "Does he still love you?"

"I think so. He said as much." Sheathing the second blade, he touched a fingertip to his lips in a gesture to accompany reliving a kiss.

She shrugged. "Then the question is why he moved to Eagle Falls, of all places. It's not a place I would go if I wanted to maintain contact with family and friends. It's a place I would go if I wanted to disappear."

"Huh." Eliot squinted at her. "I hadn't thought of that."

"That's because you are distracted by his—" In her experience, men varied much more wildly in what they found attractive in other men than women. Her sample, admittedly, was small and shallow, and Keino certainly never thought about anyone else when she touched him. "...Whatever parts you find distracting."

He huffed a light snort. "Yes, I suppose so." Stepping to her side, he sat and took over the task of applying pressure to her cut. "Would you come with me to meet him? Eldrack trusts your opinion of people, and so do I."

She hissed from the pain of his hands clamped down. "Yes, but not today. I have made promises I will keep for tonight. We can go tomorrow."

The door opened, and Colby, of all people, leaned in. He took in the sight of them and blinked. "Sorry for the interruption. Have either of you seen— Is that blood? Are you alright?"

"I'm fine," she said as he walked in and crouched by her side. "I slipped. This is minor and will heal on its own."

Colby rolled his eyes. "Don't be difficult."

Eliot snorted. "You might as well ask the sun not to set."

"This is true. I am difficult. Everyone knows this."

Colby chuckled. "I'll take you down to get this healed." Without giving her another chance to protest, he scooped her up and carted her away.

Chavali squawked and resisted the urge to struggle. He had at least five times her strength, and if he dropped her now, it would hurt. "Tomorrow," she called to Eliot.

"Come find me whenever you're ready."

Colby's ground-eating strides had them out of the room before she could confirm. "What's tomorrow?"

"This is his business to tell or not." She noticed the muscles in his face tighten a tiny bit, showing he disliked that answer. "Suffice to say that I have plans for much of the day. If you are available now, I can fit in a reading lesson. The other thing would take too long and be too draining, I think. I must see to my clan this afternoon and evening."

"Oh. Sure."

People passing them on the stairs got those looks, the ones that said there would be a story all over the tower about Colby carrying her down the stairs by lunch. They would conveniently gloss over the part about the blood. "I will need to change my clothes after this. How long do you need to find whoever you were looking for?"

"Someone wanted Portia. I was going up anyway, so I offered to check your floor on my way out. That was my last stop before concluding she's not there. I had a thought to take Karias for a ride, but he can wait until later."

Inside, she cringed at how her next request would feed the gossip fire. At least this might distract them from her alleged consorting with demons. "May I prevail upon you to collect me a cup of tea, then?"

"Yes, I can do that. Come to my room whenever you're ready." He carried her through the archway for the nineteenth floor, taking her to a large room covered with pure white tile. It would show every tiny speck of blood yet be easy to clean. Two tables with eight chairs held eight white-robed Healers, all of whom had books and folders occupying them. One of the Healers had many years on her, at least sixty of them. The rest had no more than thirty.

"Non-life-threatening," Colby announced.

"Ginny, go handle it," the elder Healer said with a flick of her wrist.

Ginny jumped out of her chair. Colby set Chavali down gently on the floor. He stayed there, letting her lean against him. The girl pushed

Chavali's skirt up to see the cut, and she noticed that Colby took a good look before politely averting his eyes.

"Hi." The girl gave her an encouraging smile. "Um, I'm going to —"

"Just do it already," Chavali grumbled.

The girl's smile faltered. "Right," Ginny said. She put her hand over the cut and took a deep breath. Her thoughts focused on a connection she had to something Other, a connection Chavali recognized from brushing against it before. The entity her soul had been bound to as Fallen provided this power to the Healers.

Heat pushed into her thigh, spreading around the cut and searing it. Leaning her head back, Chavali groaned at the deep, intense sensation that danced the line between pleasure and pain. It lasted less than a minute and left her blinking when it ended. Her clan had an herb-healer, one with only a small touch of a gift. She'd needed that woman's help once, when she became the Seer. It had felt nothing like this.

"There. Good as new." The girl gave Chavali a bright smile and offered her a hand up.

Rocked by touching that entity, as she also had been both times before, Chavali waved Ginny off. "Thank you. I need a minute to collect my wits."

"Are you alright?" Colby pulled her closer, holding her up. His brow crinkled with concern.

"I will be fine."

"Are you sure?" The girl leaned over her, biting her lip. "Did I mess it up?"

"No. It's me, not you."

"What's wrong?" The older Healer's voice crackled with concern and disapproval.

Colby smirked and looked up, shaking his head. "It's just Chavali being Chavali. She's difficult. Everyone knows this."

Chavali grinned and rolled to her side, breathing deeply to recover. "This is true."

"Isabella, make a note about Chavali," the older Healer said, crossing her arms. "She's difficult. Also, she needs to lie down after she's healed, so she can't be counted on to get up and walk out."

"Do you need help getting to your room?"

"No." She waved Colby off. "I only need a minute or so. Go, I will be along shortly."

"If you're not there in half an hour, I'm coming to look for you."

Chapter 15

Her arms filled with a sack of supplies, Chavali knocked on the farmhouse door and walked in. "It's me," she called out. She set the sack on the floor and pulled her mittens off. Thank goodness the snow had stopped. They'd still have to dig out a space for the bonfire. She hung her cloak on a hook by the door, mittens in a pocket.

"Chavaaaaaaali!" A small person ran into her leg, wrapping her arms around it and squeezing.

"I'm sorry I'm late." She ruffled Haizea's hair and braced for Danel's impact. Thank goodness she'd had that cut healed, or this visit would be much less pleasant. "I came as soon as I could." Bending down, she picked the little girl up and herded the boy into the living room.

Biholtz caught her in the doorway and hugged her. "How long can you stay?"

"Until morning. I have pressing matters to deal with tomorrow, but nothing before then. Where are Penny and Marcus?"

"Moving slower because they're old and crotchety." Marcus grinned and entered the room, followed by Penny. "Colby came by the other day. Thanks for sending him when you couldn't."

Chavali nodded. She needed to remember to thank him for taking the initiative on her behalf. "I have received the materials I require to perform the ceremony. This means we should discuss it more concretely, to be sure." Sitting on the couch, she let the children arrange themselves around her and wound up with Haizea and Danel each claiming half her lap. Danel's legs draped over Biholtz's lap.

"Ah. Yes," Marcus agreed as he sat in a chair across from her, "we should be real careful about that. Clear."

Penny perched on the arm of her husband's chair. "How will it work?"

"We must have a bonfire. I have brought everything else. Both of you and I will all need to fling blood into the fire. Joining our clan means that you promise to hold certain kinds of information close. There are things I have not told Eldrack or others because they do not need to know, and you must agree to take care with what you learn of us. I have already said this, I know, but Biholtz and I will teach you the clan tongue. Armed with it, you will discover much more."

Penny squeezed Marcus's shoulder. "We understand."

"As elders in the clan, you technically will have some authority over it. Since there will be only six of us, three of whom are children, this is largely irrelevant. As I bring others into the clan, you will have a say in whether any given candidate is acceptable. Otherwise, little else will change until the clan is larger."

"How many people do you intend to bring in?" Penny asked.

"The clan is meant to have between two hundred thirty and two hundred thirty-five members. I expect it to take the rest of my life, and possibly that of my successor, to achieve this. There's no need to hurry and induct two hundred people now; it's better to stay small until I am released from my service here." The children had only an abstract understanding of Chavali's job. She avoided using the term "Fallen" or discussing her death with them, concerned they might not grasp the gravity of it and say the wrong thing to the wrong person.

Both elders nodded. Marcus asked, "What will really change for us, then?"

Chavali took a moment to think about that. "I have no idea if you will feel anything different. Every member of the clan during my lifetime, and for several generations previous, had been born into it. Otherwise, I cannot think of anything."

"How do you know how to do the ceremony, then? Are you making this up?"

"No." Chavali grinned at Penny. "I can explain afterwards. Not before."

Penny huffed. Marcus put his hand on her knee and chuckled. "I get it. The Seer keeps the secrets. It's fine, Chavali. We're both game to do this. These kids are something special, and we'd like to watch them grow up."

"What do you say, Haizea, Danel, Biholtz?" Chavali held all three close and kissed Haizea's head. "Should we let Marcus and Penny into our clan? Should we teach them our stories and ways?"

Biholtz nodded gravely. Haizea eyed both of them up, then crossed her small arms and nodded. Danel tried to stay as serious as the two girls. He failed, letting a pleased smile spill out.

"The Blaukenev clan has thus voted unanimously to bind Marcus and Penny to our fates, and us to theirs. Is there time to make cake for tonight?"

"Cake!" Haizea shrieked. She jumped off Chavali's lap and ran from the room with her arms raised and flailing in joy.

Danel followed her, without the noise.

"I can make a cake by nightfall, yes." Penny stood with a smile. "Are there any special foods to prepare?"

"I have none of the recipes and no knowledge of such things. Whatever will make everyone happy is fine. Is it acceptable that I spend this night here?"

"Yes, of course," Marcus said as he creaked to his feet. "What are we going to do? Turn our Seer out? We'll need to dig up the snow for that fire. Biholtz, you've got a strong back. Come help me do that. I only have two shovels, or I'd make Chavali help too."

Knowing better than to suggest Marcus might be too old for such labors, Chavali retrieved her sack without comment and set to the task of mixing what needed to be mixed and crushing what needed to be crushed. She had a thought that if Eliot and Patrick sort themselves out, she might invite them into the clan also. They would need capable defenders and teachers.

The matter churned in her mind until Penny announced dinner. Chavali sat with Haizea on her lap and Biholtz and Danel in the chairs beside her. The food had some of the spices she knew, pointing to Biholtz influencing Penny's cooking. With full bellies, everyone threw on cloaks and boots and tromped outside to the pile of wood sitting in a ring of bare ground.

Clan bonfires had always been built much higher than this stack.

Although it disappointed her, she understood. Winter had another month to go, and they still needed to keep the house warm until it passed. A wagon caravan could pick up deadfall and move on. Here, they only had what could be gathered nearby, and this reason for a large fire seemed frivolous.

Chavali carried her three preparations out and scattered one over the bare wood. Because her words for this ceremony had to be delivered in the clan tongue, Marcus and Penny wouldn't understand it. She couldn't help that, only offer them cues to do their part.

"The Blaukenev clan has roamed Tilzam for hundreds of years. In the beginning, it started with one man and one woman, Estevior and Istal. Like them, we are few, lost and alone. Tonight, we begin to rebuild the clan, following in their footsteps. Istal, the First Seer, and Estevior, our Founder, had only two lights to guide their path. We have four. Like them on that first night, we add two more: those of Marcus and Penny, our beloved and trusted friends."

She took flint and steel from her pocket and struck them together near the stack, willing the bonfire to light. The first spark shriveled to nothing before reaching the wood. Her second spark leaped to the kindling and smoldered. A surge of nerves rushed through her, wondering if this meant Estevior disapproved. Taking a deep breath to stop her hands shaking, she stepped closer and pushed the third spark onto dry leaves that caught fire. Relief settled on her shoulders as the flame spread to the kindling, then to the wood.

"Like this fire, we are one, bound together. We share our lives, our hopes, our fears, our successes, our failures. We defend each other, we love each other. We are sisters and brothers. We welcome these two lights to join our own."

Taking her second preparation, she tossed a handful onto the fire and watched it roar upward, crackling and releasing a rich, earthy aroma that threatened to reduce Chavali to tears. It reminded her so strongly of home, of her family, of the dead. The wagons had always smelled of this, and she never knew it came from this particular blend of herbs and leaves and flowers.

Eager to fill the air with the scent, she threw another handful, and another, until she'd emptied the pouch. Out of the corner of her eye, she noticed Haizea crying into Biholtz's shoulder, and Danel clutching at her. If she could, she would take them in her arms and cry with them. The Seer had no such luxury.

Beckoning Penny and Marcus forward, she drew her knife and the final pouch. The spirits surrounded her at all times, yet they only pressed on her when she used them or they used her. Now, they swarmed close, summoned by words, intentions, smells, sights, and grief. She felt them roiling in the air and slithering across her flesh. She breathed them in and heard their whispering voices.

"I am the Seer of the Blaukenev clan. I am the clan, and the clan is me." Gripping the knife until her knuckles went white, she pressed the tip to her thumb. This reminded her too much of killing herself, and her hand shook because of it. She took a deep breath and forced herself to slice down her thumb and across her palm. Pressing the knife to the wound, she gathered as much blood as she could with the blade then dipped it into the pouch. With the knife, she scooped out incense and flung it with her blood at the fire.

It hit the flames, and the spirits screamed in wordless pain and rage and confusion. That shouldn't happen, but she felt the tether to the heart of the fire form as it should. Rocked by the noise only she could hear that refused to let up, she grabbed Marcus's hand and cut it the same way. "By my blood, you are bound to me, bound to the clan, bound to our ancestors, bound to our descendants."

The spirits swirled around her, still screaming. For the first time, she picked out faces, distorted as if a pane of thick, bubbly glass stood between her and them. Each flashed past, similar to all the Blaukenevs she'd ever seen. One with pale skin pushed into her view. One she swore must be Keino shoved her aside. Her breath caught, and she groped for Penny's hand. No matter how strange this had become, she had to hold on and see it through. This would not fail because the Seer lost her grip.

Her fingers closed around a wrist and she strained to see past the flickering spirits. As quickly as she could, she made the cut and spoke the words. This time, she threw the knife into the fire then threw the pouch after it. "We are one," she shouted, begging the spirits to quiet and settle. "Our clan is complete and whole, bound forever! We are Blaukenev!"

The spirits stopped. She panted, staring at the fire. Pain exploded in her head. She stumbled, suddenly dizzy. Darkness consumed her.

Chapter 16

Chavali's hair billowed out, moving in a strange wind. Pressure pushed on her body from every direction. Though she'd never been fully submerged underwater outside of a bathtub, she'd seen memories from people who had, and this resembled those in most ways. Plants with flat leaves reached upward, swaying in the breeze, and her feet sank into soft mud as she took labored steps. Despite that, the air had no murkiness or other distortion; she could see clearly in the harsh sunlight.

She pushed through a forest of tall plant columns and watched fish wriggle past her. The husk of a forgotten house lay crumbling to the side. In slow motion, she vaulted over the rock wall marking the edge of its property. Where she landed, silt roiled up and spread out. In the distance, she saw a dark shape, one she feared for no reason.

If she could hide well enough, he wouldn't find her. She spun and had to push her hair out of her face. In doing so, she noticed she no longer had the feather in her skull, which confused her. But he was coming. She needed to hide. The house might work. Digging her feet into the silt, she fought her way to the door.

An arm of rock swung out from the wall and slammed stony spikes into her side, tossing her through the water-air and sending her blood misting out. She flew until she hit the ground, smacking her head in a cloud of silt. The impact jarred her spine and sent jolts of pain out to her fingertips.

"He is coming," she whispered. Pushing herself up, she saw the dark shape in the distance becoming clearer. When he reached her, something would happen, and it would be bad. She scrambled to her feet, bleeding and limping. Fish swam to the rapidly growing cloud of blood and tasted it.

She groped in the water-air for the house, knowing it wouldn't save her now. He was coming, and he'd follow the trail she left. When he found her, bad things would happen. She grabbed the edge of the window and sliced her fingers off on invisible shards of glass. Glancing over her shoulder, she saw him coming, his cloak flaring out behind him.

Gasping for air, Chavali shot upright with a shriek. Haizea squeaked and Danel mumbled in protest. She grabbed Haizea, gathering the three-year-old in her arms and squeezing her tightly. None of that had been real. This, here, now, was real. She wheezed and gasped, unable to close her mouth or get enough air.

"What'sa matter?" Biholtz asked.

"Nothing." Forcing herself to calm down, she kissed Haizea's head and laid back on the bed. The three children snuggled up to her again in the darkness. "One of you must've invaded my dreams."

"'S'not time to get up yet." Biholtz yawned and fell asleep again.

"No, it's not." Chavali lay awake, listening to them breathe. It took every ounce of will she had not to replay the nightmare, over and over again. She needed to go see Kelly. If she couldn't sleep, she couldn't do her job. Eliot could wait until after that. She'd have breakfast first too. No running around smashing muffins and losing biscuits today, and no getting delayed by Karias.

Eventually, she drifted back to sleep and woke when the children squirmed. Early sunshine painted the room with a gentle glow. She hugged Haizea and kissed the top of her head while tousling Danel's hair. Biholtz put her arms around Chavali's neck and reminded her that a mere twelve years was enough to understand her Seer needed the affection and contact.

"I'll stay for breakfast," she told them with a contented sigh. "You can start teaching Penny and Marcus our tongue, as much as you want." So long as Blaukenevs lived, the clan lived, and so did their language. It wouldn't die on her watch. "Speak it in front of them. It'll help them learn it."

"I want you to stay, Chavali." Danel looked up at her with his big eyes.

"I want to stay. I can't. I'll visit again as soon as I can, I promise." She kissed his forehead and chivvied everyone out of the large bed. Penny had made eggs and biscuits with jam and held a steaming mug of tea ready for Chavali.

"Are you alright?" Marcus fixed her with a stern, no-nonsense stare. "The fire went out for no reason, and we had to carry you to bed." He held up his hand, healed without a scar.

Looking down at her own, Chavali forced herself to smile. She also had no scarring or other evidence of the cut last night. "It went fine."

He grunted and pointed with a forkful of egg. "I didn't ask about 'it.' I asked about you. Someone told me I'm supposed to take care of my Seer, or something like that."

Chavali sipped her tea. "I apologize for not warning anyone that I might pass out at the end." She would have, if she'd known.

Penny smacked Marcus's hand. "I want to know how you knew what to do."

Pleased to have the subject changed, Chavali smirked into her tea. "As the Seer, I have access to certain kinds of memories from my predecessors. I cannot discover what they ate for breakfast or who they loved or hated, but I can channel their knowledge of rituals and stories. I am connected to their spirits, in a manner of speaking."

"Oh my." Penny's eyes glittered with the knowledge. "What do you mean by 'spirits'?"

Chavali swallowed a bite of egg and shrugged. "It's difficult to explain and not entirely clear." Her eyes flicked to Haizea, sitting on her lap again, hoping to convey the reason for her reticence to discuss the subject now. She needed to not confuse them by suggesting, even obliquely, that she could speak directly with any of their loved ones.

"Ah." It appeared that Penny understood from the way she nodded. "It sounds like being the Seer is quite the responsibility."

"Yes, it is. According to some, it's a weight that can only be carried by the most difficult among us, which is why they chose me."

Biholtz and Penny giggled. Marcus harrumphed. Chavali grinned and shoveled her food down. She hugged everyone and left, a bounce in her step. In the morning sunshine, her nightmare seemed distant and unimportant. For once, she knew she had to go see Kelly anyway.

Hurrying down the stairs, she ignored everyone she passed.

Someone went to fetch Kelly at her request, and she waited in her Healer's office. Pacing across the room, she dredged up the nightmare, forcing herself to replay it in her head. By the time the door opened and Kelly slipped in, she'd gone through it enough to strip the emotion from it. Without that attached, it bothered her much less.

"Good morning. How did you sleep?"

"Poorly." She stopped pacing and faced Kelly, in need of distraction from her thoughts. "I had a different nightmare last night. All of it was new, from start to end. I've never seen anything like it and have no words to explain some of what happened in it."

"Oh." Kelly blinked and met Chavali's gaze with enough discomfort to notice. "Why do you think that is?"

"I don't know. Here, let me tell it to you." She explained the dream from start to finish, including every tiny detail she could think of and how she felt during each part. "This man, I know it wasn't Robin. I *know* this. If this is a warning, then there's someone out there I haven't met yet. He is coming. *He is coming.* Right before this, I did the ceremony, and it ended with stabbing pain in my head, the same as I get when I deliver a prophecy. I think this was a prophecy, one delivered the only way I could accept it while sleeping. Except that makes no sense, because I never get images with them, and nothing was purple, so it couldn't have been."

She realized she'd fallen into ranting and stopped to take a deep breath. "If this keeps happening, I will never get enough sleep. It will slowly kill me. That is the important part here."

Kelly rubbed her eyes and raked a hand through her disheveled hair, smoothing it down. "You sound a little obsessed."

"Do I?" Turning around, Chavali stared at the painting. Her feet carried her to it, and she traced a whorl with a fingertip. The seductive simplicity of the act soothed her mind. "It's been so long since I had a new dream that I've forgotten how to deal with it." She took a deep breath and moved to a spiral. "Is there an herb I can take once in a while to prevent dreams? Not all the time, just when I have a string of difficult nights."

"There are a few herbs that can help you sleep. So long as you only use them here at the tower, and not every night, I don't see a problem. I can have some sent to your room."

"Thank you. That will help until I can get a handle on this."

A swish of cloth announced Kelly standing up. "Maybe you should get a similar painting for your room. It seems to help. Could be the difference between falling back asleep and staying up all night."

If she could figure out why this pattern appealed to her so much, she could have it distilled down for best effect. "That's a good idea, yes." Tearing herself away from it, she hurried out of the office to find Eliot. It turned out to be easier than expected when he emerged from the thirteenth floor as she reached it.

"Eagle Falls called for help because a child has gone missing. I volunteered you to come with me, so you can pick a third. Kieler, Colby, or Damian?"

She shrugged. "I only know Colby." Bringing him meant hassles to deal with, but Karias would make up for it. Knowing what to expect seemed more important in this situation than avoiding him.

"Then let's take Colby. I'll go get him. You go pack. Meet in the tavern. Hurry, but don't kill yourself to get there."

Chapter 17

Chavali rode Karias, and the two men ran in the channel the horse cut through the recent snow. She would never be able to keep up with any of them on foot, and they all knew it. Eliot promised more training before he had to jog too hard for talking. At that pace and without having to stop at the Creator's Tower on the way, the journey passed swiftly.

"Stop," Eliot called out when they reached Jack's body. He doubled over and panted, hands on his knees. "One minute."

Beside him, Colby also gasped for breath, though he chose to lean against a tree. He waved Karias off. "Go on ahead. Few minutes."

The horse whickered and plunged ahead, Chavali gripping his mane. She'd filled all three in on the situation during the ride and now said only, "Do whatever seems right when we get there."

As she and Karias approached, Chavali heard loud, angry voices. In the distance, she saw torches burning in the middle of town and found that curious for late morning on a sunny day. Search parties ought to be scattered around where the missing child had last been seen, and perhaps in the woods, not clustered in the center of town. Karias loomed large enough to be obvious from a distance, and it came as no surprise that someone hurried out to greet them.

"Andrew, yes?" She took the hand Lilly's husband offered to help her down from Karias's back. At the moment, she chose to be grateful for the mittens separating her from his thoughts.

"Yes. Thank the Creator you've come. Did you bring anyone else?"

"They are on foot and will be along shortly." She searched his face and knew enough without having to be told. "The missing child is your son?"

"Yes." He covered his face and sagged. "I took him out into the woods. Not very far, just enough to show him how to set a rabbit trap. Joey saw something behind me and pointed, but when I turned to look..." He mimed a blow to the back of his head. "That's all I remember."

She yanked a mitten off with her teeth and used that hand to check for the lump on his skull. It had swelled to the size of a marble, and his thoughts revealed the truth of his account. He'd seen nothing of his attacker, not even the tip of a boot. "You should lie down."

"I can't." He leaned onto her, searching for solace. "Not while he's out there in the clutches of a monster. He must be scared to death."

She gave him a quick hug then gripped his chin and forced him to look at her. "Where is Lilly?"

"Out with the search parties. They're combing the forest. I wanted to go."

"Where were you in the woods?"

Andrew covered his face again and pointed. "Why did they take him and not me? He's just a little boy."

Chavali wanted to despise him for his weakness. Not so long ago, she'd been in the same position. Then, she'd thought and felt the same things. She knew the agony wrenching his heart. "Go home, Andrew. Make sure his home is prepared for his return and stay where you can be found easily. Do not wander, so you can greet him when he is brought back to you."

Defeated and obedient, he bobbed his head. "Yes. You're right. One of us needs to be there. Bring him home," he begged.

She nodded, unwilling to make a promise in words. As he shambled away, she laid her hand on Karias's neck. "Why take the boy, indeed," she mused. "All of that was honest and real."

Good to know. Unless we're dealing with the kind of monster that prefers children, the reason to take the son but not the father could be about making him suffer, but I doubt it. If that was the goal, they'd have taken both and forced him to watch or listen or made sure he knew who did it.

Chavali agreed. "It's about the mother, either because Andrew is not the father or because he doesn't matter. You can track by scent, yes?"

Yes. The snow may hamper me.

She saw Colby and Eliot reaching the edge of town and ideas formed in her head. "Take Eliot into the woods and follow what you can. I will use Colby as a guardian and to find you after I have had a chance to check with these people in town."

You're smarter than you look.

She snorted and pulled her hand away. "Coming from a horse,

this is not saying much."

Karias muscled his way into the snowbank, and Chavali hurried to meet the men. "Lilly's son, Joey, was taken by an unknown attacker who assaulted his father. He is five years old. There are search parties in the woods already. Eliot, you follow the horse. Colby, come with me." Without waiting for discussion, argument, or questions, she turned on her heel and rushed to the town center.

Closer to the gathering, she found Candy's husband, the merchant. Candy had mentioned his name once, and she struggled to remember it. He paced and wrung his hands, far more agitated than someone else's missing child ought to make a person.

From where they now stood, they could hear a woman speaking to the crowd, and Chavali recognized Kember's voice. "...so put those damned torches out. We'll need them if the boy's not found by nightfall. Remember, keep your children inside, with your doors and windows locked. No one goes into the woods alone and unarmed. Until we find every last one of these monsters and kill them all, we're not safe. If anyone wants to join the search at this point, come up here. The rest of you, go home and keep your families close."

Angry muttering filled the air as the crowd broke up. Chavali pointed to the merchant and slipped to his side. She wanted to take his hand, but he wore gloves. Only his face had exposed flesh.

"Oh, hello." He gave her a strained smile.

"This is awful, yes?" She noticed that Colby gave her plenty of space, which she appreciated.

"It's a disaster," the merchant whined. "I never wanted anything like this."

Listening to his words made her instantly suspicious of him. If Jack hid his nature for so long, it made sense that others also could. He and Candy had arrived recently, and what better reason for a merchant and his wife to join an isolated community than finding a place he could express his true, monstrous nature? "This will be bad for business, I expect."

He threw his hands up and walked away. "Myra will never consent to setting anything up within ten miles of here when she hears about this."

Chavali followed him, working hard to keep up with his pace. "Surely she'll understand?"

"Oh, yes." He snorted. "She'll *understand* all the way to Todan, where it's safe. What we found here? It's real, not a wish or a dream or a fantasy. Real." He whirled to jab a finger at her. "Everything we've done has been for the good of the Syndicate. Everything! We've given them our lives! We're not going to let these freaks—" He searched her face and frowned. "Who are you again?"

If he despised werewolves with so much venom, he must not be one. It could be Candy, yet she had tried to hide her command of magic. None of the stories spoke of werewolves as mages. It could still be possible but seemed farfetched. "Sean's friend. Why are you not out with the search parties?"

"Me?" He hugged himself. "I'm no good for any of that. I have to —" Stopping, he scanned the area as if he'd lost track of where he was. "Where is Andrew? Have you seen him? Someone should make sure he's alright."

"Andrew is fine." She cursed the cold as she put her hand on his arm, protected by his cloak. "He went home."

"I should go see him. He must be sick with worry." Shrugging her hand off, he hurried away.

Letting him go, Chavali watched his cloak flap until he turned a corner. "That was a very strange conversation."

"Yes, it was." Colby stepped up behind her. "Syndicate?"

"He's a merchant of some kind, but I don't know the specifics."

"There's the Continental Trade Syndicate. They negotiate with other groups for reduced fees and access, that sort of thing. They have a deal with the Order of the Creator's Path, for example. Members pay a lower rate to use the Towers."

"And what does that have to do with Eagle Falls or werewolves?"

"No idea." Colby jerked his head the way they'd come. "We should find Karias and Eliot before they get too deep into the woods."

Chavali nodded and walked beside him. "This place is vexing."

"You say that like it's a surprise or strange." He grinned and took the lead when they reached Karias's trail through the snow. They hadn't gotten far yet and weren't hard to find.

Eliot waved to them and explained. "The spot Joey was taken from has already been tromped through, but they managed to preserve tracks of some kind of beast. From what we saw of that other werewolf, I'd say the tracks match that kind of feet. They disappeared after ten steps. Vanished without a trace, and we couldn't find how the werewolf got there in the first place."

Chavali set her hand on Karias's neck. For the sake of appearances, she pretended that her footing had faltered and she needed his steadiness. "The Continental Trade Syndicate may be involved in this somehow, but it is unclear."

Too many people have muddled the scent already. I can say with certainty that a large predator was there. Where it went or came from, I have no idea. Incidentally, I'm in no way sure that I can tell the difference between a human being and a werewolf in the shape of a human being. My guess would be no. Also, thank you for being discreet.

Chavali looked down at her own boots, following her own footprint to the churned snow in their wake. "How could anything carry a child away and leave no footprints in fresh snow?"

Flight, magic, or using the environment creatively. They could have climbed the trees and moved from branch to branch, jumped down into a creek and walked up that, and so on.

Eliot looked up, his thoughts probably headed in a similar direction as Karias. "Do you see that?" He pointed up and to the side.

Looking in that direction, Colby frowned and said, "A cluster of branches doesn't seem all that unusual in a forest."

"How about a cluster of branches without any snow on them?"

Chavali peered at the spot, comparing it to the surrounding branches. Now that she knew what to look for, she scanned the area. "There. More. They went in that direction. They must have been flying?"

"This stinks of magic," Colby said. "You said that merchant's wife is a mage, and he's acting strangely."

"Perhaps." Until she saw Candy again, she had no reason to jump to conclusions. Apparently, she'd missed something and someone in Ket and had no desire to do that again here. "Given the ease with which Jack concealed his nature, it's not bizarre to imagine one or more mages also concealing theirs."

"We may have stumbled into a war," Eliot muttered.

Chavali bared her teeth. "I choose the side that does not stoop to abducting and terrorizing children."

In the distance, a wolf howled.

"Here's hoping there is one," Colby said with a sigh.

Chapter 18

They lost the trail. Whoever did this found a clearer path and took it. Karias led them deeper into the forest, hoping to pick the trail up again. They crossed the tracks of search parties without running into one. After a few hours of what seemed to be aimless wandering, Colby called a halt.

"We're not accomplishing anything, and I for one am hungry. Let's stop and think instead of exhausting ourselves like this. Chavali, I haven't really heard the whole story, so start at the beginning, and let's see if anything starts to click together."

Karias whuffed his agreement and laid down, offering all three of them a place to sit. Colby rummaged in his saddlebags and produced a cold meal of hurriedly collected bread, apples, cheese, and savory pastries. Chavali gave her apple to Karias and perched at the base of his neck. She related all the events the same way Eliot had for Eldrack at first—without mentioning Patrick.

When she finished, she took a bite of the pastry and found she preferred this particular kind cold. "The biggest question seems to be about who in the town would gain from taking this boy from this mother. If they gained nothing, they would have chosen a different child."

"I don't know much about werewolves," Colby said, "but what I do know is that followers of the Pure Seed consider them an abomination, worse than half-elves. At least an elf looks somewhat human. Wolves are animals. That's what they think."

Chavali recalled Sean using 'abomination' to describe werewolves and chose to be glad he no longer accompanied them now. They needed options, not dogma. "I know what you think of the Pure Seed." Given they'd killed him for trying to rescue a group of half-elven children, she could understand why he spat their name.

Colby nodded. "I'm not sure I buy the whole 'monster' thing. If these two men were monsters unable to control their appetites and urges, why doesn't Eagle Falls have a history of grisly murders? There should be piles of bodies, not just here, but also in the nearby villages."

"The Fallen would've noticed that by now," Eliot agreed. "That's part of the point of the Courier Circuit. We pay attention. These are simple folks who want to live simple lives, and when there's a violent murder, they talk about it for months afterwards. Longer if they can't figure out who did it."

Staring off in the distance, Chavali listened to Karias offer his suggestion and repeated it for the two men. "Could there be bodies no one knows about? Men like Ander who might be assumed to have moved on and their bodies never found?"

"It's possible," Colby said, "but the villagers would talk about it. The people who choose to live outside the main grouping are still part of the local economy. When they disappear, it makes a stir. Suddenly, there's one less source of venison or firewood, or one less strong back to handle labor, or whatever they do. In a city, no one cares. In a village of less than three hundred, it's more like your clan."

Put that way, Chavali understood it better. Everybody would be in everybody else's business, and secrets would be hard to keep. Gossip would move swiftly, and in order to be free of it, a person would have to be solitary. Public confrontations, like her slapping Keino, would be talked about for days, even weeks.

Karias's ears twitched. *Someone is coming.*

Chavali looked up and caught movement a second before she heard a branch snap. Patrick stepped out from behind a tree. He focused on Eliot, of course. His dumbstruck, utterly helpless and longing expression in that moment of candid surprise revealed so much, she wanted to slap him for being too obvious. She nudged Eliot, who sat next to her, knowing he'd have an equally stupid look on his face. Both men recovered with gestures they probably thought hid everything, and the rest of Patrick's search party stepped into the open.

"We are lost," she announced. "And have taken a break to evaluate the situation."

Patrick coughed and approached, leading four men behind him. All wore swords or axes and seemed to otherwise be average townsfolk. "We're not really finding anything. You look familiar, ma'am, but I don't think any of us knows you?"

It struck her as curious that Patrick wanted to play this game as much as Eliot did. What stake did he have in hiding their relationship? No one would care, so long as neither party abused the other. "I am

Chavali. This is Eliot and Colby. We are friends of Sean's, arrived to assist with the search."

"Ah." He stopped several feet away, his companions arraying themselves into an arc. She got the feeling they chose to be prepared to fight. Considering the situation, she took no offense.

"It seems to us that whoever took the boy has gone to great pains to obscure their trail. It also appears that both the men who have been found to be rabid animals lived out in this woods." She noticed Patrick twitched when she said "rabid animals," which made her wonder about him. Two of the other men also tried to hide negative reactions, and all three shifted subtly into more defensive stances. "It is, therefore, of some interest that Ander does, as well."

"He wouldn't harm a child." Patrick and the two other men relaxed a notch.

"I'll wager you thought that Jack would never harm a woman," Colby said.

Eliot directed his attention to his remaining food, saying nothing.

"Poor Ramelia. I saw that with my own two eyes, and I still don't believe it," one man said, shaking his head sadly. This one had had no real reaction to her comments.

"In all the stories I know on the subject, werewolves behave similarly to actual wolves, to a degree." She offered this in the hopes of provoking more reaction, as well as continuing to gnaw on the problem itself. "This would mean they have a pack of some kind. Two seems small for a pack, does it not? I would expect five or more, I think. They are also territorial, yes? Preferring to stay in the same area would mean returning to familiar places when under stress."

If Jack went to Ramelia's house for Ramelia, then the logical place to look would be that waterfall area where you were attacked before. You said those flowers point at the moon, and werewolves are supposed to be tied to the moon. There could be a connection.

Karias's thoughts echoed the path her own wandered down. She hopped to her feet. "We should go to the falls." Since Eliot had already asked her to get involved in this whole Patrick situation, she swooped down on him and took his arm. "Show us the way."

Patrick blinked down at her. "Uh, sure. I guess." His hand moved in a short series of gestures she assumed had to do with giving orders to the other men.

Interested in having a few minutes to speak with him alone, she tugged on his arm and got him moving before Karias stood and shook the snow off his legs. "I am Eliot's friend," she murmured to him. "And I know who you are. He is too flustered to speak for himself, and so I am here on his behalf."

"You— What?"

"We will speak later when there is not a child in peril and true privacy can be had. Suffice to say for now that he is madly, stupidly in love with you and would tell you everything if he could. I suspect the same holds true for you. Whatever secret you keep, unless it is about abducting children, I doubt he will reject you for it. His secret is likewise understandable and forgivable. Remember that and hold onto it."

He gulped and nodded. "I didn't have anything to do with taking Joey."

"We shall see."

"If you think I might've done it, why're you walking with me?"

She rolled her eyes. "Because Eliot is my friend. I have already said this. Pay attention. So long as you are not the culprit here, I am not leaving this town again until you and I have a serious talk. Is this clear?"

Patrick sighed. "Yes, ma'am."

"Good. Trying to kill me to avoid it will make your life difficult and quite a bit shorter. Not to mention that, as noted, Eliot is my friend, and he'll have to hate you for doing it. I would take exception to this."

He blinked several time, then chuckled. "I can see why he gets along with you."

Chavali arched an eyebrow. She heard the splashing of the waterfall ahead and chose not to respond. As they walked, the sun set, leaving only the soft glow of the full moon to guide them. They reached the path and turned the corner to find the flowers in full bloom, pointing at the bright orb in the sky, lighting up the entire grotto. The circles of melted snow around each stem had widened despite the fresh storm.

"Owen came from there." She pointed to one side of the grotto.

"Candy said he was crazed, vicious." Patrick slipped out of her grip to stoop at the edge of the clearing where she indicated.

She shrugged. "One man diving into a headfirst attack on five people does not point to mental stability."

Once again, a wolf howled in the distance. Patrick and those two men cocked their heads to listen, while everyone else looked up and around. These three men had to be werewolves. Chavali could think of no other explanation for their behavior. This, then, had to be the secret Patrick guarded from Eliot.

"Owen had a son," Patrick said with a frown. "Ander knows that. I don't recall him saying anything about the boy when he brought Candy and the body to town."

Too many people, too many signals, too many questions. Every single story Chavali knew of werewolves painted them as despicable monsters who stole children, murdered adults, or smashed wagons. Yet, as Colby said, Eagle Falls had no stack of dead bodies or legion of missing residents. At least five of them had been living here in peace for years, unbeknownst to the residents.

She looked up at the moon, wondering if all the stories she knew told an embellished truth, based upon prejudice instead of fact. Considering how she knew them, she hoped not, yet expected so. Her clan had never been full of paragons of honesty and virtue. Estevior himself always struck her as an arrogant peacock, even in the most flattering tales.

Squinting, she stepped closer to the pool to get a better look at the trees. "The snow has been disturbed there." She pointed at a tree with bare branches. "Yet there are still no footprints."

Karias stepped to the water's edge and dipped his nose in to drink. His tail twitched and he whinnied. Colby moved to his side and knelt by the edge. Reaching into the water, he retrieved a small sock, one made for a child's foot.

"There's no reason to come here," one of the probable-werewolves said. "It's a dead end. If you want to go around this, you go around it, not go near the water."

"Maybe he's up on top of the cliff," another man said, "and the sock fell into the water up there?"

Chavali moved closer to the pool. She couldn't shake the feeling they had to be close. "No, there is something here. Hidden, one way or another."

Eliot nodded his chin at the falls. "Chavali, do you know any stories with caves behind waterfalls?"

She blinked and stared at the curtain of falling water. "Yes. Several of them."

Chapter 19

"I'll go first." Pulling his large sword from its clips on his back, Colby plunged into the water and waded to the falls. At the deepest point, it reached halfway up his thighs. He ducked through the waterfall, pushing forward with a gasp. Two heartbeats later, his arm stuck out again, and he beckoned everyone else forward.

In this frigid cold, Chavali sighed at the idea of being soaked to the skin. At least they'd all be in the same condition. She watched Patrick and Eliot hop into the water at Colby's gesture. The rest of Patrick's companions followed suit. One of the other two werewolves stopped to offer her a hand stepping into the pool. Yanking her gloves off and stuffing them into a pocket to try to keep them dry, she took it.

You seem reasonable, aside from that "rabid animals" comment. Still have to find a way to keep you out of the way. Getting the feeling you three might be more trouble than— He let go when she set her second foot onto the bottom of the icy pool. "Just what we need in the middle of winter, right?" He gave her a weak smile then rushed through the waterfall.

Pulling her hood up seemed almost pointless since the water reached her waist. She gritted her teeth against the cold and did it anyway, knowing her hair would take a long time to dry later. Hurrying through, she gasped on the other side, tossing the hood off again. Karias followed her through, and she flinched away as he shook.

"Thanks," she grumbled at him, wiping her face.

The horse snorted at her and ducked his nose under her hand. *I think this is the worst criminal hideout ever. At least be sensible about it and find a waterfall with a ledge and a gap so you can come and go without getting drenched.*

"It probably has another way in and out," she murmured in response, keeping her voice down. "Otherwise, I agree with you."

The cave mouth, a rough-hewn hole in the dark, slippery rock, had barely enough room for the large horse. Light flickered deeper in, and she made haste to find it. Karias clopped in behind her, and they found the others in a twisting tunnel. The light came from sconces bolted to the tunnel walls, each a source of yellow magical light no greater than a common torch and flickering with a simple pattern.

"Mages make magical lights," Chavali muttered.

They certainly do.

They found a wide, tall cavern with a large puddle in the center. By the time Chavali reached it, Colby already knelt beside Joey, cutting the ropes binding his arms and legs. The rest of the men spread through the cave, checking behind every corner and peering at the walls for crevices that might lead deeper.

Joey saw Chavali, and the moment he could, he ran to her, tears streaming down his face. "It was a monster," he sobbed, burying his face

186

in her wet skirt.

Chavali picked him up and rested him on her hip. His wide eyes reminded her too much of Danel. She brushed his cheek with her thumb. "We will protect you from the monster, but you must tell us what it looked like."

He nodded and wrapped his arms around her neck, leaning close and sniffling. "Really big, covered with gray fur, and a wolf's face. I thought wolves were protectors, not monsters."

Though she noticed Patrick and the other two werewolves stiffen, she kept her attention on the boy and turned to leave with him. "What did it do to you? Are you hurt?"

"No, nothing. I don't remember the rope."

"Chavali, wait." Eliot's voice made her stop and look over her shoulder. He crouched on the floor beside a cleft in the wall, holding an empty flask and a small stick. "There's more back here."

"He doesn't need to see these things," Chavali said, frowning. "He needs to be away from here." Despite her words, she watched him lift a glass jar with dark residue clinging to the inside then a white plate with soot on the bottom. "We saw things like this at Ramelia's house, only they were all broken. Did this monster have a lab of some kind here?"

Patrick moved closer to Eliot, his movements disjointed and hesitant. Close enough to reach out and touch the other man, he curled his hands into fists and crossed his arms. "What kind of monster uses a lab?"

"I heard them," Joey whispered. "Talking."

Chavali kept her voice down too. "Just now?"

"No, before. They said it's been a hard winter, and there's not much food left."

"How many voices did you hear?"

His small face screwed up in concentration. "Two. Are they going to hurt Mama and Papa?"

Unwilling to confirm or deny anything of the sort, Chavali kept her face neutral. "What else did they say?"

"They said they needed food and the village has plenty, so they were going to take it and...and nobody would stop them." Joey rubbed one eye with a small fist. "They said they wanted to—" He buried his face in her neck.

"They said they wanted to kill people in the village?"

Instead of answering, he nodded and held on tighter.

Two people discussed plans to murder villagers in front of this boy. Why? They must have other places to speak on such topics. The forest certainly had plenty of space for clandestine conversations. She shook her head, confused by the behavior. If they intended to kill the boy, why wait? If they intended to let him live, why take him in the first place? Who were these two people?

Patrick's behavior could suggest discomfort with Eliot because of his condition or because he had orders to kill anyone who found this place. Were that the case, though, she would expect the other two to have similar orders and less personal conflict. Colby and Karias, as well as the three other townsfolk, might give them pause, yet they ignored a perfect chance to stage an impromptu ambush in the tunnel leading to this cave.

Joey gasped as she turned the next corner, shaking her free of her thoughts. A great furred beast stood before her, its golden eyes blinking with surprise. It towered over them both, thick with muscle and boasting sharp fangs bigger than her fingers. For a moment, Chavali stood there, her mouth gaping open. Owen had been this close, but she'd been busy trying not to die at the time, unable to take in the sight and appreciate his size and strength and beautiful horror.

The moment passed. She turned and ran back to the cave, ducking in case it reached out to swipe at either of them. "Colby!" she shrieked, knowing he'd stand the best chance against this thing. At the mouth of the cavern, she hopped over a rock and kept going, aiming for Eliot.

Behind her, she heard the werewolf growl and snap. The cavern echoed with scraping metal, and she passed Colby, already holding his large blade defensively. Eliot stepped up and grabbed her, keeping her from hitting the wall. They spun together to protect Joey, letting her see the monster burst into the cavern and stop at the mouth.

Patrick tensed and stared at the beast, his face transformed by abject hatred. Checking the other two werewolves, she saw the same thing, making her wonder a great many things.

The werewolf scanned the room then focused on Colby. It growled with a teeth-baring snarl. Colby took a step closer, and Chavali saw both man and werewolf tense. The werewolf shifted, sinking into a fighting stance, then it spun and fled, tail disappearing around the corner in a flash.

Patrick and the two other werewolves charged after it. Colby turned to check on Chavali and Joey. "Are you both alright?"

"Yes, fine. We startled it as much as it startled us. Go, follow it, all of you. I will stay with Eliot." The three townsfolk needed no further encouragement and dashed away.

"Karias, stay with them." Colby hurried out of sight.

"Many things are happening here." Chavali crossed the cavern to Karias, gesturing for him to kneel. "I think there might be two different factions of these wolfmen. This all may have been about a schism between them." When Karias obliged her, she climbed onto his back and settled Joey in front of her. "We need to reach the village before they do."

Eliot hopped onto the horse behind her, and they ducked low to get through the tunnel, Chavali's arms holding Joey close. The horse leaped out through the waterfall to find the clearing empty already. Karias kept going, finding the path and pounding down it. They overtook Colby and the three townsfolk with no obvious sign of the three werewolves. Several different voices howled in the distance as the snow flew in Karias's wake.

Karias moved faster than the wolves. His thoughts showed concentration on the path and speed, on keeping his hooves under him and spotting hazards. He slid to a stop in a shower of glistening snow, ending sideways in the middle of town. The crowd had dispersed, leaving the space between these buildings empty.

Leaping off the horse, Eliot ran to the bell on the general store and used its rope. Clanging filled the air as he yanked it over and over.

Chavali squeezed Joey. "The horse will keep you safe," she told the boy. "Hold on tight, here and here. Don't let go, except for your mother or father." She slid off the side, landing heavily on her feet and patted Karias to get his attention. "We don't know what the fight is about, so only defend villagers. Don't take sides otherwise."

Are you sure? If the werewolves are trying to kill us—

"Yes. I am sure. Avoid causing serious harm to anyone."

Very well. Colby won't hold back until he has a reason to.

"I know. Protect the boy." She gave Joey an encouraging smile and thumped Karias on the flank. Without him helping, they would be less effective. With him helping, she suspected more werewolves would die. Given her current suspicions, that seemed an undesirable outcome.

People slipped and scrambled on the ice to reach the middle of town. Chavali saw Candy's husband, Lilly's husband, Kember, and two dozen others. Lilly herself must not have returned from the search yet. The bell would hopefully bring some of those search parties in.

"Joey!" The boy's father ran to the horse.

Chavali summoned up the only thing she had left of her father: his ability to cut through a crowd with his voice. "Joey is safe! There are many werewolves headed for the village now!" Movement in the distance caught the corner of her eye, and she turned to see a small army of wolves and werewolves descending upon the village. In the lead, the largest of them bounded through the snow, and she thought it might be the one from the cave.

It made no sense. Patrick's expression had spoken of rage for the werewolf who dared to take a child. This child specifically, perhaps? The whole group of them—far larger than she expected—shouldn't be moving in concert to attack the village. Screams cut through her thoughts, and she realized the villagers had seen the wolves. The small crowd panicked and scattered in the face of terrifying monsters bearing down on them.

She stood and watched in the midst of chaos, her hand reaching for her knife and slow, steady steps taking her to Karias. Eliot's familiar presence by her side bolstered her resolve. Together, they would face this and come out of it alive, one way or another.

The wolves flooded between the buildings, disappearing from sight. Growling and barking filled the air, punctuated by screaming and wailing. Wood crunched with a bang, and Chavali thought she heard the cracking and creaking of a house collapsing. One high-pitched scream stood out for cutting off abruptly.

Candy burst into the small clearing, out of breath and projecting terror. "They're animals," she puffed. "Save yourselves!" Without pausing, she plunged between the buildings again.

Colby, his large blade slick with blood ran into the small square with the three non-wolf search party members. "They're insane," he called out.

"They're fighting among themselves," Chavali countered. "We're in the way. Defend, do not attack."

The four men slowed, faces all expressing the same surprise. "Are you—" Colby stopped himself and hurried to her side. "Yes, of course you're sure. Sorry."

Another shrill scream ended too soon, this time from the direction Candy went. Chavali wondered if it had come from her. She also wondered why the search parties hadn't returned yet. Surely, they heard the peal of the bell. Even if they had no idea what it meant, some of them should come to check if the village had burst into flames or found itself under attack of some kind.

Two women stumbled into the small square and immediately sought refuge with the group. Both collapsed, hugging each other. "One killed Daisy. I saw it myself."

"How did it happen?" Chavali spun and crouched by their side, hungry for any information, any tidbit that might explain what she couldn't reconcile.

"We turned a corner, and there it was, the scariest thing I've ever seen. It grabbed her and tore her throat out." The woman dissolved into tears.

This act sounded nothing like an accident. That creature had purposefully and intentionally murdered a woman. Why? To solve a food shortage problem? When they'd lived peacefully with the village for years? Patrick had no intention of slaughtering villagers, not for anything as banal as food. She'd watched him and felt confident about this. If this had to do with revenge for Jack, they would have acted sooner.

Candy's husband ran into sight, throwing himself around a corner and panting. "They're killing people," he gasped. "Rabid animals, hunting for easy prey."

"Come here. We'll protect you," Colby said.

The pause he spent scanning them made Chavali give him a second look. "No, I stand a better chance of hiding on my own." He hurried to the other side of the house and disappeared from sight again.

The unmistakable smell of burning wood reached Chavali, and she twisted to find the source. One of the houses on the edge of the village must have been set afire. They all could hope for it to be Ramelia's, as that would destroy nothing of significance, and it stood far enough from its neighbors that the flames shouldn't spread.

Three wolfmen chased two men through the clearing. At the edge, the wolfmen slowed to a stop, facing the group. Colby planted his feet and faced them, sword held out. Another wolfman came from the rear, running at Joey and Lilly's husband with a roar. Chavali surged to her feet and joined the husband, throwing themselves between it and the boy.

Chavali expected to crash and tumble to the ground in a mad thrash of limbs and claws. Instead, she found herself staring down a panting werewolf, its attention focused over her shoulder to the father, who had thrown his arms out to shield his son.

"I will not let you harm them." Chavali held her knife up as a feeble warding against the creature. A heartbeat passed, long enough for Chavali to catch the movement of more wolfmen nearby. Then its fur and muzzle melted away, the six-foot form shrinking to reveal a woman.

Before her stood Lilly, bundled against the weather. "Andrew," she breathed.

Andrew's mouth opened and shut as he blinked in bewilderment. Joey held onto Karias's mane, and the horse tensed for flight.

For Chavali, everything now suddenly made sense. She'd been right, which eased her conscience on a great many subjects. Lowering her blade, she stepped aside. No one needed her protection right now. As much as they had pressing matters to tend, these two needed a moment, and she hoped no one would die for letting them have it.

Lilly shook her head and reached for Andrew. "Nothing has changed. I've been this way since before we married, I swear it."

He looked at her hand, his face pinched with pain. "I...don't— Lilly... How?"

They could afford one moment. It had passed. Chavali touched Lilly's shoulder, hoping to give her a reason to hear the screams and snarls still echoing between the buildings. "How many in the other faction?"

The wolfwoman blinked and raised her nose, sniffing the air. Throwing her head back, she howled to the sky in a forceful wail of command. When she closed her mouth, she met Andrew's gaze again, her own full of pain and sorrow. "One, I think. Only one. But we don't know who it is, only who it isn't, and he or she is stronger than any of us, but not all of us together. We can't sniff them out because we lose our scent in this shape."

"Colby, stand down. There is only one wolf who needs to be fought." Chavali raised her voice so all the wolves could hear it too. "We are not here to harm anyone. We came to see Joey brought home to his mother and father safely, and that has been done. There is at least one woman dead now, by one of your kind. If it was an accident, then there can be forgiveness. If it was not, there will be justice, but it will be carried out properly, not with the swift execution of an innocent man."

All around them, the wolves shrank into their human shapes. Chavali noted Eliot's mouth falling open as he caught sight of Patrick shifting his shape. Her attention snapped to the two women they'd sheltered when one screamed and the other fainted. With a roll of her eyes, she ignored both.

Villagers stepped hesitantly into the square, some faces twisted in horror, others in wonderment, and a few grimacing with the sting of betrayal. Kember stepped forward and surveyed everyone with an unhappy frown. Her gaze settled on Lilly. "I don't know what to think right now. You say it's only one, but you've been lying to us for a long time, so you'll have to excuse me if I don't take your word for it." Gesturing to another villager, she gave the order to bind all the werewolves by their wrists.

Chavali bit back a protest. She had no authority here and had nothing else to offer these people to make them feel safer. Mere ropes likely wouldn't stop a werewolf from changing shape, but if it provided enough of an illusion to let these people calm down and get to the bottom of this mess, then it suited her well enough to keep quiet.

The wind shifted, and she caught the scent of smoke again. "There is a fire to be tended somewhere. I cannot see it, but I smell it."

Kember nodded. "Kara, grab a few people and go take care of that. Jess, you and Maris go find everybody who got hurt or killed and bring them all here to be tended. All you wolf people..." The mayor rubbed her chin. Her gaze settled on Joey and his parents. "Andrew, let's get them all inside someplace so no one has to freeze while we sort through this. Go see if Ramelia's house is still standing so we can use that."

Her order shook Andrew out of his confusion. "Right. Yes. I'll...go do that." His eyes darted to Chavali, then to Joey, and she understood his request.

"I have already promised to see him safe. Nothing has changed." She moved to Karias and put one hand on the boy's leg, the other on Karias's neck.

This is rather high up on the list of bizarre things I've witnessed.

"I agree," she muttered to the horse. For the boy, she put on a comforting smile. "Don't worry, Joey. We will figure this out."

Joey nodded, his small mouth turned down and eyes glistening with distress. He turned to watch his parents, and she noticed rage flash across his face. Before she could react, he leaped from Karias's back, his shape growing and sprouting fur as he sailed through the air.

Whirling, Chavali saw a villager looping rope over Lilly's outstretched hands. Joey the werewolf crashed into the three of them, roaring in a half-sized and higher-pitched mimic of the adult wolves. Lilly, her hands tangled in the rope, wriggled and scrabbled to separate Joey from the villager.

Not stupid enough to grab the boy, Chavali went for the villager, hauling him out of the way so the mother could gain control over her son. "I don't think we should separate them."

"Y-yes, I, er, think...you might be right," the shaken villager said.

"Joey, you can stay with your mother," she called out, hoping it helped. "No one will take her away from you."

Lilly pinned her son to the ground and snarled at him, too quietly to be overheard. The boy stopped struggling and shrank into his human shape, then burst into plaintive wailing. Andrew stood and watched, mouth opening and closing in stunned silence again. He turned and fled the square.

Chavali helped the villager to his feet, the spirits catching disorganized thoughts of shock and betrayal in their brief contact. She saw Eliot binding Patrick's wrists, the two men having a brief, quiet conversation. Colby helped collect the werewolves and caught her eye, wanting her to come with them.

"Kember," Chavali said, "the three of us wish to help sort this mess out." Out of the corner of her eye, she saw two men carrying a limp body covered in blood. From the way the two women chose to carry on, she guessed that must be Daisy's corpse.

Kember nodded. "You seem like a pretty capable person, so yes, please. I won't turn aside the help of the folks who found that boy when the rest of us couldn't. Even if he is— Go ahead and talk to anybody you need. Let me know what you find out." With that, she turned to the two hysterical women, coaxing them away from the corpse and out of the square.

Stooping beside Lilly as she comforted her son, Chavali sighed. "We will need to tie you both, but I would have you able to hold his hand."

"Thank you," Lilly said with a nod. "I appreciate your help finding him and keeping this calmer than it otherwise might have been. Joey, Chavali is going to help us, but to do that, she needs to tie our hands. If you don't struggle, it won't hurt."

Still crying, the boy nodded and let her wrap a length of rope around his wrists. When both had been tied up, she walked with them to Ramelia's house, which had no sign of fire damage. Someone had lost their home in this mess and would need help getting back on their feet. Had such a thing ever happened in her clan, everyone would have dropped everything to build a new wagon for the affected family. They'd see how it went here.

Chapter 20

Nearly a third of the village had been crammed into the small house with their hands bound. Colby and Karias stood sentry at the door, and Eliot stationed himself inside it. What struck Chavali about this gathering was their familiarity and the ease with which they shared space. Though no one showed any happiness for being here, they seemed comfortable together as a group.

"For those I have not yet met, I am Chavali. My friends and I delivered your mail a few days ago, and we have little other connection to your town. I do not care who it is that turns out to be guilty. I only wish to discover the truth of what happened here. What I know is that Ramelia was killed by a werewolf, and events unfolded in a fashion such that Jack was executed by an angry mob despite being an innocent man. Innocent of *that* crime, at any rate.

"I also know that a man named Owen attacked my friends and me for no apparent reason, seemingly in a fit of madness. His son has not yet been found, and I fear he too is lost. Further, I know that Joey was abducted by a quite large werewolf, and at least one woman was killed by a werewolf in that chaos. Who will fill in the gaps?"

Lilly cleared her throat. "Jack was our Alpha. The leader of our pack. I was his Beta, his second in command. We meet once a week in secret. At the last full moon, a new wolf joined the pack and challenged Jack. He lost and Jack let him live. At the next meeting, that wolf came back and overwhelmed Jack, putting him on his back in less than a minute. No one knows how he managed it after his first performance.

"We accepted it because that's how we do things. The new Alpha was strange, as if he'd never had a pack before. Everything he wanted to do was clumsy or stupid, or he'd ask for my ideas or opinions. Most importantly, he never showed us his human form, so we don't know who he is.

"That night Ramelia died, Jack had a plan, and he'd called for everyone to show up to a meeting. I don't know what he meant to do, and I followed him because he wouldn't tell me. I watched him go to Ramelia's house. While I waited for him to leave, I think someone knocked me senseless, because I woke up with a mouthful of leaves from the shrub I'd been lurking in. By then, as I later learned, the villagers already had Jack unconscious and halfway to the tree they hung him from. The pack had already gathered for the meeting, so none of us saw anything, and we had no idea about any of it until it was too late." She stopped and covered her face with both hands.

"You should know," Patrick said into the silence Lilly left, "that two other children went missing before Joey, both of them also ours. Neither has been found. We also have reason to believe Owen and his teenage son were taken. The Owen I knew, though, wouldn't have attacked you. In fact, the main reason I decided to settle here is because there's something about the area that makes it easier to control the change. We can keep our senses and can shift or not shift as we please, even under the full moon, though it's still harder then."

Chavali mulled these things over. "Is it common, a werewolf dramatically increasing in ability in so short a time?"

"No," Lilly said. "It was bizarre and impossible how much he'd improved. I think Jack knew how he did it and intended to expose a fraud that night." She paused, looking down at her son. "Jack told me that if we ever needed true help, we could find it in Cloverdale. When he was hung, we should have sent a message then, but I want to do it now. Can you take a message to someone there named Eldrack? He's supposed to be sympathetic and an ally."

For once, Chavali found herself surprised. She considered lying about their connection but saw no real reason to. "Eldrack is our employer. Among other things, we handle the Courier Route for him. You have his attention already with our presence here."

Palpable relief rippled away from Lilly, spreading across the entire pack. "Then you can truly help us. Since we think it must be someone newer to the village, some of us thought it might be that merchant Patrick helps with his caravan, or his wife. It can't be, though, because I've seen Candy once when I heard the new Alpha howling, and Patrick has seen Grant when I was with the new Alpha."

"That leaves someone who doesn't live with the villagers," Patrick said, "and we haven't been able to find a lair or den of any kind."

"What of Ander?"

"The hunter?" Lilly shook her head. "No, he and Jack were friends." She sighed in defeat. "Would you please tell my husband—all our spouses—that we've been faithful? We don't— Not with each other. Jack was... We all loved him. He was a good Alpha and a good man. A true friend and someone all of us knew we could count on."

Chavali nodded. "For all the good it may do, I will. I must ask all of you to remain here for now. The villagers may act rashly if you walk about freely."

"We will." Lilly swept her eyes over the pack, a queen demanding obedience from her subjects. In response, a murmur of agreement rumbled through the room. "We will not, however, remain here with our hands bound indefinitely."

"I assume it does little to hamper any of you anyway." When several of them nodded, Chavali shrugged. "So long as you stay here, I see no need for your hands to be tied." Though they could presumably handle it well enough on their own, she moved to the closest man and picked at the knot of his ropes.

"Creator watch over you and guide you to the truth."

Chavali left the house with a nod, finding Karias twitching his tail and Colby leaning against the wall. Eliot exited behind her. "We have a hunt on our hands."

Expression closed and mouth drawn down in thought, Eliot grunted his agreement.

Colby rubbed Karias's nose. "It sounds like this rogue werewolf could be anybody."

"It does, yes." Chavali scowled. Her money would have been on Candy or Grant, if only because of the presumably magical augmentation of the rogue Alpha. For either of them, though, she had no idea why they would make such an effort. What did they hope to gain by dominating a werewolf pack through magic? It made no sense. Someone else must be behind it.

"We should go speak with the rest of the villagers. By now, they've probably all told each other the story of this chaos enough times to distort it into a thing of true terror and madness. This is how gossip works, as we all well know."

Colby smirked at her. "Why, Chavali, if I didn't know better, I'd say you might be a tiny bit grateful to Sean for showing you how these things work in the big, wide world."

She sneered and walked away. "Don't be ridiculous." The three of them followed her back into the village, and she heard Karias snickering behind her.

Chapter 21

Two bodies lay in the central square now, a second woman joining the first. Karias nodded towards the store, showing where the rest of the villagers had gone. Chavali gestured for Colby to stay outside, expecting at least one person to storm off and attempt to do something stupid. To her relief, he nodded his agreement and took up the post. Eliot followed her inside, this time staying close to her.

Nearly a third of the residents packed the small space, wedged among the shelves and tables. Goods lay in piles on the floor, attesting to a hasty clearing of the surfaces to accommodate so many. Angry voices growled and shouted over each other, and small knots of people whispered and muttered among themselves.

Though she found it difficult to pick out individual voices, Chavali got the gist of the mood easily enough: shock, betrayal, anger, hurt. Andrew sat with his face in his hands. Kember argued with another woman about whether to torch the entire village and start over. Two men shouted about how much more they had to complain about than everyone else and each other. A woman and two young children huddled together, sniffling. Several people sat and stared at nothing.

"That's my husband," one woman wailed. "How did I never even suspect?"

"I've been married to a monster all these years."

"She seems so nice, I just don't understand."

"We have to kill them all before they kill us."

"They're animals, all of them!"

Chavali shoved her way to the middle of the mess. Unless she took control of the situation, this village would be a disaster. They all had a clan here, and needed to stand together, and accept the differences between them instead of railing against them. "These people," she shouted, "are your friends, your husbands, your wives, and an important part of this village." As she'd hoped, her words shut them up. Whether it came from volume, the feather in her skull, or something else, they let her speak.

"As you say, they have lived among you for so long without a problem. They each held a secret in their hearts, one they feared you would hate them for. How strange is this? How many of you have never kept a secret from the ones you love? Would it have been better had they been honest about this part of themselves? Of course. Does that change the fact that each of you cares about at least one of them? No. At least five are dead over this already. We know Jack died an innocent man, hanged by people too afraid of *what* he was to remember *who* he was."

One man jumped up and pointed at her, face twisted in fury. "I saw him rip Ramelia's throat out!"

"Did you?" Chavali crossed her arms and stared him down. "Are you sure that's what you saw? Think back. Where was the blood? And why did he take that into public? If he wanted her dead, he had many chances to kill her privately, because they met often in her house. You can suggest that a lover's quarrel went out of control, yet this still does not explain why he carried her outside of the house to kill her, nor does it condone a summary hanging."

As she spoke, the one man's hand curled into a contrary fist, then he slowly sagged as her words urged him to think instead of reacting. "No, that really doesn't make sense, I guess. I..." He looked around at his neighbors, none of whom met his eyes. "I'm not really all that sure what I saw," he muttered. He sat and hunched on himself, his cheeks tinged with pink.

"Know this: they feel at least as betrayed by you as you do by them. That does not have to keep you apart. It can be the thing that brings you together. For now, though," Chavali gestured to the door, "we still must find a murderer. This would be a good time to go home, mourn, and remember what you thought of each of those people two weeks ago, before all of this happened."

Murmurs of agreement and acquiescence buzzed in the room, broken up by the shuffling of cloth and feet on wood. The villagers stood and plodded out, heads down. Eliot patted Chavali's shoulder, offering his approval as they watched.

"The Creator herself must have sent you," Kember whispered as she stopped by Chavali's side. "Thank you for keeping my town from tearing itself apart."

Chavali nodded in acknowledgment, wondering if the mayor would be as happy when they discovered the full truth.

When the place had emptied, Eliot still sat on a table, watching her. "How early did you figure out what Patrick is?"

She turned to find his expression carefully neutral. "When we met in the woods, I suspected but had no proof. Not before this. Other things seemed more important in that cave and during the flight and fight that followed. Had there been a true chance to tell you, I would have. It still would only have been my suspicion until he changed where we saw it."

He snorted. "Somehow, your suspicions about people always turn out to be right."

"I am skilled at guessing. I can tell you without a doubt that he loves you still, very much, and he is a decent man. I will tell Eldrack this also. All you must do is the same thing the people of this town must do: accept him for what he is."

"It's...not what I expected. It's not even close to what I expected. I knew he was hiding something, but—" He shook his head. "I suppose mine is just as crazy, when you think about it."

"We are quite similar to him, in many ways." She knew what her clan would say to such a thing: werewolves are evil and this is all madness. Until she met Patrick, she would have agreed. Knowing he could feel what he so obviously felt changed a great many things in her mind. Offering Eliot a hand, she pulled him outside to collect Colby. They still had work to do here.

As expected, the big man stood sentinel in the center of the small square, beside the two bodies left to the cold until the villagers could be moved to deal with them. She had a thought to bury one in the same hole they'd removed Ramelia from. Covering her mouth and nose to block the smell of blood and waste, she crouched beside Daisy to peer at her wound. Colby and Eliot both did the same, neither appearing to be bothered by the state of it.

"One injury," Colby said, using a knife to prod the woman's ruined neck. "Quick, deadly, and messy."

Eliot nodded. "Nothing removed or otherwise mussed. Whoever grabbed her did it to kill her and nothing more."

"Someone without control would've slashed her up more than this. They would have ripped and torn whatever they could reach and kept at it until they had to stop for some reason. Likewise, an accident?" Colby shook his head. "I've seen accidental deaths, plenty of them. This looks deliberate to me. Same for the other woman."

Chavali pursed her lips and looked away from the gore. "Either these two saw something that mattered, or their deaths were convenient. This woman being killed terrified the others who saw it happen, which sent them into panicked flight. They came to us, and we then knew werewolves were killing people." She shuddered, trying to imagine the kind of depraved mind that might murder a person to cause panic. "It was most likely done for effect. Which means Colby will not wait outside anymore, because this person has little regard for life."

"Agreed. The question is, who are we looking for?"

"It irritates me," Chavali said as she stood, "that neither Candy nor Grant can be our rogue werewolf, because either is a natural suspect now. They are not well integrated into the village. Candy pretends to be less of a mage than she is. Candy knew Ramelia. Grant is frequently 'away on business,' and he employs Patrick. Neither happened to be at this meeting. There are too many connections for it to be coincidence. Yet, both have been seen when the werewolf was also seen." She growled in frustration.

The three of them stood beside Karias in silence, while a breeze sought all the openings of her cloak. She shivered and huddled inside it, pulling it tighter and thinking about everything Lilly and Patrick had said. "We suspect the werewolf had some kind of magical enhancement. Since Candy is hiding her true capability, either she is using it in a way she knows others will not approve of, or she has personal reasons to not want it known. Someone who wanted magic to defeat the leader of the local pack might exploit such a desire."

Colby straightened and nodded. "We should talk to her. Whatever reason she has to hide it, you can probably convince her to talk."

"Barring that," Eliot added, "you can just take it from her."

Having thoughts along the same lines, Chavali nodded. She saw Colby's mouth twitch with disapproval and chose to ignore it. They had no time to bicker about methods. The two bodies in the snow deserved answers, and this village deserved peace.

Chapter 22

Chavali noted minor damage to several homes as they walked to Candy and Grant's. None of it would take much time or effort to repair individually. Collectively, these people would be busy for a while. It turned out that the house next door to Candy and Grant's had been the one on fire earlier, and it needed to be torn down and rebuilt. As they turned the corner, a young couple and their two small children emerged from the charred husk, carrying singed belongings.

It tugged at her heart to see people burned out of their home. Though her clan hadn't lived long enough to see their beautiful wagons destroyed, and she hadn't watched it or seen the aftermath personally, Railan's descriptions had been enough. Never again would there be a place quite so sublime as Papá's wagon, nor with such history. Hundreds of years ago, her ancestors built and carved it, and over the centuries, they repaired it and replaced the wheels and repainted it.

For this family, they would always know that peculiar pang for the loss of their home to the consuming and chaotic force of fire. She hated them for the coincidence of timing that showed she had such a significant experience in common with strangers. Identifying with them made everything more complicated and annoying.

"Chavali," Eliot murmured with a tap on her shoulder, "you're scowling."

She straightened and brushed a hand over the beads in her hair, making them clack together on purpose for the familiarity of it. "This is my thinking face."

Eliot snorted. "Only when you're thinking about things you hate."

"He's right," Colby said. "We need your sugar, not your bile."

"I'm aware of this. I know how to handle people, thank you."

Colby's mouth twitched with a repressed smile. "Karias, keep an eye out. If the werewolf sees us now, he'll probably come to try to interrupt."

Chavali rolled her shoulders and schooled away her irritation then knocked on the door. It took a long time for anyone to answer, and as she considered repeating the knock, Grant cracked the door open and peered out. Unlike before, he wore a hat, scarf, and gloves against the cold.

"We have been asked by Kember to assist with sorting out the chaos because we are as impartial as can be found. I noticed that you and your wife were among those who did not come to the store earlier. We wish to come in and speak with you both about what you saw during the fight and panic."

"Oh." He shifted his weight and averted his gaze. "We didn't really see anything. Just tried to stay out of the way."

Inside, Chavali raised an eyebrow, but she kept it to herself. She recalled seeing each separately, and both refused an offer of safety in numbers. People who'd made a deal with the rogue werewolf might not truly fear him, though it struck her as odd that they chose to be outside their home instead of remaining inside it. Perhaps the fire next door had driven them out. "It will take only a few minutes. Two women were murdered, so even small, seemingly meaningless details may help."

"No, I really don't—"

Chavali cut him off by shoving her boot into the door. With a flick of her hand, she got Colby to push the door open. "This is not precisely a request, Grant."

Grant let go of the door, unable to prevent Colby from opening it, and stepped back with his hands up. "I'm sorry. We're both just shaken up. I'm not...excited to rehash any of it so soon. Come in."

This time, when she stepped inside their house, no rush of heat greeted her. "Was your house damaged?"

"Yes, actually." Grant retreated, leading them to the sitting room they'd used before. He pointed at a window with a jagged hole covering more than half the pane of thick glass. Boards and books and cloth lay scattered on the floor beneath it, materials that all could serve to block it until the glass could be repaired properly. "We'll have to get some tools to do anything about it. For now, I've got a kettle on for tea."

Candy sat on the couch, huddled under a blanket Grant must have been sharing with her, hair tucked up under a hat and neck wrapped in a scarf. If Chavali wanted to read the thoughts of these people, she would have to manufacture a reason to touch them. With how miserable they both looked, she might not need to.

"I would appreciate some tea. Thank you for offering." Chavali pushed her hood down and sat beside Candy.

Eliot took the chair opposite Candy. Colby leaned against the wall. To prevent Grant from boxing her in, Chavali shrugged out of her pack and set it on her other side. That would force Grant to either remain standing or to sit in the chair Colby loomed behind. Chavali approved and flashed Eliot a conspiratorial smirk.

Grant sighed as he surveyed them then disappeared into the kitchen.

"Candy." Chavali reached over and put a hand on the blanket where she guessed Candy's arm to be. "I know this is difficult to relive so soon, but we must ask you to tell us about what you saw today. Where were you when you first learned the wolves were coming?"

Candy's gaze flicked to Eliot, then Colby, then the wall. She shrugged. "Outside."

Chavali expected this kind of answer from a child or someone in shock. Although Candy appeared to be quite upset, Chavali suspected this to be false. The lucid way her eyes moved suggested subterfuge, and the shrug felt out of place.

"We can, instead, talk about how you murdered Ramelia."

As she'd hoped, this baseless accusation snapped Candy out of her feigned shock. "What? I didn't hurt her! Ramelia was my friend. I would never harm her. How dare you suggest that. I was there, and I saw Jack kill her."

Chavali remembered her saying she hadn't been there to see it, not arriving until after the fact. This new story rang more true than false, yet something still seemed off about it. "How did you come to be friends? I gather she was focused on her research into those flowers and had little time for others."

"You didn't know her at all," Candy snapped. "She was sweet, very nice. Everyone liked her. That's why it was such a shock when she was killed. She had a soft spot for Jack, but he apparently didn't feel the same."

"How did it happen? Did they have a lover's quarrel?"

"No, no, nothing like that." Candy stopped, frowned, and shifted, suddenly uncomfortable. "It doesn't matter. They're both dead. This is settled and over. There's nothing to talk about."

Grant returned with two steaming mugs, offering one to Chavali and the other to Candy. He surveyed the room, still unhappy with the seating options.

"Very well. What did you see, Grant?"

"Me? Jack killed Ramelia, plain as day. She never should have—"

"She means today," Candy spat. "While those— When the monsters were running about, killing people and smashing everything. One of them even set fire to our neighbor's house. It was utter madness. Those things should all be killed. They're a drain on the village's resources."

The final statement echoed what Joey had overheard in the cave, making it clear Candy had some involvement with the rogue werewolf, though Chavali had no idea how deep it went. "And, I expect, quite noisy, especially in the woods."

"Yes, exactly! Always snooping around in that forest, and weirdly attracted to those flowers. As if it wasn't enough of a hardship to study them in this wretched cold, with the—"

A strange, meaty thunk cut her off. Grant gurgled and clutched at his neck, mouth opening and closing while he tried to make noise. His eyes bulged and blood stained his lips.

"Karias," Colby bellowed, "attacker outside!" He grabbed his sword and stayed clear of the window.

Grant dropped to his knees. Candy's eyes and mouth went wide with horror. Eliot sprang to his feet, drawing his blades. Chavali lunged for Grant, catching him before he fell on his face. The plain hilt of a knife stuck out of his neck, and she knew he stood no chance of survival without a Healer close at hand.

"Can your magic heal?"

Candy, paralyzed with true shock and terror, stared at her husband as he bled to death in Chavali's arms. "Not again," she whimpered.

Someone outside grunted in surprised pain, then a person smashed through the window. Tight cloth, light enough in color to be pure white, covered every inch of his body, from head to toe, even over his eyes. He tumbled to the floor, sliding in a less-than-graceful landing. Red stains sprouted on his clothing, attesting to the sharpness of the glass he'd been kicked through by Karias.

The stranger—who could not possibly be a werewolf—leaped to his feet and found Eliot jumping into his path. Seeing that he'd been headed for Candy, Chavali let Grant fall to the floor, jerking the blade from his neck to use it. She grabbed Candy and yanked the woman to her feet. "Mourn later," she growled, intent on saving this woman's life long enough to get as much of the true story as she could.

Dragging Candy past the fight to the kitchen, Chavali could tell this strange man had skills far beyond hers. He whirled and danced, ducking under Colby's huge blade and meeting Eliot's with his own, both at once. Eliot's fluid grace and Colby's brute strength combined to force him away from Candy and Chavali, yet he still managed to maneuver himself to the front door while rolling past both men.

He threw the door open to find Karias's huge body there, hind hooves raised. The horse kicked him across the room, and he managed to twist just enough to avoid letting Colby behead him. Eliot slammed his sword into the floor as the stranger rolled out of the way of his blow. The man leaped to his feet with nothing between him and Chavali. She had a throwing knife. He had a sword.

Colby's blade hacked down, and the stranger somehow knew to duck to the side. It spared his life, but not his clothes, as the giant blade scraped down his arm, slicing a layer of flesh off. He hissed and gave his attention back to the two men. They slipped and slid through a deadly dance, one Chavali had no hope to match with her meager skill. She pushed Candy deeper into the kitchen.

Soft whistling snapped her attention to the tea kettle still boiling on a trivet over their hearth fire. Snatching up a towel, she grabbed the handle and sloshed the water at the man steadily backing towards her. His continuing advance toward Candy made no sense to her. In his place, she would count the mission a partial success for having killed Grant and look to retreat and try again another day.

Steaming water hit him in the back, making him stiffen and strangle down a scream. Eliot's sword stabbed through the man's leg, and he dropped to one knee. Colby stopped his blade at the man's neck.

"As you might imagine," Colby said, "we have some questions for you."

The stranger grabbed his leg and hissed in pain as Eliot pulled his sword out with a spray of blood. A flash of light shimmered around him, then he disappeared. Colby slashed his sword through the suddenly empty space. Eliot lunged with his blade. Chavali stood and blinked.

"I do not understand what just happened." She set the teapot aside and noticed Candy quivering in the corner.

Eliot crouched and swiped a finger through the blood, rubbing it on his thumb. He opened his mouth to say something then shut it and shook his head.

Colby pulled his sword out of the way and wiped his forehead with his sleeve. "It's like he used a Creator's Tower."

"That's not possible," Eliot said. "You can only do that from one tower to another. No one can just pop from anywhere, not even to a Creator's Tower."

"It had a blue flash, the same kind you see when you use a tower."

"I know, I was standing here too. I'm just saying that's not possible. There must be some other explanation. Maybe he turned invisible and ran off. I've seen invisible before. Encountered it, I mean. Teleporting, though, no, that's not— It's just not."

Chavali held out her hands. "We will tell—" Candy might not be coherent enough to explain any of this to anyone. That did not excuse carelessness. "Later." For now, she yanked Candy's sleeve out of the way and grabbed the woman's arm. "I know you were lying before. Tell me who the werewolf is that abducted Lilly's son."

Candy's thoughts jumped from Grant with blood dribbling out of his mouth to the fight to Chavali to Owen to things Chavali had to concentrate on to understand. The woman dissolved into hysterical tears as she focused on Grant's death. Chavali had no patience for her. They needed to stop that werewolf from killing anyone else, and Candy knew his identity.

She slapped Candy across the face. "Who is the werewolf?" she demanded.

It was us. Candy sobbed and sniffled, shaking her head and sucking in gasping breaths.

"'Us'? What do you mean? Who are you working with?" Chavali watched the woman's thoughts paint the picture as she struggled to accept the past few minutes. What she saw made her grab Candy's hand and yank off her wedding ring.

"Please," Candy wailed. "Please help me. I don't want to die."

"You created this," Chavali sneered. "A ring that could make you change into a werewolf. Two of them, so you and your husband could share the responsibilities and foil attempts to discover your identities. You used magic to defeat Jack, setting him up for the circumstance that led to his wrongful hanging. You tortured three children and Owen to madness and death. You took Joey, tied him up, and left him in a cave, and you tried to instigate the pack to murder the villagers. You murdered Daisy to foster panic and hate. After all this, you ask for mercy?"

"I never wanted Ramelia to be hurt. She was my friend." Candy hiccuped, sobbing through the words. "The werewolves aren't really people. They don't matter! We didn't want to hurt anyone else, but they wouldn't just let us do the research. I only wanted to study the flowers with Ramelia. That's all I ever wanted. Those stupid wolves got involved, so I studied them too, because they're connected to the flowers, but it drove them all mad, so we had to kill them. That one escaped, you saw it. He was a monster."

Eliot held up the second ring, smudged with Grant's blood. "Why those flowers? What did you think they'd be able to do that could be worth all this?"

Candy shook her head, now covering her face. "I thought they might be able to...to let us teleport goods and people without having to use the Creator's Towers. It just got out of control. We only wanted to know what it was doing to them. I had no idea how to run a werewolf pack. Neither did— Neither did Grant." She fell into weeping again.

Chavali let go of Candy's arm and stood, not hiding her distaste. "I'll explain everything to Kember."

"Wait." Colby held up both hands. "You want to just give her to the villagers? You know what they'll do. She'll be dead in a day, if it takes them that long."

"And is this wrong?" Chavali stared up at him, perversely pleased he stayed true to his usual annoying virtues. "She has taken many lives. Should she not give hers for the sake of justice?"

Colby frowned and shook his head. "It seems..."

"Unfair? Did I mention the part where she tortured children to madness, and then she put them down like animals rather than try to save them? Or perhaps we should go over the part where her actions sent Jack to the noose. She killed Owen in front of us and behaved as if she had no idea what could have caused him to attack, as if she had no idea why he might be there. She ripped out the throat of that girl lying in the center of town for *no reason.*

"What is fair, Colby? Would it make you more comfortable if, instead, she lived a life of torment in a jail? Or perhaps you'd prefer the Ket way, to send her to an island to fight madness for survival." By the end, she found herself shouting and stopped to take a breath and calm down. "Given the choice, I would kill her now, but that isn't my job or decision."

For several long moments, only Candy's sobbing broke the silence that followed.

"I agree with her," Eliot said. "We'll turn Candy over because it's not our place to decide what happens to her. The people of Eagle Falls are the ones who have suffered, and it's their right to carry out justice according to their customs. The King would agree, and so would Eldrack."

Colby sighed and nodded. "Someday, all the blood on your hands will drown you, Chavali."

Chavali snorted. "This, coming from a soldier." Stepping outside, she wanted to believe the madness here had ended. That strange teleporting man said otherwise. She strode up the cleared path, half expecting the assassin to come after her next. They'd missed something important in Ket, and now they'd missed something important here. At least they knew they'd missed it already, instead of learning about it a week too late to do anything.

In the village center, the mayor held her arm around the shoulders of an older man, murmuring and tugging him away from the two dead bodies. His body bowed and shuddering with unspent grief, he shook his head. Chavali approached and debated how to handle this situation. She had no reason to care about this particular man's pain and preferred to remain detached from the village as much as possible. At the same time, she needed to speak with Kember and could see the woman struggled with him.

Taking a deep breath, she moved in front of the man, facing him over what must be his daughter's corpse. "A werewolf did not do this," she told them both. "Someone who wanted you to blame a werewolf did this. Someone with no children of their own, someone who believed the wolves to be lesser and unworthy, someone who would sacrifice your children in the name of their goals. In this case, it is two people."

Seeing that she had their attention, she offered the man her hand. "One of them is dead already, slain as we confronted them. The other is in our custody, and we will give her to Kember." She turned to the mayor. "I encourage you to treat Candy as a dangerous individual and suggest her penalty be harsh, as is fitting for her crimes. Everything that has happened, starting with the two missing children, has been Candy and Grant's fault, either directly or indirectly. They are responsible for all the deaths."

The man took her hand, and she squeezed his while enduring the onslaught of his despair. Daisy had been the light of his life, his only family left. He had a thought to lie down and let the cold numb him until they needed another grave. In her clan, no one would stop someone his age from doing this unless he had an invaluable skill he hadn't passed on to another yet.

Kember's face hardened. "They killed Ramelia?"

Although Chavali had a sneaking suspicion the mysterious teleporting man may have performed the actual murder, she nodded. These people had no need for that detail, and spreading it might hinder Eldrack's efforts to investigate the matter. "They caused this, yes."

"Did those werewolves try to save my Daisy?"

Chavali faced his raw agony without flinching. "Yes. Not directly, but their goal has always been, and ever will be, to protect Eagle Falls." Knowing about the effect of the flowers on them, she had no doubt of this. "Sometimes, they may fail, but it will never be for lack of effort."

The man nodded and squeezed her hand. "Creator forgive us all," he mumbled. His mind flashed with disturbing things he wanted to do to Candy and Grant, and Chavali let go.

Colby entered the clearing with Candy slung over one shoulder and bawling through a gag. Under Kember's direction, they deposited her in a barn and tied her to a post. They'd keep her under watch until an official decision about her fate was made.

"We should go," Colby said as they left the barn.

"Eliot needs to speak with Patrick." Chavali crossed her arms, daring the man in question to disagree.

Eliot sighed and rubbed his face. "I have no idea what to say."

Chavali rolled her eyes and grabbed his arm. "Don't be stupid." Dragging him to Ramelia's house, she glanced aside to see Karias step up to his master and nudge him. She wondered idly if Colby's difficulty with this situation could be traced to some memory she'd discover later.

"Chavali, cut it out," Eliot said.

"Don't whine. I just had to sit through the filth in that woman's head. You get to have someone you love back. I can whine. You may not."

Eliot grumbled something unintelligible.

"What was that? It sounded like, 'Yes, Chavali, you're right, I'm needlessly overcomplicating my love life by worrying about stupid things.' In which case, I agree with you." She pushed the door of the broken house open without knocking and found everyone playing simple games on the floor to entertain the handful of children in the room. "We found your rogue alpha, and there is no longer a threat. I'll explain, but only after Patrick comes out to talk to him." She yanked Eliot into view.

"Oh." Patrick cleared his throat and blushed. "Um. Sure."

She mirrored a handful of smirks that bloomed in the room and hauled Eliot around the corner so the pair could have a semblance of privacy. "Do you need a chaperone?"

Eliot glowered. "I hate you."

"Yes. The feeling is mutual." She stepped out of sight, intending to listen and make sure Eliot didn't fumble the whole thing.

Patrick ducked his head and hurried past her, then he coughed. Eliot coughed. Feet shifted on the ground. Armor creaked. Chavali crossed her arms and kept herself from pacing or tapping her foot impatiently. She heard them breathing and knew they couldn't be doing anything other than standing there, uncomfortably avoiding staring at each other. It made her want to scream.

"So," Patrick finally said. "I didn't die in that attack on the caravan."

"I gathered that."

Patrick left a pause, which Chavali assumed involved giving Eliot an annoyed look. She would have. "I wound up getting dragged back to their camp unconscious. When I woke up, they said that since I was a merc, they'd give me a choice: either I agree to work with them for a cut, or they'd cut my throat. I felt pretty confident that I could probably maneuver them into giving me a chance to get free, so I agreed to join them, and put on a good show about how little I was actually being paid and that sort of thing."

"I guess something went wrong?"

"In the middle of the night, a rabid werewolf raged through the camp. I'm still not sure why. It killed all of them, but I managed to fight it off. Except I got bitten, and it took hold, and...and here I am. It was sheer luck that I found this place. Otherwise, I would've been just some mad werewolf roaming the lands for the next would-be hero to put down."

Patrick's voice faded to nothing, and a long silence sat between them. "This is the part where you explain how *you* died but not."

Eliot sighed, and Chavali could imagine him scratching his cheek or grabbing the nape of his neck—possibly both at once. "It's complicated."

"More complicated than getting bitten by a werewolf? Come on, Eliot. Just tell me. Is this about that woman? She's some kind of sorcerer, isn't she? Are you bound to her somehow?"

"No." Eliot grunted. "I mean, yes, she's involved, but not— Look, I can't—"

"But you *can*."

Chavali huffed in annoyance and stepped around the corner to see Eliot clenched and trying not to reject Patrick while still pushing him away. They reminded her of— In that moment, she saw herself and Keino, except that she would slap him now and storm off. "He cannot tell you because he has pledged an oath on his soul to keep this secret until he gets someone else's permission to explain it to you. This other person is not me, nor is it our companion, Colby. He was not able to secure that permission while we were gone."

Patrick blinked at her then turned back to Eliot. "You really could've just said that."

"Yes, you could have." She rolled her eyes again and left them to whatever sorts of obnoxious—and private—emotional outbursts they'd segue into. Colby looming with a pensive frown from the other side of the front stoop made her stop and wipe her face blank. At the moment, he needed not to see her bemusement and mild irritation at Eliot. She obliged his needs because...

Never mind. "Did you wish to be the one to explain all of this?"

Colby shook his head. "No, you're better at that sort of thing."

Chavali silently agreed. "This thing you struggle with, I understand it. You know I have a conscience, Colby. So does Eliot." She knew those inside could hear her and chose to use the moment rather than shying away from it. "I have told you stories of my clan, mostly about goats doing human things, in simple ways. You're not foolish or stupid enough to misunderstand the purpose of them."

"Of course, but what does that have to do with this?"

"Candy and Grant broke the most important promise of a community: everyone eats together."

He nodded with a sigh then gestured for her to go inside. "I'm fine."

She knew a lie when she saw one but chose to ignore it. With a nod, she ducked inside and told them everything she knew about what had happened and why. All of them sat and listened in silence. Rage filled the room, palpable and threatening. When she finished, she wondered if the flowers would be enough to keep them from shifting and destroying things.

"Thank you for explaining all of this," Lilly said, her words clipped and strained. "I have no doubt they'll hang her for the murders of those two women."

Chavali nodded. "This seems likely to me as well."

To her surprise, the pack moved closer together, reaching for each other, touching and being touched. One moment, she thought their pain would rip the building apart, and the next, she thought she might want to slap someone for forcing her to witness a gross display of community and closeness. It cut her deeply to see these people basking in a kind of joy she missed from her first life. This second one had precious little of it.

Lilly held her son close and managed a small smile. "You've proven yourself a capable ally. May we ask you and your friends to remain and represent us for whatever process is used to reach judgment over Candy's fate?"

More than anything, Chavali wanted to leave this place behind and bask in her own tiny clan. However, she knew the Fallen had a vested interest in the stability of Eagle Falls, and duty demanded that they represent Eldrack to the best of their ability. "Yes, of course. I'll go see about that for you." She fled the house so fast that Colby had to hop out of her way.

Chapter 23

Hours later, Chavali sat on the front stoop of Ramelia's house, watching the sun drift down behind the trees. Candy's "trial" would take place in the morning, and Kember had accepted Chavali's request to be present, with the condition that they had to stay with the pack for the night. It seemed that the one thing all here could agree on was that the three Fallen could be trusted.

She'd spent two hours talking to the villagers after that, trying to make sure no one did anything stupid overnight. At this point, she knew they'd put Candy to death tomorrow and that there would be more discussion regarding the werewolves. Eliot, of course, sat and talked with Patrick all afternoon and evening. As far as she knew, they'd gone off someplace for true privacy, and she assumed Eliot would be in better spirits when they returned.

"I sometimes wonder how it looks to you," Colby's voice rumbled from behind her. "Things like this, especially, where the color is what makes it worth watching."

Chavali snorted. "I wasn't born this way. When I became the Seer of my clan, I lost colors. I can see them in the thoughts and memories of others too. The biggest difference is the details I miss, because two colors can look the same to me."

The wood creaked as he sat beside her. "So you remember what you're missing. Does it compare well?"

"Well enough." She could tell he asked to open a deeper conversation. He'd let her into his mind and now expected her to reciprocate somehow. For several seconds, she wrestled with the impulse to tell him something that told him nothing. After what she saw in his mind, though, he deserved more than that from her.

"One of my most vivid memories is that of my sister's birth. I was six at the time. My purpose there involved only one duty: holding a blanket until someone snatched it out of my hands, then I would pick up another and hold it ready. I stood there with my brother, watching—"

"Wait. Your *brother* watched that?"

"Yes, of course."

Colby stared at her. "Where I come from, they don't let any men and boys in while babies are born. We have no place in or part of any of it. The privilege of attending a birth is reserved for women."

"Where you come from is full of idiots."

"Thanks."

She grinned. "I thought you preferred honesty."

He huffed, an answering grin creeping into the corners of his mouth. "It doesn't have to be quite so blunt."

"I respect you, Colby." She patted his shoulder. "I disagree with you about a great many things, but I respect you."

Looking down at her hand, he smiled. "Thank you. I feel the

same way."

She squeezed his shoulder and used it to help herself stand up. "I suspect tomorrow will be trying. So to speak. Come, we should eat and sleep."

He followed her inside to a large pot of stew. They sat with werewolves, watching and listening to them make the best of the situation. When Patrick and Eliot returned, well after dark, it appeared their private "conversation" had gone well. She had no chance to speak with either of them in the large group before they found a spot to settle in for the night.

For herself, Chavali elected to take a blanket outside where Karias lay on the ground near the front door. The accommodation lacked a great deal, but it let her escape the taunting the werewolves had no idea they inflicted upon her. She fell asleep without knowing where Colby chose to rest for the night.

She found herself in darkness, with some kind of heavy cloth covering her face. Though her limbs felt leaden, she reached up and pushed away canvas, the same kind her clan used for their tents. Her other arm hurt with an ache that couldn't decide if it should be sharp or dull. Blinking in the harsh light outside, she saw her wrist had a hole through it, one made by a knife. Impossibly red blood dripped out, falling only because of gravity. Her heart had already stopped beating.

Screaming, louder than anything she'd ever heard before, filled her ears. She looked up to see Papá and Pasha fighting four men, his sword and her spear flashing in the light of a fire growing among the wagons. More of her clan fought in scattered knots. There, Amets stabbed through an attacker, only to be cut to pieces himself. Auivel slashed her twin daggers in a blur, ripping up two men at once. While she dodged a third and fourth man, a dagger plunged into her gut from a distance.

Chavali watched in horror as her clan fought bravely against impossible odds. Pasha's dress whipped around her ankles, its rich, vibrant green at odds with the duller grass. Papá's dark red sash stood out against the spray of blood as an attacker cut his arm. Colors pressed on her. The sharp tang of burning paint slapped her across the face. Suddenly, she noticed the copper bite of blood in her mouth, where it had dripped down from her nose.

"No," she breathed. With every ounce of strength she had, she scrambled away from the fighting. Rolling and finding her feet, she lurched into a shambling run and hit someone. Wiry arms caught her, and she found herself staring into the baby blue eyes she would dread for the rest of her life. His lips parted, ready to speak, and she screamed. Pushing away from him, she fled and refused to look back.

Her feet carried her past a bend in the road, and she stopped dead at what she saw. Someone stood in the middle. She knew those shoulders and legs, that shaggy, black hair. Breath catching in her throat, she watched him turn to face her, his thick daggers bared and red smeared across his white shirt and dark beard. She'd never noticed the tiny flecks of gold in the brown of his eyes before.

"Keino," she whispered, unable to manage anything more.

He took one step towards her, raising his knife. Her eyes snapped open in darkness, a sharp sound dying on the wind. Strong arms held her close, and heat radiated all around her body. Wood scraped on wood nearby, and a steady heartbeat thumped in her skull.

"It's fine," Colby said, his voice deep with her ear against his chest. "Just a nightmare. No one is in any danger. Sorry she woke you."

The door slid shut, and she sat curled up on his lap, clutching his arm and noticing the rawness of her throat. His hand stroked her hair, pushing it out of her face without forcing his thoughts on her. He'd put his gloves on.

"You're safe, Chavali. Whatever it was, it can't hurt you."

She wanted to believe him. "There's nowhere to hide." The words came out as a scratchy rasp.

"Then don't hide. You're no coward. You're one of the bravest people I know."

The absurdity of his statement made her laugh. Once she started, it turned to tears, then to ridiculously hysterical sobbing that she couldn't stop. Their faces now seemed more vivid than before, as if the dream had burned them into her brain. She'd never seen Pasha in full color as an adult before.

Had Keino somehow escaped? Doubt chased her in circles. She hadn't lived long enough to see any of that, nor had she seen him die. He could be alive someplace, wandering in a daze, even now, six months later. It crossed her mind that he might have been working for the attackers, except that made no sense. Not only would it have killed a piece of him inside to turn against his clan, he would never have done anything to hurt her.

Colby kept talking, murmuring soothing words until she calmed down again. When she did quiet, she wound up staring down the road, the light of the moon reflecting off the snow. If Keino had survived, assuming her death hadn't driven him mad, he would have come looking for her as soon as she'd been revived. He would have found her by now. What did that nightmare mean? It made no sense.

None of her dreams made any sense, of course, but this one felt so much more real than any of the others. With those others, even while inside them, she had a sense they couldn't be anything more than metaphorical. Flowers could not eat her flesh. People could not be alive, trapped under ice. None of those things would happen directly. That revelation came early and made bearing them easier.

This dream, though, showed her things she knew could have happened. What she saw of her clan fighting depicted how they actually fought. Pasha's shoulder dropped like it always did when she cut with her spear. Papá's feet danced like she'd seen him do a thousand times before. Auivel, Amets, and all the rest moved and fenced and stabbed and slashed in the ways she'd seen them practice before.

The attackers had no grotesque or absurd features; they appeared to be normal men with normal weapons and normal armor. She'd smelled genuine fire, and the complexity of the scents under it reminded her of home. The wagons had all the details she remembered and even some she never paid attention to. Plants in the rooftop gardens shriveled in the heat before flames overtook them.

"Chavali, I know you don't want to, but we both need some sleep." Colby's quiet, weary voice interrupted her thoughts. "If it would help, I can take off a glove."

She shook her head, certain that, despite his intent, the offer would only make things worse. "No. But thank you for offering."

His head leaned back, and he drifted off. He'd arranged himself so his arms still held her, even in sleep, and she could stay there, warm and protected. She had no doubt he would and could leap into full alertness to defend her at need.

A fleeting thought that he might make a good clansman chased her into slumber.

Chapter 24

As expected, the trial was a quick, predictable affair. Chavali's part in the not-quite-sham gesture had been to tell the village what really happened. As with Kember, she omitted the appearance of the teleporting man, thinking this both too farfetched to be believed and irrelevant to the villagers as a whole. Suspicion brewed, though, as Candy continued to deny killing Ramelia. The villagers decided to blame Grant for that one and chose to have his body hung beside his wife so it also wouldn't profane the ground.

Chavali sat and watched as two men carried Candy out of the barn they'd used to host the spectacle. One slipped and let her fall into a manure pile on the way out. He took care to protect her head, lest she be granted the mercy of unconsciousness. This time, there would be no audience for the hanging because no one followed them out. Instead, Andrew stood to speak.

"Almost everyone is here," he said, gesturing to the half of the village present. "I'd like to know what people intend to do about the werewolves."

"They're monsters," someone grumbled from the crowd.

"We should put them all to death!"

"Banish them."

"Everything was fine two weeks ago!" Andrew put up his hands. "My wife has never once harmed me. My son has never once harmed any of your children. Were any of you listening here? Until that couple came here, none of them harmed a hair on anyone's heads. I love my wife and I love my son, and they're werewolves. What they also are is people. They think, they feel, they love, they laugh, they hurt, they cry, and yes, they rage. So do we. I've never seen anything more monstrous than the lynch mob that murdered Jack."

Multiple voices rose in both protest and agreement. Beside Chavali, Colby tensed, ready to leap into the fray and sort things out. Keeping it low to avoid attracting attention, she held out a hand to stop him. He saw unruly people about to cause trouble. She saw a community ripping apart.

Kember stood and added her voice to the shouting match, achieving nothing. These people had other faults and fractures they'd been hiding, and this one subject galvanized them to finally act.

Leaning closer, Colby muttered, "We can't let them kill each other."

"They won't."

"I'm not so sure. We could stop this."

"We won't be here tomorrow."

"Then we can help them argue more productively."

Chavali pursed her lips and scanned the body language of those in sight. She had to admit several of these people danced on the edge of throwing punches or worse. With a curt nod, she twined her fingers through the spirits, calling up an illusion of a dark cloud blowing in through the open door and flowing through them all. The cacophony quieted as people shifted from arguing to confusion.

"Melodramatic," Colby whispered.

Chavali snorted. She banished the image with a wave of her hand. "People of Eagle Falls, you face a choice." Her voice, forceful and loud enough to cut through the muttering, commanded attention. "It is clear and obvious, yet you bicker around it as if all your old grievances have bearing here. The werewolves will not leave. They are tied to this place by a mystical bond. If you do not wish to live among them, then you must leave. And this is not a decision to make as a community. It is personal. Each of you must make that choice for yourself and your family. Never mind what your neighbors think, because it is irrelevant.

"Any who wish to leave, there are several other villages within a few hours' walk, which you all know. If you are ready to leave within three hours, my companions and I will escort you to whichever village you prefer or to the Creator's Tower. Otherwise, you're on your own." She tapped Colby's thigh as she stood to make him also get up. "We do, however, live in the area. Given the history of this community, we will be paying attention, especially when people die or disappear."

After taking only one step, she thought of one more point that needed to be made. "I recommend against speaking much of werewolves. This, we also will be paying attention to." She left the barn at a brisk walk with her head held high, Colby following on her heels.

Several steps away from the building, he fell in beside her. "I've never seen dark green fog before."

Chavali huffed. "It was supposed to be black."

"Ah." He grinned then blinked at her. "Did you just admit to making a mistake?"

"Perhaps." She might have said more but saw Eliot standing outside with Patrick, both leaning against the wall of the house and laughing together. They happened to glance to the side and noticed her and Colby approaching. She waved. Eliot returned it.

"Patrick can't leave and Eliot can't stay."

It reminded her of her own predicament with the clan, though his had hours of travel involved, not minutes. "Yes. Would you like to remind him of this?"

"No."

Chavali snorted. "Coward."

He chuckled. "You didn't ask me if I *would* do it. You asked me if I *wanted* to. Go ahead inside and tell Lilly what her husband said. I'll talk to Eliot and Patrick."

With a nod, she slipped inside and related the events for the pack. "In your place, I would be wary of incidents over the next few days," she said when she'd finished. "After that, I doubt anyone will make an effort. It's difficult to say what stories they may spread. I have asked for discretion, but I can't control what comes out of their mouths."

"Thank you," Lilly said, wrapping Chavali in a warm embrace. "You've done a great service to us, and we won't forget it. If you ever need our help, you only have to ask."

The hug surprised her and made her smile. "We remain available to you as well. In Cloverdale, the tavern's bartenders know how to reach any of the three of us. I expect you will be seeing Eliot often."

Lilly drew back with a wry chuckle. "Yes, I think so." She turned to her son with a bright smile. "Joey, let's go home."

The boy's face broke into a joyful smile, and he thumped into Chavali's leg to give her a quick hug before running out the door. Other members of the pack also touched her and thanked her as they followed their new Alpha out of the makeshift jail. She stood in the empty house, noticing they'd left the house cleaner than they found it.

"Because I can't, that's why!" Patrick's raised voice caught her attention. She looked up to see him fleeing past the open door.

Nothing about this place made her ever want to return again. It seemed to turn men into idiots at an alarming rate. "No," she bellowed, "both of you come in here right now!"

Eliot froze in front of the door, caught in the act of chasing Patrick. He turned and must have found the look on her face compelling, because he hung his head and shuffled inside, keeping his eyes anywhere but on her. Patrick sighed as he trudged inside and also avoided looking at her. Colby filled the door and crossed his arms.

"I have little patience for this sort of thing on the best of days and less after putting up with the people of this village. Patrick, our employer has made it clear that my opinion about you carries weight with him. In light of that, I will now tell you the things Eliot has kept close. If you speak any of this information to anyone other than another member of our organization, you will be killed for it.

Patrick gaped at her. "You're serious. You'd do that."

"Yes, quite. Eliot is my friend, and since he loves you very much, it would hurt me to do it, but I will cut your throat if you force me to."

He gulped and nodded. "I understand."

Chavali caught Colby wiping away his surprise and questioning in favor of projecting stalwart support. Eliot slid to the floor, where he sat and stared at her with an expression that clearly questioned her judgment. She ignored him to nod at Patrick.

"We are, all three of us and more, bound to an entity that will destroy us if we betray it. This happened because we died once, and it has found a way to bring people back. Once. An organization called The Fallen pays the price for each of us, and in return, we pledge our lives to serve it for a period of five years. At the end of this time, we are free to do as we please, so long as we keep the secrecy of the Fallen."

Patrick reacted as expected, with shock and disbelief. "That's impossible," he finally managed.

"So is a werewolf controlling his shifting, so far as I understand. And yet, here we all are. What was that argument about?"

Eliot sighed. "He won't come with me."

"Of course he won't." She rolled her eyes because Eliot had, apparently, lost all his brains. "Don't be stupid. He can't leave, or he loses control, especially under the full moon. If he came with you, one of you would wind up dead. Or both. I believe we've already been told that sort of thing is a 'dire waste of resources.' You can visit him whenever you have a chance, the same as I do with my clan. Now, is there anything else I need to fix for you, or are you prepared to enjoy the last few hours you have together for now?"

When both men shook their heads, she breezed out of the house, only pausing to let Colby step aside.

Chapter 25

Twenty-seven of the villagers chose to abandon their homes rather than knowingly live alongside werewolves. It took until nightfall to get them past Candy and Grant's swaying corpses and to their chosen destination of Trennis, and to then return to Cloverdale. All three stayed quiet through the trip, and when they reached the tavern, Colby sent Karias off to tend to himself until morning.

As they crossed the wide, empty room two floors underground, Eliot stopped and put an arm out in front of Chavali. "What did you mean when you said we'd been bound to an entity?"

She raised her brow and wondered why he brought this up now. Beyond him, she noticed a figure reaching the top of the next set of stairs and grimaced at the icy glare Railan leveled at them all. Nothing good could come of such focused displeasure from Eldrack's chief and most dedicated agent.

"Later," she hissed.

"Get your asses down to see Eldrack," Railan snapped, jabbing a finger at the floor. When none of them moved, she flared her nostrils.

The puckered scar cutting across her nose rippled. "Now."

"I can explain," Eliot began.

Railan cut him off with a raised hand. "I don't care. Tell *him* why three of his agents disappeared without a word yesterday morning. Let's go." She turned on her heel and stalked down the stairs.

"He didn't know?" Colby frowned. "I thought he knew."

"Things have turned out reasonably well," Chavali muttered. "He can't be too angry with the results."

"This is about process," Eliot agreed, though his tone lacked confidence.

"Hurry up," Railan's voice called from below.

They hurried and followed her down to the thirteenth level, then into a mission briefing room. Chavali sat and fingered the beads in her hair, making them click together. Eldrack would want to hear everything, so she spent the time mentally running over all the events they'd witnessed and participated in.

By the time Eldrack walked in, Colby and Railan had also taken a seat and Eliot had fallen into pacing. Eldrack wore a faint scowl and carried a folder that he dropped onto the table. In many respects, she preferred this man to the nicer version, though it embarrassed her to have disappointed him. For some reason.

"There's dried blood on all your clothes," Eldrack said with precise, clipped words. "The sooner you explain, the sooner you can get cleaned up."

"I got a message from Eagle Falls," Eliot said, looking at his hands. "I should have brought it to you, but it said a child had gone missing, and that made me..."

"Do something stupid," Eldrack supplied. "Had you come to me, I could have told you the story of Ramelia's death wasn't right, because her throat was slit with a blade, not claws or fangs."

"Yes," Chavali said with a nod. "We know who killed her."

"We do?" Colby frowned. "She protested her innocence on that more than once."

"The man who killed Grant also killed Ramelia." Chavali waved her hands to make everyone else stop talking. "Let me explain all of this, from the beginning. First, you knew about the werewolves, yes? Before we told you in the report. You knew Jack, and had an agreement to help him if he ever asked."

Eldrack's mouth twitched, and Chavali couldn't decide how to interpret that. "Yes."

"Then let us go back to Ramelia. She studied the glowing flowers. In her studies, she attracted a friend who also found them interesting. Candy was a mage, and she wanted to study them for the possibility of using them for transportation to help her husband, a merchant who tired of paying for the use of the Creator's Towers.

"Candy found the werewolves problematic because they tended to show up around those flowers. This turns out to be because the flowers emit some kind of energy that allows them to control their urges and bodies when their curse would otherwise rule them. Patrick, by the way, is a werewolf, and I found him to be entirely trustworthy. I don't believe he is any risk to us whatsoever. Though he may not be exceptionally useful as an ally, he is one, nonetheless.

"To deal with the werewolves, Candy poured much of her power into these rings." Chavali pulled both out of her pocket and dropped them onto the desk. "I recommend they be destroyed. The wearer can take the shape of a werewolf in its most terrifying form. It's unclear whether it influences the mind as part of the shifting. The couple then managed to keep their identities secret from the pack and unseated Jack as the Alpha.

"Jack figured out who they were, I think, after they took children and experimented on them to discover how the flowers worked. For some time, Jack had been seeing Ramelia, and which is how he came to have a confrontation with Candy and Grant at her house, and an assassin killed Ramelia under all three of their noses. Candy and Grant went into a panic, got sloppy, and tried to incite a battle between the werewolves and villagers in order to create chaos."

"Stop." Eldrack had never interrupted a report so brazenly before. Curious and surprised, she shut her mouth and let him speak. "How did an assassin kill Ramelia without them knowing it?"

"I'm getting to that." Chavali related Grant's death for him. "There is more to this than one mage meddling with werewolves and flowers."

Eldrack nodded his agreement. "Tell me about Grant. The merchant."

"There is little to tell." Chavali shrugged. "Forgettable and uninteresting. I don't think we even determined what goods he traded. His wife had all the personality in that household. I believe the whole debacle was her idea. He went along with it, out of either fear or love. I suspect the latter, as I don't recall him ever seeming afraid of her. I suppose it could have been mutual interest. Sean might know more, as he claimed to have been previously acquainted."

Eldrack frowned more. "Ramelia's research had nothing to do with teleportation. She thought she'd found a new kind of energy that could be used in different ways than traditional magical or mental power. In a way, I suppose she had. How did Candy and Grant come to be there, studying that?"

Chavali sat back and thought about the question, mulling over the things she'd seen in Candy's mind. "This is not clear, and both are dead now. I didn't think to ask."

"I know Chavali can't tell," Colby said, "but the glow does look an awful lot like the one the crystals on the tops of the Creator's Towers give off. I would guess someone heard about that and sent her to investigate. Anything that appears to be connected to the Towers but isn't controlled by the Order of the Creator's Path would be of interest to all kinds of people."

Eldrack nodded again and sat. "I assume you found the child that went missing?"

"Yes." Chavali filled in the details she hadn't explained yet, telling Eldrack about everything except her nightmares. He had no need to be bothered by such things. As she'd been told multiple times, everyone here had nightmares, at least at first.

Clasping his hands together on top of his folder, Eldrack waited a few beats before speaking. Chavali had the feeling he needed to think and make decisions, and chose not to interrupt. "None of this goes into a written report, and no one talks about it. There was no mission, and you three weren't there. Of course, none of you *should* have been there." His voice took on a hard edge. "Definitely not without saying something. If you'd come to me, I might have sent more agents, or assigned someone with different skills, or, oh, I don't know, *told you that you'd be dealing with a large pack of werewolves*. Now, on top of all this, I have forms to fill out because of you three."

Eliot rubbed his face and looked away.

"It was a lapse in judgment," Chavali offered. Eliot should be able to account for himself, yet he clearly couldn't. "One created by the unusual circumstances. I'm sure it won't happen again."

"No." Eliot sighed heavily. "It won't."

"Fine." Eldrack waved them all out with a sharp flick of his wrist. "Get some rest and be ready for a new mission tomorrow."

Chavali scowled but chose not to argue with him in this state. If she went to see her clan for dinner tonight, that should be good enough. She kicked Eliot's leg to make sure he neither sulked in his chair nor started his own argument. Both he and Colby stood as she did, and they filed out.

"I think I'll go drown myself," Eliot groused as he hurried up the hallway.

"Psst." Railan passed behind them and beckoned for them to follow her into the next conference room over.

Eliot had reached the stairs already and slipped out of sight. Chavali looked up at Colby with a shrug, then they both ducked into the room. Railan shut the door softly behind them and pulled them into the far corner. "He's under some stress right now," Railan told them. "Since you're hock deep in this now, I'm going to tell you about it."

Always interested in anything she shouldn't strictly know, Chavali perked up. "What does 'hock deep' mean?"

"Never mind that. This morning, he got a letter from the

Continental Trade Syndicate. Signed, sealed, and authentic as far as we can tell. It accused him of having Grant killed by one of his operatives. We both think it's a forgery. It's impressive and stands up to every kind of scrutiny imaginable, except that Eldrack knows Myra, the person who signed it, and the wording of it...he doesn't think she wrote it but has no way to prove that."

"You got it this morning?" Colby crossed his arms with a frown. "He was only killed yesterday. How could they possibly know about it already?"

"Yes, that's also troubling." Railan sighed and leaned against the wall. "It's plausible but unlikely they actually would learn about it so soon, especially with how remote Eagle Falls is."

"You think they killed him to set Eldrack up?" Chavali considered this and shook her head. "No, that makes no sense. He and Candy discovered the flowers and studied them for this Syndicate group. She was as surprised to see someone teleport as we were, and that was the thrust of her research."

Colby shook his head. "Someone else is setting us up? Why? What could anyone possibly gain by starting a war of some kind between the Fallen and Syndicate?"

"The downfall of one or the other," Railan said. "Or weakening of both. Myra was kind enough to include a threat of reprisals that we have to take seriously. Do either of you remember seeing anything that might point to who that assassin was?"

Chavali shook her head. "Plain clothes, no unusual marks. His face was covered, and he moved very fast. This knife he threw into Grant's neck was nothing special, and he delivered it through a hole in the window they hadn't boarded up yet. This speaks to skill, which was evident in his movements. I could tell by watching him that I had no real chance to stand against him."

Railan took a deep breath and gestured to the door. "I must stress that you need to let Eldrack know when things like this happen. Even so, you did good work. Get some rest, and don't be surprised if Eldrack changes his mind about sending you out again tomorrow."

"I really did think he knew," Colby said with a sigh.

"It's done," Railan said. "Lesson learned, and let's move on from here."

Chavali nodded and left the room without further comment, the information churning in her mind. She hadn't ever paid much attention to politics before and had little interest in doing so now. Fate, it seemed, had other plans for her. If she needed to act with an understanding of such things, then she had a great deal to learn. The ability to read would make it significantly easier.

She reached the stairs and went up, Colby walking beside her. "I intend to see my clan for dinner tonight. May I come by for a lesson before then?"

"Sure. Give me an hour to clean up and—"

"Chavali!"

She turned to see a woman she recognized from passing on the stairs without ever hearing her name. "Yes?"

Breathless, the woman smiled with delight. "I'm so glad I ran into you! I heard about the faerie sparks you get your prophecies from, and I wonder if I could ask you some questions?"

Chavali blinked at her, entirely uncertain she'd heard that

correctly. "What?"

The woman gave her an understanding, sympathetic smile, with a hand up in apology. "I know it's not something most people know about, so I'm sure it's unexpected to run into someone else who's heard of them. It'd be really great if I could just take a few minutes of your time, though. You could help my research into their nature and capabilities, which could, in turn, help the Fallen on the whole."

Chavali's eyes narrowed, and she knew Sean needed to be murdered, slowly and painfully. "I don't know who told you that, but I do not commune with faerie sparks, whatever such things may be." She waved the woman off and returned her attention to Colby.

"No, really," the woman persisted, "you don't need to pretend you don't know. I understand. Everyone thinks I'm crazy too."

"An hour," Chavali said to Colby, ignoring the woman. Odds placed Sean in one of three locations, and she left Colby with a wave to check the dining hall. As expected, the woman fell in beside her. "What is your name?"

"Shyla. It's nice to meet you." Shyla stuck out her hand to shake, which Chavali looked at without touching.

"I do not commune with faerie sparks. I have never heard of them, and they sound like something a drunken mage might come up with to explain a transgression to his wife."

Shyla's hand fell along with her face. "But I heard—"

With a flick of her hand, Chavali cut Shyla off. "They lied to you."

"I thought I finally had proof." Shyla pouted, her shoulders slumping. "Where *do* the prophecies come from?"

"None of your business. Excuse me, I have things to do." Chavali elected to check with the Healers first, to get away from Shyla sooner. Outside the main reception area, she heard Sean's voice and moved closer to be in a good position to interrupt if he happened to be talking about her.

"...just really irresponsible. She's a private sort of person, and it's not unreasonable to ask that we all stop speculating about where her gifts come from. Besides, I understand that it caused her to lose people she cared about a great deal, and no one wants to be constantly prodded about that sort of thing."

"Well, I still think that if it really is caused by a faerie spark, that's an important thing to know."

Chavali didn't recognize the second male voice. She did, however, have to stop and wonder if Sean had gone mad or perhaps hit his head too hard while training.

"I wouldn't put too much stock in the prevailing opinion of whatever's behind her gift. I know for a fact she never said that and hasn't said what it really is."

They drew closer, so she slipped out and hurried up the stairs. Not only did she have no interest in allowing the other speaker a chance to direct the question to her, she had no idea what to say to Sean. For once, someone chose to protect her privacy instead of inciting more prodding. That it happened to be Sean doing this confused her. Surely, this was a sign of impending disaster, perhaps even Reunion with the Creator.

Chapter 26

When Chavali returned from a hot bath, someone sat at the foot of her bed. She stood in the doorway, frozen in the act of toweling her hair. Her Healer hadn't visited her here before, and she had no idea why that changed now.

Kelly shifted, giving the impression she'd been there long enough to think too much. "I had a feeling you wouldn't come to see me, so I took the initiative."

"I wasn't aware I'd done anything to suggest I might need intervention." Stepping inside, Chavali shut the door and chose to be grateful she'd taken clean clothes with her instead of a robe. She noticed a ceramic teapot on her table with a pouch beside it.

"You ran off with Eliot and Colby."

Chavali's lip curled. "Eldrack has already scolded all three of us for this, as has Railan. There is no need to discuss it further." She tossed the towel into her hamper and picked up her comb.

"I didn't come here to scold you."

"Then what did you come here for?"

"I heard it involved a child."

"You heard correctly, but this doesn't answer the question." Chavali leaned against her dresser, picking at snarls in her thick hair. "It is a statement designed to make me want to discuss the situation, which I'm not interested in now. I have asked Colby to provide me with a reading lesson, and then I wish to spend the evening with my clan."

"Colby is busy, so you have plenty of time right now." Kelly's pleasant smile flashed with smug victory.

"I see." Finished with her task, Chavali set the comb aside and crossed her arms. "Many things happened. Some were confusing, and I have not yet considered them enough to discuss them. At such time as I do, I will come to see you for whatever further unraveling you are capable of providing."

Kelly nodded, her face blank enough to almost cover her lack of surprise at the answer. "Did you have another new nightmare?"

Chavali crossed her arms and scowled. "Yes. I am not prepared to discuss that either."

Triumph flashed across Kelly's face, replaced by concern. "It's supposed to be getting better, not worse. Never mind discussion, tell me about this one."

"No. I have things to do. Besides, for all I know, speaking of them is the thing making it worse."

Kelly raised her brow and gave Chavali a stern stare. "That's an excuse. It's also ridiculous." She huffed and rolled her shoulders. "I thought we got past this. You know my entire job is to help you with this very thing. You agreed to let me do my job."

Right now, Chavali didn't want to talk about it. Talking about it would stoke a disastrous, flickering sense of hope that Keino had somehow managed to survive, when she knew that to be impossible. She saw him only moments before she died, unable to move. A child could have walked up and killed him, and someone much more dangerous than that had been in the tent with them both.

"On my terms," Chavali snapped. "You do not come here, walk in, and make yourself comfortable. I did not agree to that."

"Are you saying that you would've discussed this if I'd only waited outside instead?"

"No." Chavali rolled her eyes. "I'm saying that I will come see you when I'm ready to, and I do *not* appreciate being hounded."

Kelly stood and clasped her hands together, utterly failing to hide that those words hurt. "You're a very difficult person to take care of."

"I am a difficult person, period. Everyone knows this." For once, the words fell flat and hollow and bitter. Chavali's gaze drifted to the wall, and she had a thought to acquiesce. Being difficult for no reason didn't suit her or serve any useful purpose. "I dreamed of my clan. Of their deaths. It was...upsetting. I am not ready to speak of it yet. Sleep may help."

Kelly nodded and gestured to the teapot and pouch. "That will help you avoid dreaming. It's a crutch, though, not a solution. I won't give you more until I'm satisfied there's no other option."

"I understand."

The Healer moved to the door then stopped without opening it. "Can I at least ask how the clan induction went? We didn't have a chance to discuss it last time."

"Ah." She still hated doing this in her room, her sanctuary.

Despite that, she had no particular qualms about offering a few vague words about the subject. "It went well enough. I had never done it before, so I cannot say if anything went different from normal."

Kelly turned, trying too hard to conceal a smile. "Are you happy with having done it? With bringing strangers in to share your secrets."

That particular turn of phrase reminded her of Eagle Falls. In a sense, the werewolves had done the same with the villagers, though it hadn't been by choice. If she wanted to be honest, she hadn't had much of a choice either. Eldrack picked Penny and Marcus, with the caveat he'd find someone else if she deemed them unacceptable, so long as she explained why and the reason didn't amount to "they're not clan."

"I am satisfied it was the right thing to do, yes." Chavali flicked a hand to shoo her Healer away. "I wish to see them now." Expecting to spend the night with her clan, she tied the pouch to her belt.

"I look forward to seeing you soon about your dreams."

Chavali made a noncommittal noise and waved her hand again without looking. The door opened and shut, and she let out a breath as soon as she confirmed her solitude. Though Kelly had less skill than she at reading and manipulating people, she would learn, and eventually, Chavali would have difficulty hiding anything at all from her. At some point, she would have to bring Kelly into the clan, if only to protect herself and her secrets.

Chapter 27

Because she'd asked for the lesson, Chavali stopped by Colby's room to see if he really was suddenly busy. He opened his door, and she caught a curious flash of relief cross his face, chased by discomfort, and finally covered over with determined resignation.

She peered past him to see a Healer, plump and a few years older than Kelly, with her dark hair cut short. Apparently, the Healers colluded to manipulate circumstances for their Fallen, a fact she found both annoying and sensible. "Should I come back tomorrow?"

"No," Colby said, giving his Healer a dry glare. "Greta was just leaving."

The Healer pinched her lips thin and stood from his table. "Of course I was." She had a low, earthy voice. "Enjoy your reading lesson." Greta's particular emphasis on the last two words proved she'd been paying attention to gossip in the tower.

Chavali walked in as Greta walked out.

Colby shut the door, sagging against it with relief. "Sometimes," he said with a shake of his head.

"Yes, mine also. I have had little time to practice since the last lesson."

"I understand." He snorted. "Solving murders and stopping genocides are time-consuming."

Chavali shrugged and smirked as she stepped to his bookshelf and ran her finger across the spines. His first challenge of every lesson forced her to find the correct book. Since she had no color cues to work with and he rearranged them between lessons, it had foiled her every time so far.

He let her examine the letters for nearly half a minute before saying anything else. "What was your nightmare about?"

She froze, having forgotten he'd been there last night. "It's not important."

"That's not the right book. Try again." He crossed his arms. "You screamed in my ear for ten minutes."

Snatching her hand away from the books, she huffed in annoyance. "I'm sorry that your sleep was interrupted by this thing I had no control over."

"Chavali." In that moment, he sounded exactly like Keino. He inflected his exasperation the same and managed to hit the same pitch. Even the tilt of his head was the same.

She took a moment to examine him critically, wondering if that dream had meant more than it appeared to on the surface. Immediately, she berated herself for stupidity—of course it meant more than that. The metaphors usually managed to warp out of control and comprehension. This dream tried to tell her something more directly.

"Have you ever dreamed about those children you died trying to save? About them surviving, growing older, reaching adulthood?"

"Not that I can recall." Colby shrugged. "Greta suggested I not dwell on what might have been and focus on the present, so I haven't given it any thought. They died, all of them. Nothing I can do about that." His expression demanded she explain how this related to the subject.

She gave her attention to the bookcase again and picked one. The letters seemed right, though they refused to form words for her. "I dreamed that one of my clan escaped the attack, someone I cared about a great deal. The context suggested that he did so by colluding with the attackers. I think. I'm not certain. This is the conclusion I have jumped to with little basis, save the feeling I had during the dream."

He sighed and shook his head. "No, you're still mixing up the F, T, and L."

"I'm still mixing them *all* up. Is this an E?"

"No, that's a C." He moved to her side and pulled out the correct book for her, setting it in her hands. "Is there some reason you think that might be true? It's just a dream, right?"

Chavali looked down at the book and traced the letters with her fingertips. They refused to leap magically into coherence for her. Someday, she would master this skill and remember her early struggles with nostalgic fondness. "I don't know. I trust Eldrack enough to say that if anyone else survived, he doesn't know about it. Railan told me that she saw most of the attack but arrived too late to provide meaningful help. I doubt she would have held back such information."

"Which is to say that you think it's possible, but not likely."

"Yes." Frowning at the book, she saw Keino from her dream instead of the cover. It had been a long time since she saw him in color, and now her memory refused to wash away all that blood. She brushed her hand across the cover, not sure if she wanted to dispel the vision or convince it to linger.

Colby left a few, long beats of silence, then he leaned against the foot of his bed. "Tell me about him."

She looked up to see him watching her, his posture hovering between open and closed and not providing any clues about why he asked. The polite interest she saw in his face seemed forced, though she couldn't tell what lay beneath it. She should be able to tell. It bothered her that she couldn't.

Turning her attention back to the book, she opened the cover and sat at his table. "He wanted me to conform to his desires and whims. To be someone other than who I am. This was a common sentiment among my clan. They knew the previous Seer and thought I should be the same, as she was the same as the one before, and the one before that, and so on."

He cracked a grin. "But you're difficult. Everyone knows this."

"Yes, just so." As with Kelly, the statement no longer felt amusing or cheeky. It struck down to her core, leaving her wondering why she once thought it a funny thing to say. Perhaps it came down to nothing more than missing those who teased her about it so much. "I don't know what is happening to me, but it's clear that speaking of it has little to no beneficial effect. May we focus on the lesson now?"

Chapter 28

Hours later, Chavali sat nestled with her clan, her belly full. Biholtz had taken over most of the cooking duties for the household, though she still worked under Penny's supervision. As a result, the dishes resembled those they grew up with. The spices and herbs needed tweaking, but they only had so many options until spring came, and the girl did well with what she had.

"Chavali, tell us a story." Haizea lay draped over her lap, gazing up at her with adoration.

Chavali glanced around the room to make sure no one objected. "Very well," she said with a nod. "I must explain about the goats to Penny and Marcus first." Giving the two elders a smile, she began, speaking in Shappan so they could understand. "When we were a traveling clan—" It struck her that this time had passed. No longer would the Blaukenevs wander without a fixed place to call home. Not for another five years, at least. By then, it might be impossible to return to that life, especially without wagons and horses and people skilled at maintaining both.

Noticing Penny and Marcus slipping into sympathy, she cleared her throat and continued. "We kept horses and goats. Other animals proved too troublesome to bring along with the wagons, though the clan has kept dogs in the past. My Papá called horses 'beasts of burden' because they pulled our wagons, and feeding and caring for them took much effort.

"Goats, on the other hand, took care of themselves and followed us because they wanted to. They knew we would feed them our scraps and protect them from predators. From time to time, we lost some to a choice watering hole, but not often. In the clan, we have a saying, '*vurik seda ahurraz*,' which means someone is goatlike in that way: loyal so long as it requires little effort on their part. This is largely an insult.

"The Seers have always used them for stories because they're familiar and an important part of our lives. We drink their milk and make it into cheese. We use their coats for craft and sometimes the horns and other parts when one dies. Never are they slaughtered for food, except in the most dire circumstances. Primarily, this gives the small herd a sense of security, but also because they were, over time, elevated to a sort of totem animal.

"Which brings us back to the stories. There are four goats: Ekia, Mendeba, Hegoa, and Iparre." She twined her fingers through the spirits, urging them to create an image of four goats and modifying it as she told the story. "One day, they stumbled into a grotto with a clear, warm spring at the center. Finding it pleasant, each explored it in their own way.

"Ekia sniffed the edges for signs of a threat. Mendeba rooted through the bushes to check for poisoned berries. Iparre wandered to find the best place to sleep. Hegoa went to the water to drink. Beyond his reflection, which he'd seen many times before, he noticed small orange and white fish swimming beneath the surface. Uncertain how deep the pool might be, he dipped a leg in and barely scraped the bottom with his hoof.

"Dark silt swirled in the water, and he pulled his leg out to keep it from getting covered with mud. Out of the corner of his eye, he noticed something moving and managed to turn in time to see a long, dark shape thrust into the cloud of silt then snap out with an orange fish wriggling at the end. It disappeared on the other side of the pool. Hegoa watched until the silt settled again and took a drink. Nothing happened, so he walked away.

"The four goats met in the middle. Ekia said, 'I found signs of wolves, but they were old. We should be on our guard, but it seems safe to me.' Mendeba said, 'The black berries here are poisonous to us, so we shouldn't eat them. The red ones are fine.' Iparre said, 'There are nettles in the grass, so we should sleep in the ferns.'

"Hegoa thought about the long walk to get here, and how little water could be found anywhere else nearby. The grotto had only one way in, and it had berries and ferns. He didn't want to leave just because of some strange thing that eats fish in the water. Instead of warning the others about it, he said, 'The water is clear and good. There's nothing wrong with it.' "

Beside her, Haizea gasped and covered her mouth. "Bad Hegoa!"

Chavali stifled a grin as she nodded her agreement and brushed a lock of hair behind the little girl's ear. "The goats ate berries and drank water and sat in the ferns. Iparre woke in the middle of the night, restless and thirsty. She stepped into the water to bathe herself and stirred up the silt. In the moonlight, she saw nothing amiss. Something underwater grabbed her leg and yanked, pulling her. She thrashed to get free and managed to break the surface long enough to bleat and breathe.

"Ekia woke first and charged to help. He jumped into the water and locked his horns with hers. Bracing on the slippery bottom, he pulled her head out of the water, and she bleated again. Mendeba and Hegoa now woke and rushed to help. Mendeba danced on the edge of the water, trying to see what had attacked Iparre. Knowing where the water monster had come from, Hegoa stomped down hard there. The thing released Iparre, and they all scrambled out of the water.

"'How did you know where it was?' Ekia asked. Hegoa saw Iparre shaking on the ground, her leg hurt, and Mendeba trying to comfort her. He hung his head. 'I saw it before.' Ekia growled at him. 'Why did you lie?' he asked angrily. 'I wanted to stop,' Hegoa said. 'I thought it wouldn't matter because it only ate a fish.'"

"Lying to the clan is bad," Danel said with a firm nod.

Chavali ruffled his hair. "Especially about dangers. If you see strange people or things near the house, you should always tell Penny or Marcus." Though she hadn't picked that specific story for any particular reason, she realized that it summed up the situation in Eagle Falls rather well. Those people, she knew, would all be better off for knowing about the wolves in their midst.

Marcus had each of the children read a simple story from one of his books for her, to show off. Haizea and Danel both could already read better than Chavali, a fact that impressed her almost as much as it stung her pride. Biholtz urged them to hug Chavali and bundled them off to bed. As much as she wanted to go with them immediately, she preferred not to interrupt their routine. Besides, she still had half a cup of Kelly's tea left. When she finished it, she would join them.

Alone in the kitchen with Penny and Marcus, she found herself reminded of moments with her own parents. Once she became the Seer, none of those chats had gone well. Many had included yelling and pointed fingers. Several had featured her or her mother crying at some point. Trying not to let those experiences color this one, she sipped her tea and held her tongue.

"Thank you for telling that story in Shappan. The children are teaching us your language, but it's so different, and we're so old." Marcus's weathered face broke into a mischievous grin.

Penny nudged him with her shoulder. "He means we're not going to pick up on nuance anytime soon."

Smirking, Chavali waved the matter off. "It's no trouble. We all need to practice Shappan anyway." She paused and noted that the silence felt uncomfortable. "Is there anything you wish to ask me, now that you are clan?"

The older couple shared a glance, and both averted their gaze from her. "There is one thing," Penny said as she examined her teacup.

Chavali waited in an awkward silence. When they shifted and said nothing, she set her cup down and folded her hands in her lap. "I'm your Seer now. You can ask anything, and I will do my best to answer."

Marcus clasped his hands together on the table and rubbed one thumb over the other. "We've been having nightmares since the ceremony-thing. You said you've never done this before, so you can't say if that's normal, exactly. I understand that. We're kind of concerned, though."

Her attention grabbed, Chavali arched an eyebrow. "What kind of nightmares?"

"Strange things." Penny set her teacup down on its saucer without letting go of it. "It's hard to remember the early parts of the dreams. They involve fire and water, and they keep ending with us in a dark, stormy place, drowning in water that burns."

Fears about the clan sharing her own bizarre dreams disappeared. The description did seem familiar somehow, she thought. Perhaps she only thought of that strange twist on the ice dream, because nothing else came to mind. "I've had unusual nightmares too," she admitted. "I don't know if it's connected to the ceremony or not. Now that you say this, though, mine also got worse after the ceremony, which is queer. It may stop in a few days. We should wait and see."

Nodding, Penny picked up her cup and took it to the sink. "I thought you might say that. Thank the Creator it's winter, or we'd be wrecks trying to deal with that and the garden and field at the same time."

"The kids'll be a big help this spring." Marcus also stood. "I can hardly wait to sit on the porch and watch them do all the work."

Penny snorted. "Yes, dear, I'm sure that's exactly how it'll work."

"Biholtz will work herself to the bone if you let her." Chavali downed the last of her tea and brought her cup to the sink.

"Don't you worry," Penny said with a smile. "The Fallen do most of the real work for all of us. Which is fair, since you lot eat most of the food anyway."

Chapter 29

Chavali woke from a blessedly dreamless sleep when Danel's elbow pressed across her neck. She stirred enough to throw it aside. Curled against her belly, Haizea murmured a sleepy protest. Biholtz grunted when the boy's hand hit her face. Danel whined. Chavali sighed, knowing she wouldn't be able to get back to sleep now.

"I can stay for breakfast, then I have to go."

Haizea wriggled until she lay draped over Chavali's hip. "No. Stay."

Sitting up, Danel stretched and yawned. "I want Penny's pancakes."

"Mine aren't good enough?" Biholtz reached over and tickled his side. He shrieked with laughter and jumped on Chavali.

"The Seer is not a pillow," Chavali grunted, wincing as he hit a lingering bruise on her shoulder.

Ignoring her, Biholtz pounced and spread her tickling to Haizea. The large bed became a writhing, giggling pile of clan. Chavali hugged them to make them stop, a smile stuck on her face. If she could start every day this way, her life would be much more enjoyable. Their knot of joy moved to the kitchen, where Marcus and Penny puttered about already.

Marcus grabbed his coat and stomped outside in his boots while Penny stirred batter for pancakes. Chavali sat and sipped tea, above the small chaos of Biholtz chasing Danel and Haizea around the living room and bedroom. After several minutes of this, Danel ran in and slid across the wood floor in his socks to thump into Chavali's side and hit another bruise.

"Chavali!" Panting, he stared up at her, eyes wide and uncertain, all traces of mirth gone. "I saw a man through the window."

"Marcus is outside," she said with a shrug.

"It wasn't Marcus," he wailed. "It was someone else. He's shorter and wearing white, and I saw him duck behind a pile of snow."

Chavali nodded and ruffled his hair. "I'll go check." It had probably been a teenager, playing some game with others. Still, with the story she told last night, it would be wrong to dismiss what he saw. If someone truly lay in wait out there, Marcus could be in trouble. Grabbing her cloak, she stepped out through the front door, hoping the mystery person chose not to involve her in a snowball fight.

She held up a hand to shade her eyes from the glare of midmorning sun on snow. The road lay forty feet away, down a wide walk that had been shoveled down to the ground. She followed the straight, stone slab path, wondering what Marcus might be doing outside. Tending chickens seemed likely, as they had a small flock.

Halfway down the path, she passed a large snowdrift and twisted her body in response to someone lurching out from behind it. As Danel had said, the figure wore all white. Thin, smooth fabric covered him completely, from head to toe. His sword stabbed into her arm, managing to sink deep into one of her bruises. He pulled away to ready for another strike, and she noticed neat, tidy stitches across his sleeve.

"You," she breathed, knowing it had to be the same man that had killed Grant. Backing up, she gripped her wound and watched him. As Eliot had taught her, she checked him over for obvious weaknesses. His stance was firm, and he showed no sign of favoring his arm or anything else.

"It's nothing personal," he said almost apologetically, and his baritone voice tugged at her memory. In Candy's house, he'd said nothing, only grunted with pain and exertion. Where had she heard him before?

"Of course not," she sneered. Small, slow steps inched her away from him. "It never is." Soon, she'd reach the house again, and then he'd be much closer to the rest of her clan. Biholtz didn't have enough skill to stand against this man. She doubted Penny and Marcus, no matter how effective they might have been as Fallen, could manage it in their advanced years. No one else would come to help her.

Eliot had been clear that in such a situation as this, her only true recourse was to run, as far and as fast as her legs could carry her. If she saw a way to throw obstacles into his path without slowing enough to get caught, she should do it. He even made her run for practice.

At this moment, her assassin—and she knew this had to be the correct label for him—blocked the only path away from the house, and she wouldn't leave her clan to be slaughtered, not again.

Another step brought her even with the smaller channel that wound around the entire house. She stopped and so did her attacker. He drew a dagger to pair it with his longer blade. Her own knife had been left on the table in her room. That left her with only one weapon, and she doubted it would work.

"Perhaps if you explained who it is that wishes for my death so badly, we could come to an agreement."

"I'll admit this would be a lot easier if you just gave up and let me stab you. I've never had that happen before, so it would be a new experience."

With his face covered, she might as well have been speaking to a statue. He gave her nothing to work with and seemed motivated enough not to consider the possibility of her buying him off. She turned and bolted up the smaller channel, hoping he'd chase her. His dagger flew past her head, missing close enough to cut a thin scrape across her neck and shear off a thick lock of hair. She had the strange feeling an unseen force somehow deflected it.

Halfway around the house, she turned and saw him following, gaining ground on her. Although an illusion might help her, she had to spend her attention on her footing and planning for the moment when he overtook her. Her heart sank when she rounded a corner and saw Marcus dumping a bucket out next to the chicken coop. She'd led her attacker straight to him and now would have to live with whatever happened to him as a result.

Marcus looked up from his task, and his bushy gray eyebrows shot up. He caught on faster than she expected him to. With a nod and a wave, he beckoned for her to join him as he ducked behind the coop. The bucket fell from his grip as he searched for something else.

The element of surprise could make all the difference here, and she decided to take the chance. Running past him, she grabbed the bucket as the best she could find for a weapon. Marcus hefted a thick post suffering from rot. She kept going until she heard a loud crack, then whirled to go back and help him.

Though the post had broken in half, Marcus wielded its shortened length expertly, knocking the assassin's forearm hard enough to make him drop the blade. He slammed the wood into that white face and kicked him in the gut, knocking him to the ground.

Chavali rushed to his side, stunned by Marcus's prowess and kicking herself for thinking him helpless. The teleportation effect had to be activated through a ring or pendant or other possession, so she threw the bucket and watched with satisfaction as it bounced on the assassin's hands. Snatching up his dropped sword, she kicked him between his legs and stabbed down into his wrist, pinning his hand down in a manner surprisingly similar to the method she'd once used to kill herself.

Taking a cue from her, Marcus grabbed the assassin's other wrist and stepped on it. "I take it he's not invited."

"No." Panting, Chavali touched the stinging spot on her neck and found a smear of blood on her fingers. With the assassin losing strength swiftly, she crouched over him and ripped his hood off, then pressed her hand to his cheek. Like his voice, his face seemed familiar, yet she still couldn't place him.

The spirits responded to her anger, surging at the assassin and scraping at the layers of his mind. He desperately wanted to activate the ring on his finger to teleport away. Shadowy, shrouded figures inspired both fear and love in him. They needed the information he'd collected while waiting for her. He needed to kill her and others to prevent disaster.

The sharp pain in his wrist and the coppery smell of his blood awakened memories of her own death, destroying her concentration. She gritted her teeth against the ghosts of pain and fear and loss. To make it stop, she kicked at the blade. The agony lessened, becoming bearable. Both of them knew he'd soon bleed to death.

Hand still touching his cheek, she grabbed his shirt and wrenched him off the ground to growl in his face. "Who do you work for? Who sent you?"

Lines of pain creased his face, yet he giggled. His thoughts flashed on moments she guessed came from his childhood, offering her no clues. Death sat on his chest heavier than she could, and he paid her no more attention.

Throwing him back at the ground, she surged to her feet and let out a frustrated roar. Marcus continued to pin the man's other arm while she stomped her anger down. He let go when the assassin rattled with his last breath.

"Interesting blade. I've seen one like it before, I think. Can't recall where, though." Flipping the sword around, he offered her the hilt. "You should give it to Eldrack. Also take his hood and whatever we prevented him from using his hands on."

Chavali crossed her arms and stared out at nothing, forcing herself to calm down. It made her arm hurt, and she kept it close to her body in the hope Marcus would either not notice or not comment. She took the sword, knowing she needed to move quickly to save a number of lives.

Marcus crouched beside the body and held up the assassin's severed hand. "Who's after you now?"

"Who isn't?" She grabbed the hand and ripped the stone ring off it, then flung the useless hunk of meat away before it could drip gore all over her. "Things grow more complex."

"That's the way life works."

Chavali snorted. "Indeed."

Chapter 30

Chavali scooped the children into a quick hug and spared only a moment to praise Danel for his sharp eyes before rushing out to find Eldrack. As always when she needed him, she found him handling paperwork in his office. She dropped the sword, hood, and ring on his desk, all still bloody.

"Rough morning?"

She'd run all the way here and had to catch her breath. Hands on her waist, she avoided meeting Eldrack's gaze on the expectation he'd give her sympathy or annoyance. Either would be distracting at the moment.

"Someone tried to kill me. He came to Penny and Marcus's home and waited outside for me to leave. He'd been watching the house for several hours and noticed something odd about Cloverdale, especially the tavern. He'd been ordered to kill me, Eliot, Colby, and Sean by an unknown entity. His body is still in the yard. Marcus said he would set it aside if you wanted someone to examine it. More importantly, he was supposed to join a force attacking Eagle Falls this evening once he'd dispatched us.

"This man was Ramelia's killer. He hid in her closet, only to find Jack, and Candy and Grant in the house with them before he'd had a chance to carry out his mission. When they argued, he took advantage of a distraction to throw a knife at Ramelia's throat, which seems to be his preferred method of killing. Then he teleported away in the ensuing chaos. Again with Grant, he threw a knife and would have left us similarly confused had he not come inside to complete his mission. Both he and I have no idea why he missed when he threw his knife at me."

She stopped and noticed the office spinning drunkenly. Dropping into a chair, she saw his face full of alarm. The novelty of it made her laugh.

"Chavali, your arm is bleeding." He stood and carefully avoided touching her flesh to examine the wound.

"Afraid I will find things I should not in your thoughts?" His attention to the injury made it hurt again.

"This needs a Healer." He reached across the bloody things on his desk to grab something on the edge.

"I will take that as a yes."

"Chavali, I run the entire Fallen organization," he said patiently. "Of course there are things in my thoughts you shouldn't know about. Don't worry about Eagle Falls. I'll send a team to warn and assist the werewolves."

She curled around her arm, holding it and cringing against the pain that seemed twice as sharp as the original injury. "I should go."

"No, you should sit. Someone is coming to tend to you here."

"To Eagle Falls. I should go to Eagle Falls."

"Chavali, you just got back, you've been having debilitating nightmares, and you were almost killed this morning. As irritating as I found your unscheduled mission, I think you've earned a few days of rest."

She quirked an eyebrow at him. "How do you know about the nightmares?"

He echoed the expression. "Do you really think that you can wake up screaming several nights in a row without me finding out about it?"

"This place is worse than a wagon full of old women."

Eldrack chuckled. "Yes, it is." The door opened, and an elder Healer swept in. He smiled at the woman and pointed to Chavali. "Thank you for coming directly to me with this. It's time now for you to allow yourself to be healed and to rest."

Chavali noticed the warmth between Eldrack and this Healer she hadn't met before. The two of them appeared to be similarly aged, in their fifties, so she suspected this might be his Healer. They'd undoubtedly known each other for many years. "I woke only an hour ago. I do not need rest."

The Healer stepped in the way so she couldn't see Eldrack anymore. "Someone told me you're difficult, Chavali."

Eldrack cleared his throat. It may have concealed a laugh.

The Healer's lips twitched in veiled amusement as she examined Chavali's arm. "How long ago were you stabbed? You've lost a lot of blood."

Thinking had become more difficult. Chavali shrugged. "I do not know."

"Mmhmm." To heal her, the woman pushed her sleeve out of the way and clamped a hand over the wound. Her thoughts betrayed a close relationship with Eldrack that faded into the background as she summoned the grace to heal.

As before, heat seared through her arm. She blinked and found herself lying on the floor, looking up at the Healer's worried frown. *I don't understand what went wrong, but at least she's not dead.*

"Nothing went wrong," Chavali snapped irritably. She batted the Healer's hand away and rolled to her side in an effort to get up.

"Then what happened?" Eldrack stood behind the chair he must have moved out of the way to accommodate her, leaning on it.

"The same thing that happened when I was inducted as Fallen."

Eldrack nodded to his Healer, and she stood to give Chavali space. She touched Eldrack's arm, and Chavali wondered if Fallen often had a second meaning, that of *falling* in love with one's Healer. Having someone dedicated to one's health and well-being could easily lead to such a bond, especially if the Healer chose not to resent her Fallen. For whatever reason, these women all seemed at peace with their duties. Chavali would hate that job.

"Can you explain it? At the time, I thought it wouldn't affect anything else."

Chavali flicked her eyes to his Healer, who would keep Eldrack's secrets for him but had made no such promise to her. "No."

"She's secretive and surly," Eldrack said with a chuckle. "I think she'll be fine." He laid his hand over his Healer's and squeezed it.

The Healer smirked. "I can tell when I'm not wanted. Take care of yourself."

When she'd left the room and closed the door, Chavali sat up. "I keep brushing against the entity that is the patron of the Fallen. I think it's interacting with my connection to the spirits."

"'The entity'?" Eldrack cocked his head to the side. "Chavali. It's the Creator."

Staring up at him, she wondered why that thought had never once occurred to her. Though she'd spent little time considering it, the Creator should have been her first guess. Not that it made sense, of course; the Creator had banished everyone from Herself. But, what else could it possibly be? Did she think some *other* god had come along and offered its power in exchange for fealty?

She scowled, annoyed at herself for not figuring that out on her own. "Of course." Pulling herself to her feet with the aid of the chair, she took a deep breath. Her dizziness faded. "I am going to Eagle Falls."

Eldrack pursed his lips and gave her what she assumed he intended to be a stern glare. "No, you're not. Your fighting ability is minimal. You have no place in a battle. You've done a good job with Eliot's problem and with unraveling the mess at Eagle Falls, but you're not a warrior. In fact, since you've done so well with that type of investigative effort, I'll be sending you on missions in the future to utilize those skills. This is not one of them."

She met his glare with her own. "Those people know me. They trust me, and they will listen to me. I do not care who you send. None of them will be able to command and prepare them half as well as I can."

Returning to his chair, Eldrack sat and regarded her. "Why does it matter? You've done your job there. You've bled for them and have your own clan to worry about. Let others handle it."

The question took her off guard, forcing her to wonder the same thing. Clan mattered. No one else did or should. In her current position, she was required to care about any and all Fallen she ran across, at least enough to help them in any way they truly needed. Then, in Ket, she'd helped a random stranger who had unexpectedly helped her in return. Eliot and Colby had earned her respect. Penny and Marcus had become clan.

Strangers, it turned out, could become allies, friends, and even family. This concept made her lip curl. It felt wrong, yet denying it would be lying to herself. Unlike some people, she avoided that as much as possible. The truth...Joey had reminded her of Danel. She respected Lilly. She wanted to keep Patrick safe for Eliot. And, most of all, if she could step in and help people avoid the fate that had befallen her own clan, she knew she had to.

Even with all of that, she had to admit that part of her reason for demanding to go came from Eldrack telling her not to. If he'd asked her instead of ordering, she might have chosen to think about it or not decide until she found out who else would be in the team.

"I believe that my presence would be of great benefit to the ability of whatever Fallen you choose to send, in that my previous interactions with the townsfolk will make them disposed towards believing there is a threat. This will make them easier to persuade into action. Thus, some injuries and deaths can be avoided by virtue of having more time for and assistance with preparation for the assault."

As she spoke, Eldrack's eyebrows climbed upwards until he grinned at her, the bastard. "I see. In that case, if you really want to go, I won't stop you. Just take care with yourself. You're still not a warrior." He picked up the ring to examine it and pointed to the door. "Be in the tavern in half an hour. I should be able to rouse a decent force by then, enough to handle the kind of numbers anyone would send to attack a tiny village."

"Thank you." Chavali nodded and left.

Chapter 31

One conversation convinced Kember and Lilly both of the danger, then Chavali assigned herself to the task of collecting noncombatant villagers and taking them to the cave behind the waterfall. Eldrack had sent one Healer in case of dire injuries, and she went into the cave with them for her own safety. Along the way, Chavali and several werewolves did their best to conceal signs of so many passing through. Ander, the hunter, appeared in the midst of it and recruited himself into the cause by promising to watch over the villagers and stand as a last line of defense for them.

Chavali returned to the village to find it buzzing with activity. Colby and Teryk worked with Karias to construct a hasty barricade of fallen trees for archers and mages to perch behind. Portia, Algie, and three other women laid magical traps on the ground in front of the barricade. Eliot, Harris, and a handful of other Fallen constructed crude mechanical traps in the area with branches and sharpened stakes.

Having no skill or talent with this type of preparation, Chavali allowed herself to be directed and wound up ripping strips of cloth and soaking them in alcohol. She then wound the small strips around thin packets that would, according to the Fallen man who gave them to her, "blow up nicely" when attached to arrows. Under his instruction, she tied them to two dozen arrows and set those where they'd be in easy reach, both at the barricade and the house they'd fall back to if necessary.

Several other small tasks occupied her for the next few agonizing hours. Waiting had never bothered her so much as it did now. This delay carried the promise of pain and death and struggle, and she wanted to get on with it already to meet her fate or not. Everyone else, she noticed, seemed at ease. Colby and Teryk chatted amiably with a few other Fallen of similar build. She overheard them grumbling about being tasked with helping werewolves. Colby told them off for it, and Teryk reminded everyone they had orders to follow.

Eliot sat with Harris. The latter kept the former from worrying too much about Patrick, who'd volunteered to be among the lookout group. Harris glanced at her often, and she heard more bawdy jokes than she had imagined existed, including several that made no sense to her. Eliot laughed, though, suggesting she lacked context for them, or perhaps vocabulary.

Algie hummed contentedly by himself, his body weaving in time to a rhythm only he knew and his fingers tangling yarn in a complicated pattern. His efforts seemed to be producing a woven scarf. The rest of the Fallen and the werewolves had scattered themselves around the spots they'd take up at the first sign of the enemy.

Eventually, Chavali gave up the pretense of gracious waiting in favor of pacing. No one interrupted or bothered her, though she noticed several of them—including Eliot, Lilly, and Colby—watching her. After a few minutes, their staring irritated her and she stopped with her arms crossed to glare at nothing.

Harris slipped up to her side and put an arm around her shoulders. "Relax," he murmured into her ear. "You're making everyone else tense." He grinned and waggled his eyebrows at her. "I could help."

She shrugged out from under his arm. "I will assume that was meant as a joke."

"Whatever works." Flashing her a bright smile, he let his hand fall and patted her bottom.

"If you do that again, I'll cut your hand off and turn it into a trophy." She bared her teeth at him.

His smile filled with mischief. "Would you keep it on a necklace? Then it might have a chance to grab your—"

The first howl cut through the air, sending defenders scrambling to their positions. Chavali stuck her tongue out at Harris as she hurried to join the mages and archers in the wedge-shaped barricade. He grinned and echoed the gesture, turning it lewd.

"Scamp," she muttered under her breath. He had, however, managed to leech the unease from her. For that, she let him see the corners of her mouth twitch up before ducking into the protected structure. Karias cut off his view of her by using his massive bulk to form the final wall. Everyone else ducked behind buildings, waiting in the shadows for a chance to take their enemy from behind.

Another howl rang out. Lilly, standing nearby, frowned. "It's a large force. They may outnumber us by more than two to one."

"If only we knew *who* they are," another Fallen said, "we'd know whether to be worried or not."

Chavali took a deep breath, utterly out of her depth. Once in her life, her clan had been attacked by a significant force, and she'd seen none of it until that nightmare. Worse, her clan had lost. In this case, she had no idea if these numbers matched Eldrack's expectations. She tried to concentrate on the matter of the fighting itself, instead of dwelling on all that could go wrong.

More howls filled the air. Lilly thumped a fist on a hollow log, the best they could come up with on short notice for an inconspicuous warning sound. At that signal, Chavali took a deep breath and twined her fingers through the spirits. Others had set small illusions to cover traps. She set the village on fire.

Under her direction, flames sprang up at the bases of the nearby buildings, running between them in chaotic, crisscrossing lines. She sculpted smoke to curl upwards and disperse and added a touch of crackling. The illusory flames wove a seemingly random pattern across the snow in every direction and licked at the walls of ten different buildings. For good measure, she added another two feet of height to their barricade with fake logs, nearly transparent from inside it, yet quite solid from the outside. All of it had to be within her sight, which limited the believability. Portia and Algie still felt this would be the best use of her talent: protecting the mages and archers.

Wolves broke the cover of the trees, running at full speed. Five raced across the short span of open ground, tails out straight for speed. Behind them, a rank of men in armor and dark cloaks dashed out, bows out and firing. One wolf stumbled and fell under the deadly rain, sides heaving and blood staining the snow. Only a single feathered shaft stuck out of its flank, offering hope for escape and survival.

Colby and Teryk both watched the scene and held up their hands to dissuade anyone from charging out to rescue the wolf or challenge the enemy. It meant they had to watch the wolf struggle to its feet while the men shot directly at it. Lilly growled in frustration along with other wolves, filling the area with a rumbling, angry hum.

The wolf shifted to its terrifying wolfman form, the change forcing the arrows out of its body and healing its wounds over. Instead of running away, though, it charged the enemy and they dropped their bows in favor of drawing blades.

"No," Lilly moaned, too quiet to be heard from such a distance. "There are too many, come back." She covered her face and took deep breaths.

Chavali thought the wolf still had an advantage against five men, in the form of claws and fangs and regeneration. She thought wrong. Each man moved with the same smooth, practiced precision Eliot employed. They'd all been trained well enough to give five men an edge over one werewolf. The wolf went down in a flurry of blood and flying snow, cut to pieces.

One man hefted his blade and plunged it down where the werewolf's neck must be, then another reached down and lifted a woman's head by the hair. He held it up for them to see, blood and gore dripping from the neck, face still twitching. The man's mouth twisted into a defiant snarl and he hurled it at the village. As a group, the five men hooted their superiority.

"Flank," Colby hissed, and he pointed to the side.

Turning that way, Chavali saw movement in the trees and nudged Portia. She wanted to be able to do more than watch and maintain her illusions. After watching the brutal efficiency of their foes, she didn't dare try.

Portia nodded and raised her hand to send death that way. "Mages, watch the flank. Archers, cover the open ground."

Two Fallen and ten villagers raised their bows, arrows held loose to await targets.

"We will kill them all," Lilly growled, "and send their heads home to their families."

The running wolves had circled around the flaming barricade and now joined Lilly. Three men and one woman panted as they leaned against the wall.

"Not sure what happened to Patrick," one of the wolves said. "Got separated and lost contact."

"He's smart," Lilly said through clenched teeth. "He'll be fine."

Chavali's eyes flicked to Eliot, and she thanked the spirits that he perched too far away to overhear the exchange. If he knew, she expected he'd do something stupid to try to rescue his lover, whether Patrick needed it or not. Instead, everyone waited. The enemy chose not to approach or otherwise show itself.

"They're getting into position," Portia muttered. "Trying to find ways to use the terrain to their advantage without taking long enough to let us entrench or flee. If they're smart, they'll either come in one to three massive waves, or they'll try to surround us in clusters of five to ten. Here's hoping they choose to use whatever magic they can early instead of holding it for later."

"Why would that help us?"

"We're still fresh. If we know it's coming, we can counter it. Later, we'll be hard-pressed to come up with the power."

Feeling this moment a poor one for learning about the workings of magic, Chavali chose to nod and not pursue the subject. "Is there nothing we can do to stop them from gaining what advantage they can find?"

Algie giggled at her. "What would you do? Run out and get your head cut off too?"

She bared her teeth at him. "You could."

Portia pushed Algie aside. "If we move now, we risk revealing the surprises we've set up. That's why we didn't charge out to rescue one wolf who stopped to fight when she should have fled."

"Watch your mouth," Lilly snarled. Only now did Chavali notice the five wolves rocking on their feet and flexing their fingers. All of them looked ready to fly into a manic rage at the slightest provocation. Their bestial natures longed to burst free, and only those flowers held them in check now.

Portia stared Lilly down. "Accept reality."

Chavali raised a hand. "Never mind. We're all testy now, yes? Perhaps they wait longer to let us fret than anything else. This is what I would do. They showed us their might and killed one of ours mercilessly in front of us. Now, they sit and gather and wait for us to fall apart, to let grief and anger overwhelm our better judgment."

"She's right." Lilly bared her teeth. "Shut up and settle down. Suza would want us to avenge her, yes, but not at the cost of all our lives. We wait and let them come. Think about all the things you'll do to them when they're begging for mercy." Her wolves murmured, passing the message along.

Chavali wished she could sit down to wait. Despite Lilly's orders, the wolves still moved restlessly. The Fallen managed to stand still, yet they also fidgeted. Eliot tapped a booted foot. Colby adjusted his gloved grip on his sword. Teryk drummed his fingers on the chainmail covering his leg. Harris shook his hands out again and again. All this movement without acting made her want to scream.

"Come on," Portia muttered. "Come on, come on, come on."

"They're quite rude, keeping us waiting." Algie cocked his head to one side, lifting his hand and staring at it as he swished his fingers through the air. "Ah, do you feel that? Brace yourselves. They're coming."

Chapter 32

"Call it out for us, Algie." Portia raised her hand, again ready to use it for violence.

"I sense...five." Algie lost all the giggles and smiles in favor of, for once, being serious. "No, six. One is trying to hide himself. He's probably invisible. They have a dozen or so half-mages."

Chavali blinked at Algie. "What are you talking about?"

"Mages, dear. They have six full mages and thirteen people with lesser magical talents mixed in among the force. I can sense them from a certain distance away."

"I had no idea you could be so useful."

Portia snorted. "He has his moments."

Algie giggled, high and bright. "That way." He pointed behind them. Anyone coming from that direction would see all the defenders waiting to ambush attackers coming from the road, the fields, or the side they expected to be flanked from. "They've sent all the full mages to the rear, and they'll be in range of most things shortly."

"Rennet, you and I should go that way to head them off." Portia gestured to a short woman wearing tight-fitting leathers and a fur-lined cloak.

"Wait." Chavali put her hand up to stop both women. "No one else is running off to meet the enemy. Why should you?"

Portia flashed her a grin. "Because we're not going out to get killed." She patted Karias on the flank, and both women squeezed out beside him. They darted out of sight.

"They'll be fine," Algie said. He squeezed Chavali's shoulder.

She shrugged away from his hand, knowing he'd leave it there if she only glared at it. "Perhaps. You can sense them, yes? Can you tell which mage is which?"

"Only if I pay attention. Which I won't be able to do for long." He nodded with his chin towards the flank side.

Several men dressed in the same white suits as her assassin skulked towards the barricade. They seemed to think their appearance and manner concealed them, which struck her as absurd. If they stood still, they would blend with the snow. Moving, they stuck out to anyone watching. Perhaps they thought no one would be watching. If so, that made them idiots.

"Should we do something, or let them come?"

Algie wiggled his fingers and sniffed as if someone held flowers under his nose. "Can you extend your illusion to mark them somehow? That would be highly useful."

Peering out over the top of the barricade, she judged the distance and nodded. "When they get closer. I'll keep an eye on them."

"Excellent!" He clapped his hands together and grinned.

Focusing on the group of men, she sent the flames inching

towards them, readying to track and match their movements when they got close enough. It would be the easiest way to mark them.

Thunder cracked the air, making her jump. Algie's hand on her shoulder made her want to squirm.

"Don't panic. Large-scale battle can be very loud."

"I'm not panicking," she snapped. "Stop touching me." She turned her attention back to the would-be flankers and counted six of them. They crept up, moving together in slow, deliberate movements.

The trees rumbled, then the noise resolved into a billowing war cry. Made by at least a hundred voices at once, it rolled across the fields and slammed into the village with enough force to rattle windows. On its heels, a tide of men flowed from the trees. They moved at speed, in an arc wide enough to flush rabbits into the arms of the mages.

But Chavali wasn't supposed to be watching that. She trusted the others to handle it, no matter how ridiculous the odds seemed. Between werewolves, Fallen, and a handful of brave villagers, they had maybe six dozen. This attacking force surely had enough people to test the limit of how large an army could successfully assemble without intervention by the Creator's Towers.

Such a massive force for such a small village had to mean they came for extermination, not subjugation. Her assassin's dying thoughts had provided no reason for this kind of overwhelming assault. Either they came to kill werewolves, or they came because of the flowers and Ramelia and Candy's research into them. Both possibilities struck her as equally terrible and probable.

Counting the masked flankers again, she found only five. One had slipped away while the oncoming horde distracted her. They moved closer and closer, darting from one pile of snow to another. She covered her ears and directed her fire to leap to the oncoming flankers, highlighting their presence with dancing flames on their arms and legs. One noticed immediately and dropped to the ground, rolling to put them out. The erratic movement made it difficult for her to keep them on his body, and he sprang to his feet again.

"The fire is fake," he bellowed.

Explosions rocked the ground as the incoming army set off traps. The archers standing inside the barricade with Chavali fired at the enemy. Screams announced the success of their tactics. Fallen and werewolves broke their cover to converge on the flankers. Chavali banished her fire from the flankers, as those men couldn't hide with so many paying them direct attention.

"Three mages have gone down," Algie shouted. "Hopefully, the two hurrying towards us are our lovely Portia and Rennet. As soon as they return, I'm going out to join the front line."

It surprised Chavali that he should announce his intentions so plainly. "How can I best help?"

He smiled at her, languid and careless. "Pay attention, defend this space, and be clever." Taking her further off guard, he seized her hand and kissed it. His thoughts swirled in a mass of chaos she had no time to decipher before he flung it away.

Rennet rolled in through Karias's legs, cradling her hand with a grimace of pain. Portia held a corner of her cloak to her forehead as she edged past him. Algie giggled and ran off.

"We convinced them to try a different approach," Portia said. She pulled her cloak aside to reveal a still-bleeding gash.

"It's bad," Rennet said, "and they're coming this way. We needed backup or we'd have stayed out there."

Portia pressed a different corner to her head. "We should've brought more Healers. Mine would've strapped on armor and charged out with me if she knew about this."

"If anyone is seriously injured, Karias can evacuate them." Chavali reached out and patted the horse's flank. "The traps are working, at least."

She saw a werewolf take a dagger to the throat. It clutched at the knife, ripping it out with a gasping gurgle. The werewolf's flesh healed as Chavali watched. The Fallen had no such ability to heal, so she focused her attention on them.

Colby and Teryk fought side-by-side with two other Fallen men of similar stature at the edge of the field. The four of them, all wielding large blades, struggled against the skill of their opponents and had to fall back step by step to avoid being swarmed. Eliot and Harris stayed with the flankers, finding themselves matched for skill, even with help.

"Archers, they need help there," she pointed to Colby. "They are being overwhelmed." Others heard her as well, and a force of ten werewolves joined them. More Fallen and werewolves covered the road, catching the enemy by surprise.

Behind her, she heard someone spit out a curse. She whirled to see a white-clad flanker inside their barricade, stabbing Portia in the side. Lightning arced from Rennet's hand to his chest, jolting him. Chavali threw her shoulder at the man, knocking his sword aside with her smaller blade.

He hit the log and grabbed her hair, pulling her along as he rolled to the side. Not strong enough to resist, she threw her weight into the roll. It knocked him off balance and put his head where Karias stomped on it with a hind hoof. She winced at the sickening crack his skull made then turned away to not watch as Karias stomped again.

"Portia, are you alright?"

"I'll live," she grunted. "For now."

"Chavali." Rennet gripped her arm and pulled her to her feet. "You should go. Get Eldrack to send us more Healers."

She frowned. "It'll take too long to get there and back. The fight will be over long before then."

"No offense, but your being here or not isn't going to turn the tide one way or the other."

"She'll never get through." Portia leaned against the wall and peered over the top. Her free hand grabbed for power and lobbed it out. "It'll have to wait until they're routed."

Aware she had few skills useful for a battle such as this one, Chavali nevertheless let her annoyance at being reminded of it show in a curl of her lip. "When it is done, whoever is most injured should go, to be tended as soon as possible. For now—" She happened to look towards the battlefield and saw a clump of men headed straight for their barricade at full speed. "Archers!"

At her command, the archers turned their attention to the dozen men charging them and fired. Rennet flung out another bolt of lightning, and Portia managed to toss a ball of fire at their feet. Two made it through unscathed and kept going, leaping at the wall. They discovered the illusion of the top few feet awkwardly and hung over the true edge instead of clinging to the side, ready to climb. Chavali shouldered past the archer who'd managed to evade one man's clumsily swung blade. The attacker had enough time to lift his head and take stock of his situation. She refused to allow herself to hesitate. Slamming her knife into his neck, she ripped it across his throat.

The man stared at her as he lost his grip and fell out of sight. Beside him, his companion fared no better, slipping off the wall with arrows sticking out of his face. Chavali blocked out what she'd just done and refocused on those farther away, some of whom had suffered nothing worse than being knocked off their feet. They'd seen everything and now knew about the illusion.

She gulped. Her heart raced as they rolled to their feet and more joined them. "Shoot. Now. As fast and as many as you can before they reach us." She darted to the side and watched the arrows fly. One villager suddenly sprouted an arrow from his chest. He fell over, gasping, and the rest ducked down.

"Great," one of the two Fallen archers grumbled, "they're shooting back."

If they stayed here, they'd be overrun. "Out," Chavali snapped. "To the house. I'll distract them." The moment those words fell out of her mouth, she wondered at the madness that must have inspired them. Perhaps she could tell them a story or insult them. Or climb onto that giant white horse to provide an easy alternate target.

The archers hurried out. Portia summoned up magical smoke, and Rennet gave her a shoulder to lean on. They limped away together, listening to the sound of armored attackers closing in on the barricade.

Chavali smacked Karias on the hindquarters. "You're my assistant." She waited impatiently while he leaned down enough for her to grab his mane and hop onto his back.

This is a very bad idea.

"Quit whining and charge them." She banished all her illusions with a flick of her wrist and held on tightly.

This would be much more effective with Colby. He plunged into the acrid smoke to the sound of coughing and wheezing from the attackers.

Her bloody knife still in hand, Chavali covered her mouth and tried to lean with Karias as he pounded through the smoke. He danced to the left and planted his front hooves then kicked out with his hind legs. Landing, he reared up and lashed out with the front. His hooves slammed into someone's chest. He knocked men aside, and she felt a sharp sting across her leg.

He was right. Colby would do this as Karias's partner, not as his burden. She had to tell these people a story to do any good. With a moment's consideration, she realized that might actually help, so long as she kept it short.

"You monsters," she cried out. "They're all dead! Just let me go."

If you mean that we should get scarce, thump me twice on the neck.

She patted his neck as hard as she dared, and he pivoted then leaped. When he needed to, Karias could move. The horse jumped over bodies and shouldered his way past attackers still on their feet. Overhead, clouds swirled in faster than should happen, and Chavali guessed what the remaining enemy mages had chosen to do with their power.

Thundering across the field in a rapidly escalating snowstorm, Karias reached the cover of trees with a stream of attackers following in his wake. No one, it seemed, would be allowed to escape, not even a lone woman on an excessively large and fast horse.

I need to get to Colby and do what we do best. Karias gave no other warning before twisting his body and pitching her into a snowbank. She clawed her way up and out of the pile of snow to see the horse plunge into the fray once more. He knocked two attackers aside, and both saw Chavali as she struggled free.

Chapter 33

From what she'd seen so far, one of these men outmatched her in skill. Two would make short work of her. Chavali flailed in the snow, cursing the stupid horse for wanting to give her a soft landing. She still had her knife, at least, and held it up as they drew closer. The bastards took their time and wore dark grins of anticipation, watching as she exhausted herself fighting the snow.

They stopped several feet away and sheathed their swords, which she took as an insult. The one with the full, dark beard nudged the other with an elbow and shared some undoubtedly crude joke that both chuckled at.

"Tell you what," the bearded man said with a smirk. "It's a shame to let so much spirit go to waste. If you do what we say, we won't kill you. We'll let you go when we're done."

She knew exactly what they meant. Only a fool wouldn't. "If you come near me, I will cut off whatever is closest."

He chuckled. "There's no need for that kind of thing."

"I disagree." She lurched to her feet, knowing they still had every advantage but unwilling to surrender. The Seer of the Blaukenev clan did not give up, not without a fight. She had no Keino or Colby or Eliot or Harris to rescue her and so would have to rescue herself.

With her free hand, she twined her fingers through the spirits and produced a crackling swirl of darkness in her palm. For good measure, the white hot sparks flung out tendrils that crawled up her arm and cast shadows to give her face sharp lines. "Thank you for giving me enough time to re-center myself. Now, I am ready to devour your souls."

The anticipation, the cocky grins, and the relaxed stances all disappeared as both men started with shock and reached for their weapons. Chavali threw herself at one, slamming the illusion into his chest while she drove her dagger into the first flash of bare flesh she caught sight of: his neck. Surprise and fear made him much easier prey. Aware that the other man hadn't fled, she rolled off her prey and cackled, the illusion drawing a bright, white spark out of the first man and engulfing it.

Rooted in place, the bearded man watched in horror as she pretended to eat his partner's soul. The other man gasped and bled for only a handful of heartbeats before he shuddered and went still. Chavali stood again, playing the part by acting as if she'd tasted something delicious.

The bearded man's mouth opened and shut. Incoherent sounds burbled out.

"Tell you what," she purred. "It's a *shame* to let so much spirit go to *waste*."

He paled and ran. When he burst out of the trees, she sagged in relief and dismissed the illusion. She scowled at the fresh corpse. So much death today, and for what? Someone wanted to kill werewolves, or thought they could protect the secret of the flowers. Perhaps both. Idiots. Well-financed idiots.

Who could afford to send this many well-trained men someplace on short notice? She stooped beside the dead man and rifled through his pockets, finding nothing. How inconsiderate of him not to carry anything identifying himself for her to take to Eldrack. Checking his clothes, she forced herself to examine the bloodstained clasp holding his cloak around his ravaged neck. She didn't recognize the symbol emblazoned on it.

Grimacing in distaste, she pulled the clasp off and rubbed it on a clean spot then tucked it into her pocket. She stood again and wondered how best to employ herself. Though she'd been helpful while standing with the archers, a small army stood between her and them now, and she had no hope of getting through while the fighting continued. If the bearded man recovered his wits and rallied a group to come back and kill her, she needed to be elsewhere.

She looked around and decided to head for the cave. If nothing else, it would be safe. At this point, with the road nearby, she knew how to get there. Hurrying up the road, she hoped someone would come soon after the battle ended. Wounded would need care. She could, at the least, wrap bandages until the Healer could tend the worst injuries.

Striking down the path to the cave, she ran until she heard a man groaning. He sounded close, and she wondered if the werewolves had caught someone before they joined the group in the village. The allure of answers for her questions sent her off the path, hopping through the snow to find him.

She found him on the ground, huddled against a tree trunk, cradling his charred and blackened arm, heaving labored breaths mixed with whimpers of pain. His armor appeared otherwise intact, and she saw no other blood.

"Patrick?" Hurrying the last few feet, she dropped to her knees beside him. "What happened?"

"Oh, thank the Creator." He grimaced and struggled to force each strained word out. "I thought I'd die alone out here."

She pulled her cloak off and draped it over him. "I have to work with Eliot and will not allow you to force him to wallow in self-pity or kill himself over your corpse. Can you not shift and heal this?"

"No. I can't heal what fire does. I can shift, but it won't help."

"It would keep you warm."

He managed a weak chuckle. "I suppose so. Is it over?"

"No, they're still fighting. As it turns out, I am not an especially effective warrior. Someone who wished to protect me deposited me nearby against my will."

"I guess that's lucky for me."

"It seems so. Do you think you can walk to the cave for the Healer?"

"Let's find out." He pushed off the ground with his good arm and let her help him use the tree to get to his feet. The effort left him panting and leaning against the tree. "If we go really slow, I can manage it."

"We don't have time for really slow. Come, you're a werewolf. A big, bad monster. You can't let your arm being burned to a crisp stop you. We must move, so we will move. Imagine there's an army chasing us. I can provide an illusion to help."

Patrick laughed, and then he cried as she forced him to move faster. Along the way, Chavali noticed how much her leg hurt, though it didn't seem to be life-threatening. Someone must have clipped her with a sword during Karias's mad ride. Both in pain, they stumbled into the clearing with the waterfall. Five armored women in cloaks identifying them as members of the attacking force stood among the flowers, and all turned to see Chavali and Patrick freeze too late to go unnoticed. Chavali scanned each woman and thought their clothes and armor seemed dry. The people in the cave might still be safe.

"Ah, refugees." The speaker crouched over a clump of the flowers, one gloved finger touching the point on a petal. "Interesting that you should come here. It means, of course, that we can't let you live. I suspect that's a foregone conclusion for the gentleman, but if you could stand still, that would save everyone a lot of time and effort."

Chavali had managed against two by luck and nerve. She had no hope against five, and Patrick would be of no help. If she revealed those in the cave, they would all die. Ander's help would be useful, yet he'd shown his skill to be from a distance, not up close.

She needed a reason for them to let her live and to ignore Patrick.

"Is that the wisest course of action? Indiscriminate slaughter? You have no idea who and what you are killing here." With an effort of will, she packed her fear into a tight ball and ignored it. This had to be done. Whatever disaster it caused in the future wouldn't matter if she failed to survive today.

The leader quirked an eyebrow. "Werewolves—"

"Don't be stupid," Chavali snapped, cutting her off. "If you think werewolves and glowing flowers are the most interesting thing in Eagle Falls, then you're a bigger idiot than you look."

The leader planted her fists on her hips. "I don't think—"

"That much is clear."

"Just who do you think you are?"

"Someone willing to negotiate if you can pull your head out of your ass for five minutes."

The woman scowled at her. Her four flunkies shifted into varying stances intended to intimidate. "Exactly what do you think you have that's worth negotiating for?"

Chavali stifled a gulp. Speaking these words aloud to people she knew nothing about drove counter to everything she believed in. She did it anyway. "I owe no allegiance to this place, save this one man. My skills are for sale. I am an oracle, a seer of the future and deliverer of prophecy. Your masters can profit from my ability, so long as I do too."

Sneering, the woman took a step closer. "A bold claim, and I expect you can't perform on command, so one without any evidence. You're outnumbered and outmatched, and you just happen to be a great gift from the Creator? I don't think so."

Hauling Patrick closer, Chavali set him down beside a blooming flower. If it helped control his bestial nature, she had hopes it could help him heal his arm somehow. The two things seemed connected in her mind. As she set him down, he rolled enough to crush a flower, and a puff of blue sparkles burst into the air. It made her sneeze.

She wiped her mouth and nose. "As I said: idiots, all of you."

"I should kill you for your impertinence."

"And I should kill you for the crime of despoiling this sacred grove by daring to be such morons within it. Go." She flicked her hand imperiously at the path as she straightened again. "I gave you a chance. Now you will have to run home to your masters and tell them of the prize you let slip through your fingers."

The woman's scowl soured so much, Chavali wondered if she'd pushed too hard. "Fine. Bring her. Kill him."

Raising an eyebrow, Chavali crossed her arms. "I will not work for them if their lackey's first act is to slay someone I care about."

Frustrated rage simmered in the tiny twitches of the woman's mouth and forehead. "Bring them both," she growled. Leading the way, she swept out of the clearing.

Two women stooped to pick Patrick up and carry him together. The third grabbed Chavali's arm. The fourth brought up the rear. Chavali yanked her arm away and glowered.

"Do not treat me like a prisoner. I come willingly and will have this known to your masters." A glance behind assured her that Patrick received reasonable treatment. In light of that, she marched along, smothering the pain with every other step. At some point, Patrick would lose control, and he would kill or infect these women. If she could keep him from also turning on herself, that could be their way out.

She wanted to get at their thoughts. They all wore full suits of chainmail armor with clothing underneath and gloves. Only their faces remained bare, and she had no reason to casually or accidentally touch one in such an intimate way.

They reached the road and left Eagle Falls behind, moving as fast as Chavali could go towards the Creator's Tower. She looked up and saw clear skies swiftly darkening to night, the storm cloud not visible over the treetops. In that direction, so far away it might as well be a thousand miles, Colby and Eliot fought for their lives and the lives of others. They'd be fine. She had to believe that. Her own survival seemed questionable, as did Patrick's, but not theirs.

Behind her, the errant moans of the injured werewolf changed subtly. Had she not spent several minutes walking with nothing but his voice to hear, she might have missed it. His voice had taken on a different edge, one less about pain. She had little cause to hope for the best yet did so anyway, silently begging the spirits to somehow intervene and force him to shift.

It happened. Ripping and grunting and gurgling and growling made both Chavali and her escort stop and look. Patrick stood in all his werewolf glory, muzzle covered in blood, a body already at his feet. One arm hung limp, blistered and furless. The other picked up a second woman and delivered her to his mouth while she struggled to pull her sword out. His jaws snapped together over her hip and ripped.

Chavali blanched at the raw violence and fled. The leader and her escort both did the same, leaving the one in the rear to face Patrick on her own. As much as Chavali feared the werewolf had gone out of control and would chase them down, she saw an opening to take down her escort and seized it.

Throwing herself at the woman, she knocked them both off the road and into the snow. She drew her knife as she tumbled. Her escort squawked and hit the snow in surprise yet still managed to twist out of the way of the blade. The pair of them wrestled in the snow, each trying to best the other, until the escort managed to punch Chavali in the face. Stunned by the blow, Chavali blinked stupidly.

Rising to her knees, the escort pulled her sword out and held it up. Chavali paled and cringed, waiting for the blow she had little hope of evading or surviving. The woman's eyes flicked upward and flared wide. Dropping her sword, she scrambled to flee.

Chavali glanced behind herself and saw nothing but trees and snow. She pounced on the distracted and panicking escort, pressing her knife to the woman's throat and slapping a hand on her cheek. The woman went still, though she breathed fast and shallow.

Creator, if you're there, please help me. I've been a faithful servant—

"No, you haven't," Chavali said. "A faithful servant of the Creator does not murder helpless villagers because someone told you to. A faithful servant of the Creator will, however, tell me who your masters are."

The woman's mind went blank, stunned into silence. Then it filled with too many thoughts to follow. She panicked again, wondering if Chavali could read her mind, wondering if the Creator had sent her as a test, wondering if she had failed.

Chavali took a deep breath. The werewolf ripping people apart nearby made concentration difficult. "It's not too late for you." She wished someone had said this woman's name or that she'd think of it. "Tell me what I need to know, and you will be shown mercy. Who are your masters?"

I work for the Continental Trade Syndicate. We all do. "M-Myra. Orders." *Karyl has them.*

Checking the road, Chavali saw no sign of Karyl, the leader. She'd run off and probably kept going. As much as that woman would be a better source of information, this one knew enough. Even if Karyl returned, Chavali had little hope of stopping her in a fair fight anyway, giving her even less reason to chase her down.

"Where can I find Myra?"

The escort's head filled with images of buildings and rooms and an older woman with the same feel of "clerk" that Eldrack had. "Todan. S-she's in Todan." *Please don't kill me.*

Knowing this woman bore some responsibility for the attack on Eagle Falls, Chavali gritted her teeth and pressed the blade hard enough to prick her skin and draw blood. Looking into the woman's eyes and hearing her thoughts as they spiraled around her desire to live made Chavali hesitate.

Chavali also desperately wanted to live. Once, she'd sacrificed that desire. Never again, if she could help it. This woman had done little, and nothing worth a death sentence. Her spasming thoughts showed snippets from her life. She'd worked as a caravan guard, defending her employers from brigands and the odd wild creature. She'd protected her younger brothers from bullies. She'd done her job faithfully and been sent on this assignment to follow Karyl's orders without knowing what they'd be prior to arriving.

Most importantly, no matter how she behaved, it sickened her to know what their force had gone to Eagle Falls to do. She understood fighting enemies, defending the weak, even championing her employer. The order to slaughter everyone, whether they resisted or not, gnawed at her even now. And she begged in her mind without blubbering out loud.

Sitting up on the woman's abdomen, Chavali turned to see Patrick in his human form, on his knees and holding his head. The three women lay scattered in pieces, a gory testament to his brutal efficiency, even with one— Actually,his arm looked much better now, with fresh, pink skin. Perhaps she'd been right about the flowers.

"Patrick, go home."

"I did this," he sobbed.

"They came here to kill us. You defended yourself. Go home. Tell them I'm fine. Go find Eliot and let him hold you and fuss over your arm."

Patrick wiped his face and nodded. He seemed steadier on his feet as he turned and shambled back down the road. She watched him until he rounded a bend and disappeared from sight. Her attention returned to her prisoner, who remained still and cooperative.

Bending down enough to touch the woman's face again, she stared into her eyes. "Go. Speak to no one about this. Then you will have paid your debt."

"I swear." *I won't fail you, my Creator. Whatever this woman says, I'll believe. From your hand to her mouth to my heart.*

"Good. You can call me Chastity."

Evelin seems like such a bland name in the face of that. She smiled.

Chavali stood and helped her to her feet. Perhaps the Fallen had just gained a new agent, one who would never know who she truly worked for. "I hope you can keep your job, Evelin. She always has uses for people with important duties."

Tears glistened on the verge of spilling down Evelin's cheeks. "I hope so too."

Fishing out the chain she wore around her neck, Chavali slid her

Seer's pendant out of the way in favor of her Fallen ring. "Should you meet anyone who shows you a ring like this one, with this symbol, if they invoke my name, trust them as if they were me."

"I will."

Chapter 34

Chavali stood in Todan for the first time in her life and found it stank too much for her sensibilities. Ket had overwhelmed her nose with its stench too. This city, bigger and more tightly packed, seemed a hundred times worse. She hurried on her way, following the directions she'd seen in Evelin's mind.

Magical lights wreathed the center of the city in a golden glow, showing how packed the streets were in the fading daylight. Chavali limped at the speed of the crowd, hugging herself against the chill breeze slithering between all the people and cursing the loss of her cloak. She cut across the crowd to lurch into her target building and pushed her way through the front door. Warmth washed over her, and she shivered from the abrupt change.

Now that she stood here, in a place holding this person who wanted her dead so badly, it occurred to her to wonder why she'd been stupid enough to rush here on her own. She could have waited until morning. She could have gone to Eldrack and told him and let him deal with it or send someone else. She could have returned to Eagle Falls, to check on Colby and Eliot and everyone else, then ridden here on Karias.

Rich, dark wood and thick, heavy velvet decorated the ostentatious lobby. Three people stepped out of a side hallway at the top of a wide, sweeping stair, chatting. It surprised her to recognize them all. For a moment, she paused and stared at the three having a quiet, neutral conversation, wondering what business brought Eldrack and Railan to Myra's door.

A letter with a threat came to mind, one issued by Myra about Grant's death. Chavali's eyes narrowed, and she stormed up the stairs. "How dare you?" she growled.

All three jerked with surprise and gave her their attention. Eldrack frowned and opened his mouth.

Chavali flung a hand up to cut him off. "You send an assassin to murder a man and accuse us of doing it? You send an army to slaughter *children*? What did Ramelia do to your precious Syndicate that she had to be slain? What did Jack do to deserve being framed for it?"

Railan held out an arm to keep her from assaulting Myra. "This isn't the time—"

"This is precisely the time!" Chavali stopped short lest she accidentally wind up at the mercy of the telepath's mind. She still glared daggers at Myra. This vile woman deserved a slap—and much worse—ten times more than Sean ever could. "All of this blood is on your hands. All of it."

Myra sighed. "Eldrack, control your agent."

His jaws clenched, Eldrack grabbed Chavali around the waist and hauled her back with more strength than she expected from the aging clerk. "The matter has been closed. You shouldn't have come here."

Straining against him, Chavali bared her teeth. "I followed the river of blood."

"It's not that simple." Eldrack hustled her down the stairs. "There are more lives at stake than a single village, and all the truly guilty parties have been punished."

"They sent an army!"

"Can you prove that?"

His question took the fire out of her rage. She had nothing. No, she had that cloak pin. Pulling it out of her pocket, she shoved it at him.

He examined the clasp with a frown. "This isn't the Syndicate's symbol."

All hope for justice fled. If that man's only marking offered no proof, then the rest of that army also had nothing. Those men might never be identified. Their families might never know what happened to them. Her lip curled.

Railan stood with Myra, quietly bowing her head and shaking hands, smoothing ruffled feathers and making excuses.

Crossing her arms, Chavali studied Myra. She would remember this woman and find a way to right this wrong. When Eldrack shoved Chavali at the door, she tossed it open and strode through. Her scowl frightened a young man on the street into scuttling away.

"I understand. Believe me, I do." Eldrack's face softened into weary sympathy. "It's difficult to accept what feels like defeat."

"Defeat," she spat. "As if this is about markers on a board."

"For someone who doesn't care about anyone but clan, you're taking this very personally. Was someone you know killed by this army?"

"I don't know. The battle still raged when I left."

Eldrack turned as the door opened again, and Railan joined them, her mouth thin. He sighed. "If they need help sorting out the aftermath, we'll go straight to Eagle Falls and—"

"No, they need more Healers. The force they fought is large."

"I'll go," Railan said with a curt nod. "You two get home and send Healers if Karias hasn't already handled that end."

They collected horses from a stable, and Chavali rode with Eldrack to the nearby Creator's Tower. She couldn't remember exactly how she'd crossed the distance on foot. The time between leaving Evelin and reaching Todan had passed her by somehow. Had she been in a daze?

At the Tower, they walked the horses in. Railan pressed the lever on the giant floor map for their home Tower. A swirl of energy pulled on her stomach and whisked them to that other Tower in a flash of light.

As she passed the two guardians on her way out, Chavali recognized the Commander without his helm on. He chatted with the other Creator's Path guardian on duty, and both turned to see who had come through. Her eyes met his. His brow twitched. She remembered him talking to someone else a lifetime ago when they started out on the Courier Circuit.

That someone else had been her assassin. She saw him briefly that day. Tired and hungry, she'd been too irritated to pay attention. Her assassin arrived and spoke to the Commander. What day had that been? The day Ramelia died? The assassin ran off down the path to Eagle Falls. Now, the Syndicate had his body, and she had no proof. She doubted the Commander would admit to dispatching that man with the forgettable face to murder a woman about a flower.

She forced her reaction away, finding it easy in this numbing cold. The Commander would never know she'd figured it out until the day she wanted him to.

Railan distracted her by climbing into the saddle and kicking her horse into a gallop.

"I want to go to the village." The need to check on Eliot and Colby and Patrick and Harris and Portia filled her.

"No." Eldrack took her arm gently and guided her to his horse. "Chavali, you're cold and hurt. You need to get home and be healed and rest."

"I need to know."

"You will. If you could see yourself, you'd understand why I won't let you go."

She looked down at her hands and thought they seemed normal enough. The blood stains and spatter probably did make her seem in worse condition than she felt, and her leg still stung. Letting Eldrack guide her, they climbed onto his horse and returned to Cloverdale. He ushered her through the tavern, where she noticed everyone staring at her, and down to her room.

He left her there, shutting her in. She wanted to know. She needed to know. If her leaving had killed one of them, she would never forgive herself. Unable to consider sleeping, she paced. When that grew tiresome without tiring her, she moved into the hallway and wandered down the length of it.

Someone familiar stood at the entrance to the study—a tall broad-shouldered man that she mistook for Colby until he turned and faced her. She froze, as she'd done in her dream. Here, now, he stood with his two daggers, light smears across his white shirt and dark beard. His eyes held so much pain. This time, he appeared without color.

"Keino?"

"I'm sorry," he said. His voice echoed strangely in her ears, as if he spoke underwater.

"For which thing?"

His lips moved. The sound came out too garbled to understand.

She grabbed her head, feeling a splitting ache coming on. "I don't understand." When he tried again to tell her something, she picked out a few words and flushed, realizing what he must be saying. In life, he often told her he'd always be by her side. "You're dead," she breathed.

He reached out. His hand passed through her arm.

"The nightmares." She sank to the floor, holding her head. "It's you. You're doing it somehow. Stop. You have to stop, Keino. It's killing me."

Several more words came out of his mouth. The only one she understood was "try."

Chapter 35

Chavali opened her eyes to a dimly lit room. Once again, she'd lost time. She didn't remember falling asleep, let alone coming up to Penny and Marcus's house. Yet, here she lay, in the large bed she sometimes shared with the children. A crack between the two curtains put a thin slice of bright light on the blanket covering her body.

Her dreams had been...almost normal. Aside from that one where she ran into Keino and asked him to help her, nothing had disturbed her sleep, even without Kelly's herbs. Maybe her Healer was right, and it had all been an expression of her mind trying to accept the fact she'd been dead. Asking Keino for help could have been what she needed to justify letting it go.

Flipping the covers aside, she found herself in a fresh, clean dress, one with no slashes or blood. Either she managed it before she fell asleep or Biholtz did it for her to spare the sheets. Her leg felt fine, offering a third possibility: Healers. She rubbed her face and listened to her stomach gurgle.

Once she opened the door, she heard Danel's voice speaking in the odd cadence of reading aloud. He struggled with a word, and a familiar voice helped him with it. She stopped at the living room and leaned against the doorway, smiling at Colby with the boy on his leg and a book in their hands. Both seemed comfortable with the arrangement.

"Chavali!" Haizea ran and thumped into her leg, wrapping her small arms around it. "We saved biscuits."

"I appreciate that."

Danel lit up with a smile and jumped off Colby's lap to join them. "And juice!"

Colby clasped his hands together and smiled at her. "I came up because I heard you wanted to know how it all went."

She recalled saying that to Eldrack and chose to be pleased he'd thought to pass the message along. "This is kind of you."

"Five of the villagers were killed, and three wolves, but not Patrick or Lilly. Portia had a near miss. We were able to get the Healer to her side in time to save her. The rest of us got beat up, some badly. The armorer is going to be busy with repairs for a while. Mine in particular had to be scrapped, and it'll be at least a week before my new suit is ready."

"Did you take any prisoners?" She brushed Haizea's hair, finding it soothing.

"No. When several turned and ran, we let them go. Karias had a cut to the leg, so he couldn't have caught them anyway."

Danel and Haizea both turned their big eyes on Colby. "Is the big horse going to live?"

"Yes, he's fine." Colby gave both of them friendly, open smiles. "A Healer came and fixed him up."

The urge to go tell the stupid horse exactly what he left her to filled Chavali. She pushed it away. He hadn't known any of those men would see her. "I'm glad to see you've been fixed up as well, and it's good the Fallen lost no one." The village would be mourning for some time, she thought. Perhaps she would visit when the snow melted.

Colby stood with a nod, tall enough for his short hair to brush the ceiling. "I should go. You have your clan to see and all that."

"You can stay if you wish. Friends are welcome here."

"I, um." His foot tapped, he looked away, and he clasped his hands together. "I'm glad you're alright too. When Karias returned without you, I worried a little bit."

"He gave me no real choice in the matter. I would have preferred to return with him. It turned out well enough, though." Her belly rumbled again. Curiosity about his behavior would have to wait. "Have you eaten recently? I'm sure it would be no trouble to have you stay for what I consider a meal and what you would call a snack."

He chuckled. "Sure, I can stay. We can all teach Chavali to read."

Chavali groaned. Danel and Haizea cheered and pulled her to the kitchen. Biholtz, Penny, and Marcus welcomed her into the warm, cheerful room, and she basked in the embrace of family and friends.

About the Authors

Lee French lives in Olympia, WA with two kids, two bicycles, and too much stuff. She is an avid gamer and member of the Myth-Weavers online RPG community, where she is known for her fondness for Angry Ninja Squirrels of Doom. In addition to spending much time there, she also trains year-round for the one-week of glorious madness that is RAGBRAI, has a nice flower garden with one dragon and absolutely no lawn gnomes, and tries in vain every year to grow vegetables that don't get devoured by neighborhood wildlife.

She is an active member of the Northwest Independent Writer's Association and one of two Municipal Liaisons for the Olympia region of NaNoWriMo.

Erik Kort abides in the glorious Pacific Northwest, otherwise known as Mirkwood-Without-The-Giant-Spiders, though the normal spiders often grow too numerous for his comfort. He is defended from all eight-legged threats by his brave and overly tolerant wife, and is mocked by his obligatory writer's cat. When not writing, Erik comforts the elderly, guides youths through vast wildernesses, and smuggles more books into his library of increasingly alarming size.

Thanks for reading! If you liked this book, please take a minute to post a review of it wherever you buy your books.

www.ingramcontent.com/pod-product-compliance
Lightning Source LLC
Chambersburg PA
CBHW070914260626
47162CB00007B/2666